Victory!

Ci Ci Soleil

Victory!

A NOVEL

Beach Reads Press

Copyright © 2022 Beach Reads Press

All rights reserved. Published in the United States by Beach Reads Press

Victory! is a work of fiction. Any similarity to actual persons, living or dead, events or places, is purely coincidental.

ISBN: 979-8-9850660-1-2

Author: Ci Ci Soleil

Book cover design: Savannah DePaz

Book cover art: Danielle Hennis

Beach Reads Press
PO Box 103
Carrboro, NC 27516
BeachReadsBooks.com

FOREWORD

Victory! is a novel in the form of magical realism. Once I was gifted with the story of Quila, I spent the next five years reading and studying, engaging in workshops, working with colleagues far wiser than I am, trying to understand both what Quila would face and how I could even begin to understand her world, much less depict it, given my own biases. The afterword to this book will give you a deeper window into the inception of the story, but also serves as a spoiler for the twists and turns of the tale. While the story engages and entertains, the issues dealt with in the book are all too real and all too devastating to society: structural racism, predatory incarceration of Black men, systematic destruction of the Black family, the war on drugs, addiction and family dysfunction, poverty, and a world of "isms" that creates chasms between us. A series of book club discussion questions are provided to foster dialogue and deeper understanding of the issues - and possibly offer insights into your own communities.

For Ruben, Alexander and Ethan. You are my Victory.

Chapter 1

Quila ran down the street, her heart thumping in her ears. She could hear her feet pounding on the pavement, even in her sneakers.

They called fuckin' sneakers for a reason—because they supposed to be quiet! she thought as she ran.

She was sure he would hear her, be able to follow her, track her, the sound of her escape was so loud. She pulled the baggie from the hidden pocket of her jacket and pitched it down a sewer drain as she dashed past. *Get rid of it. Get rid of it!*

Why I have to breathe so loud?

She ran fast. "Like a deer," Grandma Mayme always said. Quila wasn't sure what a deer was. She'd seen plastic ones decorating people's yards, sure, but see one for real? Here in the city? Not hardly.

In shit Christmas stories those suckers fuckin' fly. You can fly inside a book. On what I deliverin' I could fuckin' fly, sure, but damn deer don't fly. Not in this city.

Mayme said they melted away like snow in the spring, invisible inside of five seconds. Fast. Like her. "Quila run like a deer," Mayme had said. She sure could use that ability now. She sure could.

That dude a cop. Had to be. This a sting. Just a bust. And if I get arrested again, I be dust.

Better it was a Blue who found she was delivering Red on his territory. Or maybe not. That was a dust sentence too.

Shit. Behind bars or wearing bullets. The bars be safer, but if the Blues want you dead no bars gonna' save you. They find you. Shit! Where the winning angle here?

She felt the searing pain of a stitch in her side.

Run faster!

She flashed in anger at herself. She just couldn't get her breath. *Damn.* "Asthma," the kiddie doctor had told her. *Asked Rashida to stop smoking when I jus' a girl. And Grandma Mayme too, but did they? Shit no.*

And Quila herself had started at way too early. Picked up half-smoked cigarettes lying in the ash tray. Or she carefully snuffed out the sticks left burning on the beer can after Rashida had passed out. Her mother often smoked three at a time, forgetting that she had one burning already, having abandoned it in another room. Quila and her brothers learned that these were precious resources. Either the kids would calm Rashida down with a half-smoked cigarette when her panic attacks would start up, or when they were sure that she was really out, they would squirrel them away for their own private stash. Mama was flush in cigarettes and drugs after she'd gotten her monthly check, but by the end of the month all hell could break loose. Quila was hooked before she was fourteen. Hell, she lived in clouds of smoke at home, what was the difference whether she lit up or not? What was the difference whether it was cigarettes or pot?

Well, the weed make you feel a lot better. Really mellow you out. But, shit, what it done to my lungs already?

On a bright, sunny day in spring she was gasping for air. She made a quick turn at the corner to take cover down a side street and then she stopped short.

Shit. There they be. Right in front of me. A pack of Blues.

She stood there, looking at them, her breath ragged.

He was calm as he stood there. "So, Quila. I see you on my land again." Jaquan acted as though he was a lord with all his followers surrounding him. His boys took a step forward together, but she knew Jaquan wasn't the real leader. The real leaders didn't deign to patrol the streets—that was for underlings in the power structure. Yet, Jaquan was the leader of this ten-block area, and that made him king as far as he was concerned. She knew him well. She'd had to pay his toll before. He had his boys behind him. His family. His blood brothers. They would die for him, kill for him at a command. Or a whisper. Or their own whim. None of them showed their guns but all would be armed. All would be hungry for a kill, even for the sheer entertainment value of it, to liven up an otherwise uneventful afternoon. Beautiful days could be so boring. A lot of dust was made from sheer boredom. Quila knew she'd better talk fast.

"Damn, J. You scared me! But I'm glad to see ya'. I got a damn cop on my tail, sure because I was walkin' while Black that I was droppin' a deal. Ain't no justice in this town!"

"You be right 'bout that. No justice in this town. But you sure you weren't droppin' no deal?" Jaquan asked, amused. "Cause Walkah ain't no pig undercover. He a Blue brother. And he say you been dealing for the Reds on my land." Jaquan held up his phone to indicate the text he'd received with the report from his brothers on the street.

"No, no, man! No way. After Nashon was dusted two years ago, I got out. Just tryin' to live my life. And, uh, how's Malejah?" She searched for the name of Jaquan's younger sister, who she barely remembered from high school.

"She dust. Dropped rather than delivered, you know?" He shrugged. "Shit happens, I guess." He pulled his Glock out of his jacket. "Now, me an princess here don't want to have get busy, but Quila, you know the rules…"

"J, you know you my best man. I would never deal on you land. You know how I feel about you."

"Yeah, yeah. And you were good to me. For a while there, you were good to me. So good I let you go three or four times now, but you ain' been good to me for a long time. So, I ain' got much to calm down my trigger finger."

Quila looked at Jaquan and quickly to the faces of the brothers on either side of him. They were smirking. It was over. There was nothing she could promise him that would alter his decision. It was over. His Glock flashed in the bright sunshine.

She almost felt the revving before she heard it, a roar louder than her racing heart as the car screamed around the corner and skidded to a stop. She recognized the blue Escalade as Deyonte, her half-brother. So, word had gotten to him, and he had come for her.

Come to save me. Shit! Miracles happened. Sure, he should. I deliverin' for him anyway.

Now, all she had to do was to get in that car. He had bulletproof glass, reinforced side panels.

Damn thing a fuckin' tank inside there. I could drop a 'cid as he drive 'way, he have some in the back. I earned it. I more than earned it.

She turned to give him a glance as he got out of the car and saw his three-hundred-dollar high top tennis she hit the pavement. Saw the top of his head. He was wearing those hot designer sunglasses. Man, he looked badass in those. And his red jacket.

He look like a young Michael Jackson, before all the surgery took him away from knowing who he was. Shit, my brother one bad ass dude.

She took two steps backwards, just slowly to make her way to the other side of the car while Deyonte sweet-talked a deal with the Blues. Quila could feel her body start to relax. It was going to be all right. Elation flooded her as she knew she would sleep in her own bed tonight, not in the city morgue.

Another day, another death avoided. Shit. Life be good.

Then she heard the click, ominous like a night sky that was somehow red rather than black, like when thunder rumbled in the distance and made the walls vibrate in some kind of demon-inspired low roll. It was like the Devil was hunting you and wanted to devour you live. The glint of sun on silver spurred her to turn and sprint as fast as she could. There would be no talking this afternoon. She turned her back on Jaquan, knowing she should never turn her back on Jaquan or any man like him. The crack came like peels of thunder. The lightning bolt of reality hit Deyonte. She saw his left shoulder jerk back as the bullet hit him in the chest, then his right leg crumble as one hit him in the thigh. A third bullet went into the side of his head as he fell. She could see a fountain of blood fly up. Still, she was running to the car, to safety. His boys had drawn and were shooting back. She could tell from the screams of pain and rage that casualties were counted on both sides. Then she felt the stab in her back. Hot, searing pain. It tore through her, worse than withdrawal, with a savage tear that left her breathless. Still she ran, but her feet felt like she was running through a blizzard in winter—like when your pants weren't thick enough to keep out the cold and by the time you made it home you could hardly feel your legs anymore. Her chin felt wet. She put her hand to her mouth and pulled it away… covered in red. Then she coughed and the blood flew out of her mouth. Another searing red-hot plug of metal bit into her lower back. She could feel her arms fling outward. The last thing she saw was a slice of the clear blue sky that shone between the tops of the derelict buildings that grew on either side of the narrow street. The last thing she said was, *Heaven, help me!* But the last thing she thought of was Victory. Victory wasn't going to die this way. When she was dust it would come with an obit, not a sidebar crime news story that didn't even draw readers past the headline. Three scrolls down at least. Quila was surprised at how much time she had to think as the pain wound through her, reaching for her heart. As the pavement of the street neared closer and closer, as the darkness closed in, in her own voice she heard the shout of, "Victory!" and when she felt her head crack against the dark and dirty macadam, she knew no more.

Chapter 2

She was slow coming to. The whiteness of it all was blinding. She took in a breath. She could breathe. It was easier to breathe. Like the asthma had let go, its pinching grasp relinquishing its hold on a million tiny balloons in her lungs that only knew how to be half-inflated.

Well, it always easier to breathe when I ain't runnin'.

She certainly wasn't running now. The brightness was almost too painful to bear.

Where am I?

Then she thought, *Where was I?*

She remembered the street fight. The pop-pop-pop of the Glocks, Ravens, and Rugers had been ringing in her ears. But they weren't ringing in her ears now. No, not that, but she could hear something. She listened hard and finally decided that it was that very faint crap you hear in the background of White people's lives. Songs, once popular, now played by orchestras that couldn't get people to show up for whatever that shit was that orchestras played. She guessed that like all musicians, they had to eat, too, so they made that garbage that wasn't quite music and it ended up in shopping malls and doctors' offices, elevators and the agencies where those mandatory counseling sessions took place.

Oh my god, I ain't dead.

It hit her hard. The memory of it all, like that time she'd been thrown into the wall by one of her mama's boyfriends for coming downstairs to see what all the crying was about. It had been her mama crying and that boyfriend, she never learnt his name, didn't like an audience. She remembered the sounds. She remembered the searing pain ripping through her chest. The taste and the sight of blood. Her blood. She moved her hand, almost surprised that she could.

I in the hospital. That damn muzak going to drive me crazy and I fuckin' trapped here!

Her hand moved a bit more. She needed to feel the wound, see how bad it was. Her hand moved to her chest. *Damn. I still in emergency. I still wearin' my clothes. Woke up too fuckin' soon.* She had expected to be in a hospital bed, in a hospital gown. Maybe in ICU, where it was quiet. She'd been there once, the ER; man, that place was loud. This was not the ER. ERs didn't play muzak. Nah, their soundtrack was the drama of other people's lives.

Her hand felt her chest. She reached further. Searched out the wound. She found nothing. She moved her other hand, slowly, almost as if afraid of what she would find, moved it up to her face. No tubes. No wires. She felt her face and her chest. No bandages. She tried to open her eyes just a little bit more. The brightness dimmed ever so slightly. But the muzak got louder. The tune bothered her. She didn't know it. No one ever made muzak out of Black people's jams. Nah, that was just White people shit. Old White people shit at that. Might as well be Klan jive for all she knew. Country muzak. She tried to puzzle out why she couldn't find bandages. She had taken at least four bullets. Of course, she'd have bandages all over her.

Must be the painkillers makin' me fuzzed up. But you get the good stuff in the hospital. Not street-cut stuff.

Then she realized the truth and it made her heart beat faster. At least it should have made her heart beat faster. She wasn't sure what she felt. As her hands moved over her body, she realized that she wasn't in the hospital at all. So, she *had* made it into the back of Deyonte's ride, and he'd high tailed it out of there in that tank and she'd probably dropped two or three 'cid in celebration! The street war was just a bad dream.

Then wherever I be, whatever happened to me in between… okay, I startin' to come down.

She felt a sense of relief that the ER was just a hallucination.

You do that. See shit. Feel shit when you comin' down, she told herself, waiting for the reassurance to make her feel better.

She couldn't quite feel her body. She hoped it wasn't going to be too hard of a landing. The shit she'd been talking, well, landings could be rough. A cough startled her. It wasn't a normal cough, like you hear someone on the subway. It was cough like someone was hacking up a lung. It went on and on, drowning out the muzak with its own disturbing crescendo. Finally, it calmed down to a raggedy breath. She opened one eye and looked sideways towards the sound. She blinked a few times as her surroundings started to come into focus. There was a man sitting next to her, some dude, thin as a rail. Pale as all get out. He wasn't young but he surely wasn't as old as that haggard look on his face. He started up again, his whole body wracked with the cough that was overtaking him. Instinctively she leaned away from him and surprised herself that she could. She blinked a couple more times as her own hands came into focus; they were resting on her lap now. She marveled at her hands for a while. Then she looked at her clothes.

Yep. Same ones.

She stared straight ahead of her and saw the ugliest painting she had ever seen. She couldn't quite make it out, but it gave her the creeps.

Looking around, her ability to focus returning to her, her senses once more starting to feed her information, she realized that she was sitting in a chair. On a small table next to her were magazines about food, home decorating, parenting. No sign of Beyoncé. No powerful form of Serena. Forget anything about new twist-out styles. Just White people magazines. She heard a whimper and a sniff. Following the sound, her eyes landed on a man sitting in another chair. He was scratching. First one hand, and then the other. Now his arm. Then his shoulder, as if he were chasing an impossible itch that was snaking its way around his body. He looked at her, full panic in his eyes. He whimpered again. Then his hands dove for his leg, and he started scratching again. He used one hand to scratch the other with a vicious intensity. He held out his hands to her and Quila nervously looked down at them, afraid at what she was going to see, but to her surprise she couldn't see anything, even the scratch marks that had to be there from the man's own fingernails.

He looked at her plaintively. "Help me! Can you help me?" His voice was a raggedy whisper.

"What on you hands? I don't see nothin'."

Hollow-eyed, he began to scratch at his chest, slowly at first but then digging increasingly deeper. "It burns," he mumbled and sunk back into his chair, staring at nothing as he continued to scratch away at his face.

Collecting herself, Quila looked around the room. She jumped at the sight of another man, young. He was scratching too. Scratching hard, chasing that invisible itch around his body. His eyes held pure fear. She turned her head at the sound of another ragged breath. A brother was sitting in the corner curled up in a fetal position, his hands scratching wildly.

Clearly, she was in some type of a waiting room where people were coming down real hard. It was full of people, mostly men, which she thought was weird, young and old. One really old dude who looked like a lumpy sweet potato was in a corner looking like he was trying to hide. He was in a rumpled suit with a fat-ass red tie, and he kept covering his ears with his hands and whimpering, looking wildly about him at something only he could see. He would scratch intermittently, then he'd put his hands over his eyes and murmur something rhythmic and repetitive that it took her a while to make out. She finally decided he was rapid-fire saying, "I didn't I didn't I didn't I didn't", but she couldn't tell if it was in denial or in remorse. He'd scratch wildly, then he'd cover his ears again. He looked terrified.

She looked back at the scratchers and then down at herself. Whatever shit they were dealing with hadn't bit her yet, although withdrawal could also do that to you. No wounds even. She took a deep breath, enjoying the sensation of being able to do so.

Back at the social worker's office. Mandatory counseling. Again. Shit. They gonna' give me no end a shit for this.

Obviously, she had tripped out in celebration of her miraculous escape. But someone must have gotten tired of her and dumped her off, probably at some ER. Well, that was better than in some alley. And now she had come to in rehab. She must be coming down, but she wasn't itchy. She took in her surroundings. She realized she was becoming accustomed to the light now because the painful brightness was gone at last, leaving just that dim haze that gives off not quite enough illumination to really see how dirty the place was. A realization clicked in her head.

Bedbugs, she thought. *The place infested with bedbugs.*

Chapter 3

"Tequila Williams."

The sound made Quila turn her head, everything in slow motion. More than see, she could sense a door opening, but it was fuzzy over there.

"Tequila Williams." The voice was gentle but insistent.

She moved forward, feeling like she was stumbling, moving towards the sound of her name. She used to play a game with Victory like this when they were kids. Vicky would invite her over to swim and they would call out some stupid singsong rhymey white-ass name that Vicky loved, all while keeping their eyes closed and trying to track each other through the water by sound alone.

Oh yeah, Marco Polo. That be it.

Now it was like she was playing Marco Polo, but on dry land, and to the sound of her own name.

Why everything so damn fuzzy?

She moved towards the sound, feeling like she was pitching, falling forward, but she was glad to get away from the scratching dudes. They gave her the creeps. Must be coming off heroin. She'd known people who'd done that coming down, going through withdrawal. None of them had made it. But they scratched at their imaginary itch until they didn't have any skin left.

She followed the sound of her name and went through a doorway feeling like she had walked into another world. Or perhaps back into a world she once knew. It was an office. From what she could tell, it had to be in some high-rise in a bigger city than she'd ever been to. It must be a cloudy day because outside the glass wall was so foggy that she couldn't see anything. Curiously, there was a door in the glass wall. A glass door that looked like it led to no place. She couldn't say why, but it creeped her out. It looked cold. It radiated heat; an icy hot mirage that gave her the chills. As she stumbled forward, she noticed that in the middle of the office was a sleek, ultra-contemporary desk, the kind she had seen pictures of in those impossible catalogues over at Victory's house. The kind of furniture that real people could never afford. She looked over to her left towards an open black granite fire pit: flames rose out of a sea of clear glass beads, leaving not even a whisper of sound. Who the hell had a fire pit in their office? The walls, those that weren't clear glass, were deeply red. Not cranberry, not crimson, but so dark and with so much depth she thought that if she touched them her hand would sink in and disappear. Maybe forever. She definitely did not want to touch them.

Suddenly she noticed a chair next to her. It looked uncomfortable. Uninviting even. Then she heard a man's voice clearing his throat. She looked up and saw a man sitting behind the desk—had she not noticed him before, or had he just come in? Maybe through the icy-hot door? She wasn't sure. She wasn't sure of anything around here. She studied the man. He was lean. His suit was like nothing Quila had ever seen; it was so fine. He was what Victory would have drooled over as "strikingly handsome", which she supposed might be true for a White dude. She wasn't too sure about the mustache and goatee, but anyone would have looked good in that suit. He reeked of money. *No, not money,* she corrected herself. *Power.* His hair was longish, almost down below his jaw line, a rich brown, and slightly curly, all slicked back. An earring glinted in one ear. A diamond. *A big ass diamond,* she reflected. This was one dude who thought he was a badass for sure.

"Welcome, Tequila."

"Quila. It just Quila."

Nodding slightly, sizing her up, he acquiesced. "Quila."

She figured she should say something. This dude might have influence with a parole officer. "Uh… nice office." She tried to sound cool, but she heard the stammer in her voice, and then heard herself say before she even realized it, "But what up with them weird-ass tunes?" She could still hear them in the background.

"Oh, it's my muzak. I love it," he said with a smile. "It's once-upon-a-time-big-hit tunes… now with all the life sucked out of them. Inspired. Simply inspired. Please, sit down." He gestured in invitation.

"I can turn them down while we, ah, visit." The tunes instantly stopped.

She looked suspiciously at the unwelcoming chair and then took a seat, not knowing what else to do and not feeling like she had any kind of a choice. But then again, she knew what to do. You played the White man's game until you got a chance to come up for air. They would have a 'meaningful discussion'. A talk about her life. About how she was on the wrong track. Very quietly she growled low in her own throat. *None of these counselors never fuckin' understand that there ain't no other path for anyone like me. I don't live in no world of 'choices'. That be Victory's rich white-ass world. Me? I jus' a ghetto kid with a dead addicted mother and absolutely no choices what-ever.* So she sat down. It was the only choice she had.

She was relieved to find the chair was more comfortable than it looked, but she didn't want to be there. She would give a lot to not have to be there. Maybe she could walk out, run away, but all there was outside the door was that room, that waiting room full of those scratching people.

"Good, usually that takes longer."

"Longer? Longer for what?"

"To sit down," he answered plainly. The silence stretched.

Quila thought about all the weirdos in the waiting room.

Oh my god, she thought. *This be some new kinda' rehab. Well, shit. I gone and landed myself in some new rehab. Better then jail. What was I on?*

Before the last street corner deal she had pulled a small bit for her own personal use. The client she was carrying for was so fucked up he would

15

likely not notice that some was missing. Besides, street heroin, the shit she could afford, was so toxic these days. You couldn't get any that wasn't laced with fentanyl, and that was a death sentence as often as not. A great high—just to crash you into the low of your life. The *six-foot-under-low* they called it. Gimmie's stock was nearly always pure, or as pure as you could get. No shit was pure. The damn Mexicans saw to that, greedy bastards. That was why she carried in the first place—she could nick some of the best quality shit that she was likely to get her hands on, and Gimmie usually didn't beat her for it if she treated him right. But if she woke up here, fuzzy like this, with nothing making sense, with nothing being clear, it must have been cut with something. Then reality dawned on her.

Oh shit. Victory found me. That damn do-gooder put me up in one of them expensive rehabs. Found me. She must done it… brought me here. Oh shit. Not again. That girls tryin' to save me again. At least there be damn good food in Victory's places. And clean sheets.

She looked at the well-dressed dude. "Where be this? You my doctor?"

The man smiled enigmatically. "Hmm! Doctor, I like the sound of that." He raised his eyebrows and nodded. "Doctor. Yeah, sure. If that works for you, it works for me."

"Ain't you straight up," Quila quipped, feeling this was a very strange way to start that whole doctor-patient relationship thing. This place looked way cool, but maybe it wasn't one of Victory's high priced let's save poor little Tequila' interventions that she seemed to love so much. Then Quila remembered the bedbugs. Victory would never have put her in a place with bedbugs.

This doctor dude looked too old. No, maybe he looked young. She stared at him, finding it very hard to place his age at all. Well, maybe he was one of those trainees who hadn't finished school yet, here to 'learn' on her, in an internship. She got a lot of that at the drug counseling centers. Inexperienced freebies. And the family counseling centers. The underfunded clinics took a lot of students—it was the only way to staff the place. But hey, when you didn't pay, you got what you paid for.

Food gonna' suck somethin' awful, she thought to herself, now wishing that this had been one of Victory's stunts. "Great. So, uh. What up with them?" She jerked her thumb over her shoulder, indicating the waiting room.

"Them? Oh, I suppose a variety of things."

She thought about the people sitting on the other side of the door, young and old, just sitting, no talking, no ear buds stuck to their heads. Mostly just staring at the floor or at their hands as they scratched themselves. "What 'bout the itchy ones?" She paused. "Is that, ugh, catching?"

"Oh, you mean the *violators*. Nah, that's not contagious. No worries. Not for you anyway. Not for that."

"Violators?"

"Yes, rule breakers."

"So, what they do?" Then she thought she probably shouldn't use that sneering tone with him. She thought of the old man sitting out there trying to scratch his face off. What the hell kind of violation could you make as an old man? "Jaywalk?"

"Jaywalk?" the man asked curiously. "Oh, no, they broke the rules. It gets itchy when you get that stuff on you."

"What stuff? I didn't see no 'stuff' on them. No redness…" Her voice trailed off until she spoke so quietly, as if to herself. "No rash, no scratch mark…" She scratched one hand with the other. "Not even from they own hands."

Despite hardly even murmuring that last thought, the man seemed to have no problem hearing her. "Oh no, it wouldn't be visible to *you,*" he explained. "But we don't usually wear the stains of our sins on our skin, now do we? They're pretty hard to see. Takes a trained eye." He gave her a wink.

Quila was amazed at how detached and clinical he sounded. "Stains of…. what? You say… *sins?*"

17

"Yes, sins. They're violators. Broke a rule. It's itchy stuff when you get that on your hands. It sticks with you."

"What do? What do they have on they hands? They was nothin' there."

"Blood, of course." He said it as though he was stating the obvious.

"They have *blood* on they hands?"

"The stain of blood, yes. It's itchy." He was very patient as he explained this fact, as if to someone who was too young to truly grasp the point.

"Blood... you mean, they, they *kill* someone?"

"Yes, precisely. Exactly. With either word or deed."

"And the *sin*... that would be that... um... why they are... what you call them? Violators?"

"Violators, yes. They broke the rule. You call it a Commandment where you're from."

"A commandment? Like those commandment thingies? From the movies?"

"Oh, is that where *you* learned about them? Yes, the sixth Commandment *thingy* to be exact...Thou Shalt Not Kill. Actually, it was much higher on the list, but your kind screwed that up too. I think you've heard of that. Of course, number eight was always a favorite of mine as well."

"Number eight?"

"Yes, false witness."

"False witness?"

"Sure, you've heard of that as lying about someone. Telling fibs."

"Huh?"

"Cappin."

"Oh. Bet."

"Sure. Bet. Number eight. Somewhere in your glorious and yet short-lived life I'm sure you heard about number six and number eight. Surely someplace other than a movie?"

Quila started to become distinctly uncomfortable with the way he said *short lived*. Maybe they had picked her up and taken her to a hospital?

Maybe she had been tripping for a long time? Maybe she had almost bit it this time? Close, but not dead. Thank god for Narcan. She had come back from the edge. Thing was, she couldn't remember actually taking that heroin. And Gimmie had told her the next time she stole from him he was gonna' do her. Truth was, she was afraid of Gimmie and she believed him. She had intended to just do the deal and get the hell out of there. She didn't remember taking a pinch… but she didn't always remember. Then it struck her and she looked at the man in the million-dollar suit again. That was it, she *had* woken up in rehab. But this wasn't one of Victory's cushy 'get to know you, you're OK, I'm OK' kind of places.

Oh, Lord help me! I be in one of them religious we-gonna'-save-you charity places where they gonna' pray over me and dip me in water and talk to me about Jesus. Oh shit.

"Not exactly," the Well-Dressed-Man answered.

"Not exactly what?" Quila ventured nervously.

"Not exactly dip you in water or pray over you. We're past that point once you get here."

"Where is… here?" *Wait a minute*, she thought. *I didn't say that out loud.*

"You don't need to. Not here." He had an amused look on his face.

Not quite willing to give up the power of her voice and absolutely not ready to ask how he could read her mind so effectively, she asked, "And who those people out there?"

"Oh, they're waiting to see me, just like you were. I'll get them sorted out."

"Who they be?"

"Today? Mostly soldiers, both professional and self-appointed. Some innocents. The, uh, gentleman in a suit became a politician. Did he ever make number eight his personal tool." The Well-Dressed-Man laughed in a way that sounded uncomfortably confident. It gave Quila the shivers.

"What up with the eyes and ears thing?

"Oh that? I'm sure he's just spiritually pissing himself. You see, his ears hear all the lies he told but his eyes see the truth." He chuckled. "I would guess that's an uncomfortable place to be. At least it is when you lied like he did." He leaned back in his chair with a satisfied look on his face. "And all that blood is really itchy." The well-dressed man just looked at her.

Oh man, this be some shit trip I havin'. She looked around her again. "Can I ask you a question?"

"Another one?"

She rolled her eyes. That was all too like Victory's obnoxious older brother. Always thought he was some kind of comedian. "Those guys are violators?"

"Broke the rule."

"So, they broke your rule," she repeated, "and now they *itchy*?"

"Yes, that's about right."

"That totally unfair," she said indignantly.

He raised his eyebrows. "How so?"

"Well, didn't they have to kill? That was they job. How can you punish them for doing they job?"

"I'm not punishing them. I mean I might, but certainly not right now. I haven't even seen them yet. You were first on my list. Of course, it's that politician I'm really looking forward to sitting with. He's going to have an interesting next step."

"But... but... that just not fair." And then she added, "I was first on the list?" That made her distinctly uneasy.

"What's not fair? I didn't make up the rules and as far as I know you were told the rules. *Thou shalt not kill.* That's the rule. Believe me, it's not because we mind having those here who get killed. You have it all wrong—the innocents, they're actually very nice to work with. Very pleasant. The women and children. The scared young soldiers mowed down before they ever get to pull a trigger. But the violators, they are... well, they're more trouble. Not as pleasant." He mused, looking away from her, reminiscing on something she didn't want to know about.

"But they… defending they country," she gasped. "Or, uh, they territory."

"Don't blame me if you make up wars to justify killing. Or street wars. Or religious ones. Or political ones. I didn't make up war. You invented it. We told you 'don't kill'. It's itchy. The stuff doesn't come off well. It's sticky. Yes, they suffer with it here. They suffered with it where you come from."

"Suffer with what?"

"You're a slow one, aren't you? The *blood*. It bothers them when they get here but at least they can finally see it. It's quite bothersome there, where you come from."

"Where I come from?" She could pull up dim, far off memories of a dingy apartment. Of want. Of hunger. Of loneliness. Of jealousy. Of not fitting in. And a whole lot of fear. Mostly emotions rather than concrete things, but then again, there weren't many concrete things in her life.

"Yes, I'm sure you've heard of it. It's called different things in different cultures, different millennia. I believe for some of you it's called PTSD."

"Post trauma… somethin'…"

"Post-traumatic stress disorder."

"Yeah. Yeah. Heard of that."

"I'll bet you have. They're violators. It's itchy stuff to get on you. Don't kill. It's itchy. It doesn't come off well. We told you. If you don't follow, don't do what you're told, it's no skin off my nose."

Quila was silent for a long time. The man didn't say anything. At last she ventured, "Can I ask you a question?" He raised his eyebrows and proffered his hand in invitation.

"So the military… they just screwed and yet they good guys. What about, like, what about the… serial killers? And the… the… mass murderers? I mean, what happen to them? They must itch…." She thought about the men in the waiting room. And men like Jaquan, and her brother

21

Deyonte, who had killed dozens in street wars. "…Itch really badly." She loved Deyonte. He and Rasheed were probably the only men she'd ever really loved. She wanted Deyonte to get an inpatient stay like she was getting. One of those scared straight experiences that would get him going down a road to a non-ghetto life. But she couldn't imagine it. He was gang and guns all through. He didn't want to take the road to a normal life. He wanted to own the road, even if he had to pave it with blood to do so.

"The blood bathers? Don't know. I never see them." He shrugged.

"You mean, they don't come here? Wherever here is?"

"Not here. Not to me."

"Then where they go?" Then she laughed, "Well, at least maybe I not in hell, I mean if the mass murderers and serial killers ain't here."

He didn't laugh.

She stopped laughing, feeling her joke hit the dirt and just lie there.

"They don't go much of anyplace," he said nonchalantly, examining his nails.

"You mean, they just… just stick around?" She felt some hope for Deyonte.

"No. Not really. They don't stay and they don't go anyplace. They just… aren't." He started to show his first signs of impatience.

"Aren't?"

"Do you really want to have this existential conversation with me? We do have business to talk about."

"What you mean by 'aren't'?"

He sighed. "The guys out there," he said jerking his head toward the door. "They have blood on their hands, whether by word, inciting violence with lies like that politician, or by deed. They're violators. It weighs heavy on them, particularly as they reach the end." He looked at her and then shook his head, as if reminding himself to be patient. "People who kill get splashed with the blood they let—spiritually splashed. People who kill through others get wet with much more blood. When you do bad it multiplies. We try to warn you, try to tell you because blood is poisonous to you. It suffocates the soul. A little bit, well that eats away at you… you know, remorse, regret. Where you come from it's itchy from the inside—bad dreams, bad thoughts, hallucinations. It drives them to do whatever they can to forget, make it go away. But it doesn't. And in the end, it just gets itchier. But the blood bathers…." Here he laughed in a most uncomfortable, almost a hungry way. "Them? They relish in it. Makes them feel powerful, to kill, but it gets all over them. They can't see it, of course, none of them can. But they can *feel* it. As they get near the end their soul can't breathe... so it just *ceases*. You could say they suffocate themselves. We tell you not to do it." He shrugged again. "It's endlessly entertaining how you just don't listen." He looked at her for a long time.

As the silence between them grew she thought about all the times she knew better… *and just didn't listen.* All her reasons seemed so hollow now. She knew it was bad company she was keeping. *But I'll belong* she had told herself. *They'll protect me* she had believed. *They're like a family.* "I really fucked myself, didn't I?"

He smiled again. "Well, that's what I wanted to see you about, now isn't it? I thought we might review your life. Check out your decisions. Weigh your choices. We have some decisions to make… about you."

She knew they were going to schedule her for the treatment therapy. She hoped it was that cognitive-behavioral stuff. She'd had that shit before and she knew exactly how to play them. Then, she felt this creepy sensation down her back. It was cold around her shoulders. Without realizing that she said it aloud she heard her own voice say, "Damn. I got this feelin' like I bit it."

The Well-Dressed Man leaned toward her across his fancy desk. "Bet."

She looked at him and after a moment, laughed nervously. Her life, according to Dr. Suit, was over. She was dead. But of course, she was. When you left the life, the streets, your gang, you were dead. Sometimes they even mourned you, whether you sat in rehab or were extradited to jail in another state or were lying stone cold in some city morgue. As long as you weren't coming back, you were dead.

Wasn't worth much anyway. No shit chance of escaping the gutters, was there? Might as well be here as be there. But where is here?

Chapter 4

She looked at the Well-Dressed Man. "Oh, I get it. You a joker. Ha, ha, ha. Dead. Good joke. You mean I ain't on the street." She slumped back in her chair. "Everybody gotta be a damn comedian."

"Damn comedian," he repeated. "I rather like that. Probably have been called that before, now that I think about it." He leaned back in his chair and stroked his sculpted goatee thoughtfully.

"And you ain't my rehab counselor. Nah, you my new parole officer, bet?"

"Well, that's one way of looking at it. Not quite, of course, but that's not a bad joke. You know, I think I might like you. Usually, your type is so dully predictable, but you might turn out to be rather amusing." He laughed in a way that made her skin feel all crawly, like those people out in the waiting room. "No," he went on, "we're here to review and weigh the value of your life. It's pretty much set in stone, not unlike the one which will be set above your resting place. Quite permanent, quite un-erasable." He chuckled, "Not that your stone is very large, but it was, I suppose, a nice gesture for her to make."

"Who? What you talkin' 'bout? My resting place?"

"My dear, I suggest you take a look at yourself. A good look." He nodded towards a mirror which had suddenly appeared on the wall.

Quila got up, walked over towards where he'd gestured. She was a little afraid to see how she looked. She wasn't sure when she had showered last, and if she'd been trippin' for a few days and woke up a prisoner in rehab or some weird-ass type of jail then she thought she might look like one of those horror movie posters. At first her reflection was rather blurry, but she squinted and stared at herself and gradually she became clear. She was still wearing what she remembered from the street deal where Deyonte and Jaquan were dead set on settling it once and for all. "What the hell?" She picked at a red blob. It looked like she'd spilled catsup in big globs on her jacket. She was always doing that. She was quite the messy eater.

"Not catsup, my dear..." the voice said from over at the desk.

Quila wished he would stop reading her mind like that, but she took a closer look. Then she put her hands on the front of the jacket. She could feel a side of the zipper in each hand. As she grabbed the jacket opening more tightly and could feel the teeth of the zipper threads bite into her skin, slowly she pulled the front of her jacket open. She had catsup on her shirt as well. Then she looked more closely. Her brows knitting, she lifted up her shirt. Blue grayish looking ragged wounds, like holes, were crusted with blood.

"I'm not joking. And you are dead, Tequila Williams. You were shot several times. Some even after you were dead, although that seems like a waste of ammunition to me. But hey, we don't question the living."

"I bit it." Her voice was slow as she tried to process that information. She was dead. Really dead. That was a lot of bullet holes. She lowered her shirt and turned back around slowly. "Why they do that?"

"Don't know. I only question the dead. And Tequila Williams, I have some questions for you." He gave her an oily smile. "Come, sit down. I have some things I'd like to review with you."

She really wanted to run back through the door to the waiting room, but a quick glance told her that it had disappeared. Moving almost against her will she made her way back over to the chair and sat down.

"That's good. That's right. Have a seat. Let's see, where should we start?"

She blinked. He was looking at her intently, like he wanted an answer. "Uh… at the start?" She had heard Vicky's mother say that about a million times. It seemed like a good answer.

"No, I don't think so. Not at the start."

It figures that be an answer that only work for White folk.

"Let's start at the end. I always find that retracing the steps is a most interesting path to pursue."

Involuntarily, her hand went to her torso, where she was now acutely aware of the holes in her body.

"Not that recent. I think that whole scene is pretty clear. But maybe a bit further back. He turned his chair sideways, facing his fire pit. "If you'd be so kind as to look at my cloud."

She turned her head and above the firepit was now a mass of whiteness congealing into a thickness, like a screen. Then images started to take shape. She could see herself. And someone else running to catch up with her.

"Boring. Let's move on, shall we. Maybe this one?" The cloud image would come into focus with a scene, then go fuzzy as he looked for what he wanted to show her, then come into focus again.

"Oh my god. That Victory."

"Who?"

"Victory. Well, her mama name her some stupid Frenchie name. *Victoire*. But no one call her that 'cept her mama. She just go by Victory. Or Vic. Or Tori, depending on who talkin' to her."

"Victory? Say, that was the last thing you uttered. So that was her name?" He looked harder at the screen. "And that's who she is? She seems to be in your story, well, rather a lot. Hmm… she's cute."

"Of course she cute. She got a nose job at fifteen. And anything else she ever want. Them folk got it all."

"What's her interest in you?"

27

"Damn if I know. She dog my heels since I be jus' a kid. Always tryin' to save me, I guess."

"Save you? From what?"

Quila snorted. "Probably this." She opened her jacket wide.

"Well then, let's see her in action, shall we?" He had a most uncomfortable smirk on his face. "Let's try this one."

Quila didn't have any choice but to look at the shapes moving in the cloud. She could see herself coming into focus, walking down the street. She remembered this day. It was about two years ago. She was on her way to see Jaquan. They were an item back then.

Victory was running up the street. "Quila! Quila!" She tapped Quila on the shoulder. "Oh my god, it's you!" She hugged Quila hard and didn't let go for an awkwardly long time. "Slaps running into you! What have you been up to? Oh, we have to catch up. Hey, let's get a coffee. My treat." Same old Victory, she grabbed Quila by the arm and dragged her into a nearby Starbucks. This was not the kind of place Quila usually went. She must have looked bewildered, because after Vicky ordered some impossibly complicated drink she turned to Quila and said, "Oh, do you caffeine?"

"Huh?"

"She'll take an iced caramel macchiato, whip, drizzle, but non-fat." They got their drinks and then Victory dragged Quila over to a small round table. "So, I haven't seen you since, well, since maybe a year ago, I guess." Quila remembered that. She'd been at the mall and run into Victory, who had corralled her and made her go shopping. Then she picked out an outfit for Quila. Then she'd taken them to lunch.

"Uh, I don't want you buyin' me no clothes today, Vic."

"Listen to you! You must be working downtown. Last time I saw you, you were interested in social work. Is that what you're doing now? Oh, Mom will cry when she hears that."

Quila could just see Miss Tiffany with tears streaking down her face. The very thought of Quila redeemed, a part of society, doing good, saving others, that would be a real religious experience for Miss Tiffany. She thought it best if she kept the conversation on Victory and not on Quila's current gig. *And,* she reminded herself, *speak like White folk.* That was easy enough to do, as long as you didn't do it in front of the brothers. Particularly the Blues. That kind of shit really pissed them off. "So, Vic, what are you doing here? Last I knew, you were in college… someplace."

"I was. I graduated. I'm now in the Peace Corps, stationed in Morocco. I work with children in a pediatric physical therapy unit. I'm home now because my grandmother passed away. I came for her funeral."

"Oh, I remember Miss Maude. She was…"

"Difficult, I know. She was a relic of another era. Quila…." Here Victory put her hand over Quila's own. "I hope you can find it in your heart to forgive her. She had her good points. In her own way she was a good person. But she wasn't a very enlightened person. That was always a real struggle for Mother."

Quila remembered Miss Maude questioning her daughter-in-law why she let precious Victoire play with that little Black girl? *That little… girl is going to ruin my granddaughter*, Maude insisted, although she'd used much uglier words. She spoke about Quila like she wasn't even there. Why was Tiffany trying to save a Black girl? *That isn't a White person's job. Leave them to themselves.* Quila could still hear those words ring in her ears.

"I remember her saying I was gonna' get you hooked on drugs." Quila looked at the young woman sitting across from her. Victory's flinch showed that she remembered it as well. "She sure blamed me for Jeremy's problems."

Victory's face contorted in pain. She looked like she had to take a deep breath before she could speak again. "If she only knew the truth. I don't think Mom could ever tell Gran in a way that she understood. Grannie Maude couldn't believe anything about Jeremy that was less than perfect." She turned and, with a faraway look in her eyes, added, "And Jeremy…" She took another deep breath in. "Indeed, less than perfect."

29

Quila thought that was a pretty honest assessment of the situation. A little generous even. She had never been totally sure whether Miss Tiffany had loved her, or whether she had loved her as a charity case. A project to work on. An antidote to whatever sins she felt she needed to atone for. Or maybe just a way to annoy her overbearing mother-in-law? But no doubt about it, Miss Tiffany surely loved her son. He could do no wrong. The whole family worshiped that boy, and it rotted him to his core. Quila felt a bitterness towards Grannie Maude, which dredged up the memories of Miss Tiffany standing up for the little girl against the formidable family matriarch. Quila remembered shaking as she watched Miss Tiffany take on her husband's mother, something Quila had never been able to do with her own mother, and that defiance was a powerful thing to behold. Quila defied her elders, sure, but it was a furtive, sneaking thing, ducking out a window at night and climbing down to run around the streets with her brothers. She might have covertly claimed her independence, but she never had the courage back then to proclaim it to anyone. A girl could end up dead that way. Of course, that was then, and this was now. Now she could throw a mouthful at anyone when she wanted to. She gave Victory a long look, unable to put all that she was feeling into words. "She and Miss Tiffany had some real fights, that was sure," was all she could manage to say. She sipped the cold coffee drink. It was good, if awfully sweet. She didn't usually drink coffee with ice in it. Or whip cream on it. Or with that syrup drizzled on top.

Victory laughed. "My mother, taking on the old guard and defending me and my best friend. Gran was formidable. That took a lot of courage on Mom's part. I'm glad I could come home. It's been complicated for poor Tiffany." She took a thoughtful sip of her coffee. "Oh Quila, we need to do a better job of staying in touch. I want to make sure I get your email address. Are you on WhatsApp or WeChat? Or 4Us or Kan-ECT?" She looked at Quila expectantly. When she didn't get an answer, Victory went on, "Say, why don't you come back to the house with me? I know Mother would love to see you. Hear all your news! Find out what's going on with you."

Going back to Victory's house was about the last thing that Quila wanted to do. She thought fast. "Oh, thanks, but I can't right now. I'm meeting someone. I have plans. And Grandma is expecting me before that."

"I'm so glad to hear that Miss Mayme is still alive! Huh, for some reason I thought she had passed. So glad I was wrong! How is she?" Vic looked so expectantly happy, waiting for the update.

Quila paused. Today was Waleed's birthday, the day she made her annual visit to see him. Grandma Mayme would be there too, as always. Once a year Quila stole some flowers out of the public gardens and carefully laid them over the metal plaque that marked their shared grave. She would sit there and tell them both about all the things that had happened in the past year, the things she could remember. Like when Devan had been shot dead by Biggie back when they were only nineteen. Seemed like ages ago now. Devan's little boy was eight already. He'd threatened Queenie back in high school but she wouldn't get the abortion. She kept that little boy. Said she needed at least one person in this world to love her. Quila had been smarter. She'd never let anyone stick his baby inside of her. She'd never let anything like that stick.

"Quila? How is Miss Mayme?"

"She's not too well, to be honest." Quila took another sip of her ridiculous coffee.

"Oh, I'm sorry. She must be, well, she must be pretty old by now? Please tell her I said hi. I understand, of course, that you have to go and see her." They were quiet for a few moments. "Quila, did you ever find… your mother? I remember how we looked and looked back in high school."

"Nah. She never showed up again. One time, people said they saw her right after we graduated high school, but the boys and I never saw her." Quila shrugged. "I guess she had 'bout the same interest in being a mom as ever. I think she'd had enough. Or maybe she just could never get enough,

31

and it pushed her over the edge. It was hard on Mayme, though, to hear she was around and never see her daughter. Never have Rashida come back and rescue her from us." Quila took a deep breath. "I don't think it was her though. She would have come home if she was around. She would've needed a safe place to stay, if nothing else. I think she'd been gone a long, long time. Gone. Never found."

"I'm so sorry. So, uh…" Victory was obviously looking for something more positive to talk about. "What are you doing now? Working downtown? With children? You always wanted to work with children."

"Actually, I think that was you, Vic. You always wanted to work with children. Like those ladies worked with you. What were their names? Uh…." Quila bit her lip. She hated it when she forgot stuff.

"Fannie and Grace! I remember them. Wow, I hadn't thought about them in just, well, just forever." Victory sat back and smiled. "What a difference they made for me starting when, well, we must have been like three or four when they started to work with me. Followed me all through grade school. What a difference they made for all of us." She was looking pointedly at Quila. "You, too. So, do you work with kids now?"

"I try to not work with kids if I can help it. I do work downtown, but I'm just a courier. I carry, uh, important, expensive stuff between clients."

"Oh, you work for a delivery service! And, uh, how about community college? How did that work out?"

Quila spared her once-upon-a-time friend and shook her head. "Nope. I'm in the blue-collar world, you'd say."

"Oh, sure." It was obvious that Victory was trying to sound bright. "I hope it offers good benefits.".

A slow, sarcastic smile crept across Quila's face. "Yeah, great benefits. It has great benefits."

"So, uh, after you visit Miss Mayme, you said you had plans?"

"Yeah, I'm seeing my boyfriend."

Victory looked most excited to explore this topic. "Boyfriend? Lucky you. I have no such person in my life. It's hard in Morocco. Peace Corps is almost all women, and I work with disabled kids, which is, of course, super meaningful. But I never get to meet anybody. It's kind of lonely to be honest. You know, my mom and dad met in Peace Corps. I'm not sure what I expected." She smiled a little sadly, and then brightened. "So, what's your man's name?"

Quila smiled back at Victory. The girl had always been completely boy crazy in school. Thinking of Vic being without a man of the hour was kind of hard for Quila to wrap her mind around, actually. "I'm with a guy named Jaquan and he's…"

"THE Jaquan? That boy who was a senior when we were freshman in high school?"

Quila nodded her head.

"Oh Quila, honey, not Jaquan. He's bad news! He was dealing in the bathrooms back then. I can only imagine what he's got his hands into now. Wasn't he involved with a gang? Quila, you've got to get out of there. He'll be the death of you. Come back with me. Let Tiffany see what she can do. Or Daddy."

Quila wrenched her hand away from Victory's grasp. "I love Jaquan." It felt weird to hear her voice say it. When she told him her voice always had great conviction, but now it rang hollow in front of such a different audience and when telling a lie convincingly didn't equate with saving your life.

"But he's in a gang. Quila, that's so dangerous. And your brother's involved in, well, a different gang … still… I mean, isn't he? Isn't that a little bit like Romeo and Juliet? You know that ended badly."

"Who?" Quila found it sickening how Vicky could look so earnest when she said shit like that. Who cared about some Latinx dude and his White girlfriend? She knew nothing 'bout those people and Victory knew nothing 'bout nothing. What was dangerous was coming from a family that was allied Red and sleeping with one of the leaders of the Blues. Being in a gang wasn't

33

dangerous. Crossing gangs was just playing roulette every day, your life hanging in the balance if you got caught on the wrong side of the color line. But if you could play both sides, you could bargain to save your brother's life. It left you stuck in the middle, but Deyonte was still alive. Jaquan had let him go, for Quila. Quila felt her face get hot. "Don't you be tellin' me what to do or who to date. You such a goodie-two-shoes, Vic. Stop trying to save me. I don't need your White Savior act." She felt a flush of embarrassment, remembering when Victory had arranged for her to go to that rehab place—more swank than she'd ever seen the likes of. She checked out A.M.A. And then later on Vic had signed her up for community college. Even went with her to classes a couple of times. It was like having a babysitter… as a grown up. Then she left to go to someplace far away. "You go off to hell and back… or wherever you goin'." In her frustration she slipped back to her more everyday vernacular, forgetting to speak like Victory.

"Morocco. It's in Africa."

"Africa? You in Africa?" Quila felt frozen. *Of course, Victory got to go to Africa.*

Victory nodded, her head bobbing up and down like one of those hyper little dogs rich people had.

Quila got a hold of herself. "Yeah right, you go save those little African butts but you leave my ass alone. Believe it or not, I'm saving little African butts here, too."

"Quila…"

"I'm not like you, Vic. I don't have your choices. I never had your chances. I got these streets. This town."

"You could have different choices. Let me help you!"

"You know nothin' 'bout it. You go and tell your mama that I'm a social worker. That I done good. She'll sleep better. An let me live my life." Quila stood up to leave.

"You don't have to lie about it. It's okay… together we can…"

Quila turned on her former friend, the goody-two-shoes-girl that now she couldn't fathom how they'd ever gotten along. "And just what did I ever gain from being good? That's your privileged white ass, Vic. That's not my life. Good got me hungry. Good got me orphaned. There ain't no escape from my world through *good*. Victory—the first time in my life I got regular meals was my six months in jail. And a bed to sleep in that wasn't a bug infested couch. And my bed, that I wouldn't come home and find some stranger in, 'cause my grandma had rented my room out for the week so she could afford her medicines. Good never brought me nothin'." Everyone in Starbucks had gone quiet and were staring at the two girls now. Quila ignored the tear in Victory's eye. There was no way that chick could ever understand her. Could ever imagine Quila's life, much less live it. They came from different worlds.

"No. You were always my best friend growing up. I'm not going to leave you here. You've got to come with me." Victory grabbed her arm, but Quila wrenched free.

"Bitch, leave off. I ain't yo' charity project no more. I ain't you ticket into heaven."

"No… Quila, please…"

"You don't need to cry over me, bitch." Quila got up and left the table. She couldn't figure out why, but she felt tears streaming down her face as she ran out of the coffee shop.

The Well-Dressed Man leaned back in his chair. "So dramatic, Tequila. You've really got a flair for the sensational. Even in the way you think."

"Maybe in the way I die…"

"Humph." He laughed. "Indeed. You know, this is interesting. This friend of yours. The one who is, shall we say, hell bent on saving you? She keeps showing up in your story, but she doesn't show up in any of my rosters. Tell me about her."

"She ain't my friend."

35

"She shows up in nearly every important detail of your life. My little fire cloud only shows the key elements, so she must be *something* to you. And her name was the last word you spoke."

"Yeah, what about it? If you some type of supernatural parole officer or maybe my crypt-keeper therapist, I thought you was going to show me my court cases. The couple of arrests. The fight in jail."

"Oh that. Boring. Predictable. Routine."

"Was worth it. I got to stay two extra months. More of a home than I ever had."

"Funny," he said, scrolling through more scenes in the cloud, "these images make it look like you kind of had a home over at…"

"Don't you say her name."

"Why not?"

"I don't like it when you say her name."

The Well-Dressed Man chuckled. "To be honest, you seemed a little overwhelmed by your circumstances back there."

"I was doin' all right."

"You were off to meet a man who regularly threatened you. Occasionally beat you. You were carrying for him at this point, right?"

She nodded. "You just couldn't say no to him. There was no give and take with him. He just take, take, take."

"I see. And then you run into Victory and she offers to help you. I'm curious. My read on this whole situation is that you're actually kind of scared here. So, tell me, when you saw an escape route, when it popped up right in front of you, why didn't you climb on board that train and get the hell out of town? After all, you'd been asking for just that. An escape. As you fell asleep at night, you'd cry and…"

"You listen to me! I don't need her white-ass privilege to save me."

The Well-Dressed Man leaned toward Quila. "Not two months after this you narrowly missed going down in yet another deal gone bad. Then six months later you OD'd."

"I managed okay after that."

"You were living on the street for a while there."

"So? I was livin."

"And you were shot dead less than eighteen months later."

"I did all right," she shot back at him. Then added a bit uncomfortably, "Up 'til then."

He looked at her and laughed. "Pride. I love pride. Particularly false pride. It's the bread and butter of my world. Brings so much food through my doors, don't you know? But of course, you know that."

"I be a living, breathing example, huh?" Too late she realized that the sneer in her voice might not help her in the situation she found herself.

He looked at her intently. Almost hungrily. "I would say you're an unliving, non-breathing example of it actually, but maybe I'm just getting hung up on technical details. Let's go back to Victory."

Quila rolled her eyes.

"Oh, that's right—you don't like to hear her name. I suppose I could call her 'Miss Goody-Two-Shoes'. While that doesn't seem to be in your particular vernacular, it was your choice of, well, was that supposed to be an insult?"

Quila was sure he was smirking. She fidgeted in her chair. "It was something that Miss Tiffany always said. Man, those bitches was always tryin' to save me. One thing after another. They was always tryin' to make me White."

"Oh, was that what they were doing? Interesting. So, when Victory failed with you, she decided to work on the whole of Africa? Goody-two shoes indeed."

"Naw, she didn't go to Africa because I failed as her pet project. Naw." Quila thought that would be really messed up. "She and her mama wanted me to go to college. Shit, like that was gonna' happen."

"Not in a million years." The Well-Dressed Man shook his head. "But you spoke White to her."

"I did not."

"Sure, you did. Shall I rewind and we look at that scene again?"

Quila stared him down and took a deep breath just to show him she could. She mimicked how Victory would have spoken. "Spare me. Although I can see the delight in your eyes, let's move on, shall we?"

"Sure, if you insist, but don't pretend you can't code switch."

Now it was Quila's turn to sound derisive. "Of course, I can. How do you think I managed to stay alive for so long? The streets aren't an easy place to navigate."

"Interesting. You know, Quila, I think you're quite a bit smarter than you let anyone see. There is, or there was, a lot more to you than meets the eye." He drummed his fingers on the table. "Interesting."

Chapter 5

"Let's take another look, shall we? I'm sure we can find something amusing here. Oh, yes, I think this will be most entertaining." He cued up another vision of her life, with a high school hallway coming into view.

"Oh, not her. I hate her." Quila turned away.

"I could do this forever, you know. Or it could just feel like forever. Your choice."

She turned back towards the white billowing cloud and saw an image of her fifteen-year-old-self walking down the hallway, hair in braids, tight to her head and flowing down the back of her neck, and giant hoop earrings. She said something that she couldn't quite make out, but remembered as being very rude, to another girl in long braided extensions, wildly painted gel nails, and an expensive spangly jacket. As Quila walked away the other girl shoved a fist behind her back and then slowly began to smile. She scuttled down the hall until she found who she was looking for—her twin, donning similar extensions, nails, and jacket. She whispered into her doppelganger's ear and they both doubled up with laughter.

"That Tamoya ain't nothin but a bitch," Quila sneered as she watched the images.

In the cloud, Tamoya walked up to Victory. "Tori, honey. Let me borrow your phone."

"What for?" Victory sounded more than a bit nervous.

"'Cause Jamoya and I want to take a picture. For you."

Victory looked at them, confusion written across her face.

Tamoya gave an exaggerated sigh. "Of us. For you. For summer. You know, girl, something to remember us by. I just gotta' go and find her. I'll bring it right back. I'll meet you right back here. Ten minutes, tops." Tamoya gave her a big smile and leaned in over the smaller girl. She reached out her hand, her nails more than two inches long and every one a different base color. All were decorated with intricate designs. Some even had crystal sparkles resting on the paint. "C'mon! Hand it over!"

Victory cowed and her hand shook a little as she handed over her phone. "You promise not to break it?"

"I would never break your phone. You cool, girl." Tamoya had to firmly twist the phone out of Victory's grasp. "You run and get some lunch."

Victory watched Tamoya walk away and then hurried off towards the cafeteria. Soon the cloud image showed her coming back to the hallway. There was no sign of Tamoya. Then a yell broke through the air. Victory heard it. Everyone heard it.

"You bitch! Jus' you wait. I gonna' get you. We gonna' settle this once and for all. Like right now."

It was Quila. She came around the corner looking at her phone, heading up fast to Victory.

Victory looked a bit like a cornered rabbit. "Quila, what's happening? What's got you so high key?"

"Look at this, Vicky. Look at this shit."

Victory took Quila's phone, blinking as she stared at the message, now long gone. "Oh my god, Quila. I didn't send you a snapchat. I know that's my phone that sent it, but that wasn't me. I didn't do that!" Victory gave Quila an earnest look. "Whatever that was. I haven't gotten my phone back yet."

Quila looked down at her. "I know you didn't, girl. That not like you. But you loaned your phone to them bitches, and that was a dumb ass move, Vic. A dumb ass move."

40

Victory leaned around Quila's shoulder and looked behind her friend. "And speak of the twin devils, there they are."

Tamoya and Jamoya came around the corner barely able to stand up, they were laughing so hard.

"Uh, Quila. Just what did they send you?" Victory asked.

Quila gave her a hard look. "I'm not gonna' dignify it by telling you. Your mama would call it vulgar. I can just hear her voice in my head. *Vulgar.*" She looked at the girls coming towards her. "We gonna' settle this. Once and for all. Right here." She turned to Victory. "Vic, you hold these." She took out her oversize hoop earrings.

"We didn't say nothin' to you that you didn't deserve, you 'ho," Jamoya taunted.

Quila turned back to Victory. "Here, you hold my phone."

Victory took the phone and then three quick steps back. A boy's voice shouted *Fight! Fight! Fight!* and almost instantaneously a chorus of voices joined them, people rushing in to make a circle. Victory was pushed to the front. As the three girls went at it, teenagers were screaming, some with encouragement, some telling them to stop, many chanting *Fight! Fight!* Victory cried out as she watched her own phone hit the floor and break apart, having been dropped by one of the twins. Then a long braided hair extension fell on her shoulder as grabbing hands pulled free anything they could get a hold of. Victory startled as something hit her in the face. She shook herself and looked down. It was a long artificial nail, painted in a spectacular array of colors and glinting with a little crystal. She wormed her way through the crowd and took off running for the principal's office.

The Well-Dressed Man turned to look at Quila. "There's kind of a lot of that sort of thing here to review, but entertaining as that was," he yawned, "I'm not sure there's much to learn there."

"Why do you keep throwing *her* in my face?"

"Her? I believe that's the first time we've reviewed your relationship with the, uh, twins."

"I don't mean them bitches. I beat the shit outta' them. Them fakers never bothered me no more. I mean Vic. It's her privileged white ass over and over again. Like I didn't have enough of that before. Always dangling the life I didn't have in front of me. Always two thousand steps ahead and I never was gonna' catch up. I hate that bitch."

"Hmmmm?"

"You know, like hot breakfast. I mean whoever in the world eat a hot breakfast? We was lucky to get anything at all, but over at Victory's it was always hot breakfast. That rich folk food. And dessert. Like who ever eat dessert? Grandma Mayme never had enough food for all a mama's kids. Shit, we each got to eat two nights and then it was our turn to just go ta' bed 'cause we had to take turns going hungry. Then after Miss Tiffany learnt about that she brought us a Thanksgiving dinner every year. And a Christmas one. And one at Easter. And we ate like the rich folk for a day. But Vicky's family ate like that every day. Man, no one I knew ate like that."

"You sound jealous. Jealousy is so delicious."

"Jealous? Naw, shit, I'm not jealous."

"Sure, you are. Her food. Her home. Her clothes. Her nose job. How'd you get that phone anyway?"

"Devan was my man. He give it to me."

"Hmmm, he doesn't seem to show up much," the man said as he studied the cloud.

"Nah, he bit it at nineteen. He talk too much. It cost him."

"But Victory seems to have a supporting role to the movie of your life."

Quila jumped in her chair. "Don't you show me no more of her. It just wasn't fair. She had everything, everything handed to her. I was just some hand-me-down little pet."

He raised his eyebrows and stared at her.

Quila stared him down until she started to squirm in her chair. "That how Biggie told it. He call me Tori's little pet. I hate that bitch."

"Interesting. Victory does seem to come into your story a lot, doesn't she? But that's not my doing, that's yours. Believe me, having to watch Little-Miss-Goody-Two-Shoes is no pleasure. I wondered if you were making that float to the top just to torment *me* with it. Ironic, when torment is supposed to be up my alley." He laughed again and Quila felt a shiver down her spine.

"Why we have to do this? Look at all this shit? There ain't no point to this."

"Point? Perhaps not, but it is protocol. We always follow protocol."

"You told me I be dead. I bit it. It's over. One and done."

He turned to look at her, gazing at Quila over his fingertips. "It's not one and done, my dear. Nothing, and I mean nothing, is for free. You get away with nothing in life. The bill always comes due. The protocol is to weigh your life and see how you lived it. To see what you're worth."

Quila was afraid to ask but she heard herself utter the words anyway. "An I got a… a big bill?" She desperately tried to think of all the things she had done, and those that she had left undone. While she'd been a delivery mule, she'd never once pulled a trigger. While she'd stolen clothes and food from stores when she needed them, she'd never showed up when the others broke into a house or a business. She didn't even keep the edge when asked. Small time fights. Wasted opportunities. That could leave you with a big bill?

"You? Nah." He shook his head. "You were small time. Hardly worth my effort. Now Mister Number Eight out there—he's got a big bill. Incited hatred and violence. Acted through others. Made policy to institutionalize prejudice and hatred. Did deals to make his friends rich. Thought he got away Scot free." The mirth in his voice was evident. She thought he almost looked… excited. "He's got a big bill."

Chapter 6

"Then why you want me? I think you should just let me go. Like a small fish, too small to bother with." Quila didn't actually have much hope he'd take her suggestion but under the circumstances, she was doing the best she could. She'd had to fast-talk her way out of a lot of tight situations, but this guy was like dealing with the devil. A prickly sensation started on the back of her neck. Feeling much more wary, she sat up and looked at the man across the desk. He was back to scrolling through the cloud.

"No 'one and done'. No one gets away. Let's look at another one. Three's our regulated minimum here so let's see if we can find a good one. Oh, this might be promising. Say, how old are you here?"

She looked at the images reflected on the cloud. "Oh, I know that day. I was in seventh grade. What is that? Thirteen? Yeah, about that."

"Looks like a nice place. Where are you?"

"Oh, that be Victory's house. Yeah, swank. Nice crib."

"Spend a lot of time there?" He was looking straight at her.

"Uh, yeah. Back then. Not later. But back then."

"Why was that? I mean, if you hated Victory so much?"

"I didn't hate her. Not then. We, uh, grew different. Went different ways. Before Devan came along, when we was back in middle school me and Vic was pretty tight. Her mama wanted more than anything to save me. She wanted to see me go to college." Quila snorted in disbelief. "All through

45

elementary school and middle school she have me come home with Victory most every day. We do our homework together."

"Oh, I see. She was kind of like another mother to you."

"Nah. I never had no mother. She was a nice lady who wanted to feel good about her White privilege and deal with her weird guilt about bein' White by helping a poor Black kid. But I was beyond help. There was no way to climb over the walls and get out."

"No way? Hmmm. Interesting. So, you were caught in a trap. Interesting. Well, I'm curious about this day of yours that popped up. Shall we?"

A woman in her late thirties or early forties was sitting at the table in a beautiful modern kitchen, going over papers. The back door opened and in walked a girl, her blonde hair in a pigtail. Behind her was a taller girl, much thinner, with her curly black hair in big puffball pigtails at the top of her head.

Hi kids! How was your day?"

"Good, Mom," Victory said as she grabbed a banana out of the bowl.

"It was good, Miss Tiffany," young Quila replied.

"Go ahead, Quila. You can have a piece of fruit. Fruit's good for you! The bananas should be ripe. They were a little green yesterday." Tiffany curled her lip a bit as she described the green banana. "They're too starchy for me when they're green." She got up and took her empty glass over to the dishwasher, where she started to load up the dishes left in the sink.

Quila took an orange out of the bowl but didn't say anything.

"Do you like oranges better?" Tiffany chattered away as Quila shot Victory a look. She wanted the banana. She hated feeling the label though. She could hear the teasing from school ringing in her head, "Bananas for Quila 'cause she's a monkey!" Quila didn't say anything, but she nodded her head.

"Well then, I'll make sure I buy more oranges from now on. Do you like navels or maybe blood oranges?"

46

"What a blood orange?"

Tiffany stopped loading the dishes and looked at Quila for a moment. "It's just another type. A bit sweeter. They have kind of a reddish color on the inside. But if you like oranges, then you'd probably love a blood orange. I'll pick some up next time I'm at the store."

Quila thought about what it must be like to be able to just 'pick up at the store' whatever you wanted. Grandma Mayme counted her pennies. Victory's mom never counted anything. Quila wondered if her own mom ever counted anything. She probably counted tricks for a while, but once she got so soaked into the drugs, who knew what she counted then? She'd been gone for years. They couldn't even find out whether she was dead or alive. She was just a missing person. That was the worst part—not knowing. That she was out there someplace. Or she wasn't. Maybe Quila could find her. Or maybe she was no place to be found.

"So, today was the big social studies Civil War speech day. You've been upstairs in Victoire's room practicing all week long. How did it go?" Tiffany leaned over the kitchen island and looked at the girls.

"It was okay," said Victory. "You know, it was kinda' fun, actually. I liked being a northern abolitionist. It gave me a chance to stand up in front of the class and yell—and not get in trouble for it." Vicky laughed and her mother chuckled along with her.

"Yes, I could hear you practicing the yelling all way the downstairs before you left for school. And how about you, Quila? How'd it go?"

"All right."

"I never heard you practice. What point of view did you take?"

"I spoke as a slave. Against slavery."

"Oh my!" Tiffany was clearly taken aback. "That must have been interesting. Or hard. How was that, honey? I imagine it was… well maybe, kind of traumatic? Or, uh, triggering?"

Quila looked at her orange and then looked up at Ms. Tiffany. "It was great," she said with confidence. "In fact, the teacher pull me aside at the end of class and said I had the most powerful speech of the entire room."

Tiffany's eye's widened. "Oh, honey! That's wonderful!" She came over and enveloped Quila in a big hug. "I'm so proud of you! That's just wonderful. And what did you say to your teacher?"

"What do you mean?" Quila's face was smushed against Tiffany's chest and it was hard to talk without getting her fuzzy sweater in her mouth.

Tiffany pulled back and looked at Quila. She was still smiling. "Well, you must have said something. It's such a nice thing for the teacher to pull you aside like that. Or wait, she didn't say it in front of the whole class, did she?"

"Oh no. Just to me. Just to me."

"Oh, well, that's good!" Tiffany gave a short laugh. "You wouldn't want her to say, 'Hey everybody, Quila just blew the curve by giving the most powerful speech of all. She gets an A-plus!' When I was in middle school, that was a sure way to make everybody hate you instantly. Better that they don't know. It's middle school, after all."

"Yeah, it's middle school," Quila repeated.

Victory threw her peel in the trash can. "C'mon, let's go upstairs. Mom, we have some homework to do."

"Oh, well, let it never be said that I stood between you girls and homework! Hop along. And oh, Quila, are you staying for dinner tonight?"

Quila had taken five steps toward the door already, but she stopped and turned around. "Yeah, sure. I give my grandma a call."

"Terrific! I'll whip up a quick cake. We can celebrate you giving the most powerful speech of the class!"

"That be nice. Thank you, Ms. Tiffany."

As Quila and Victory walked into the bedroom, Vicky shut the door behind them and tossed her backpack on her bed. She unzipped it and pulled out her notebook. Quila set hers, a match to Victory's and purchased by Tiffany, on a chair. Vicky lay down on the floor with her notebook and spread her homework out around her. Quila followed suit and mirrored her friend. They worked in silence for a while, the orange sitting untouched on the floor beside Quila.

"Are you gonna' eat that?" Victory asked.

Quila looked up, then looked at the orange. "Probably not."

"Then why'd you take it?" Victory didn't look like she was judging Quila, but she did look curious.

"I wanted to take a piece of fruit."

"But you like bananas. I didn't think you liked oranges."

"I don't like oranges very much. Grandma does though."

"Oh. Okay." Victory looked down at her homework again. They worked in silence for a while. Finally, she asked, "Why did you lie to my mother?"

"About the orange?" Quila did not look up.

"No. About the teacher."

Quila looked up. "Whatdaya' mean?"

"She never said that to you. Bell rang and we all just walked out."

"So?"

"So, you were kinda' hard to hear. I know how good your speech was. I know yours was way better than anybody else's. I mean, I've heard you practice it for a week. But you whispered it in the class, like you were scared."

Quila looked down at her paper. She had no idea how to do these math problems in front of her. The minus signs and the plus signs with the numbers were confusing and she couldn't remember what cancelled out what or what added to the other.

"So, why did you lie?"

Quila looked up at her friend and shrugged. She could tell Vicky. She could tell Vicky anything. "I wanted the praise. For once I wanted someone to hug me and tell me I did a good job. I wanted someone to say somethin'

49

nice 'bout my schoolwork. If I told my Grandma she wouldn't even hear me. She nod and say, 'oh that nice' but she never turn away from the television show. I get my own dinner. I eat cereal most nights, when we have it, 'cause that all I know how to make. That all we have… when we have that. Grandma don't even make dinner no more. She say it make her too dizzy. And now your mama makin' me a cake!"

Vicky looked thoughtful. "Was it hard to lie?"

Quila shook her head. "Not anymore."

Chapter 7

"Well now, I rather liked that one. Really illustrates you during your formative years. So, is that when you learned to lie?"

"Shit, no. I figured that out much earlier. Like when the big boys come lookin' for my brother, Deyonte. I learned early on to lie and say he wasn't home. They was gonna' kill him, so he stayed alive because I sent them away. Or lie so I wouldn't get beaten. Mostly I lied so that I wouldn't get something. This time I lied to get something. And I got cake for it." She couldn't help but smile. "Up 'til this point lying only saved me from bad stuff, but this time it brought me good stuff. I still remember that cake. That was a good cake. She sent me home with all the leftovers and my grandma and my brothers all got some. That was some good cake."

"Interesting. Here you are talking about cake and not about how much you hate *Victoire*."

"Not *Vic-twah*. Her name be Victory."

"Victory." He nodded. "Maybe we should go back a bit further?"

"You da boss, baby."

"Glad you're figuring that out. You know, I have a theory that you don't hate her at all. You don't actually even resent her. Jealous, yes, but I'm getting the idea that you love her. She's like a sister to you. You are reflections of one another. Night and day, sure, but like a sister to you."

Quila squirmed in her chair. She felt a lot of emotions that were vague and uncomfortable. A lot of anger that she had gotten stuck with her crap life and a mom who disappeared, leaving a grandma who was too sick to care for the kids, all while privilege and wealth was dangled in front of her. She couldn't have Victory's life, she just stood at the edges of it, catching a crumb here and snatching one there. And she hated her own life, that was true. But the hate didn't extend to Vicky, not really. It bled up to the edges and there it melted away at the only true friendship that Quila had ever known. It was still there, up to that last cup of weird-ass coffee, even though Quila had done everything to spit on the relationship.

"Let's test that theory, shall we? I think this one looks interesting." He looked at the cloud as the images sharpened and came into focus. "You're young here. Maybe kindergarten? Maybe six?"

Quila looked up and at the image. She nodded. "I think I was seven."

"Who's the boy?"

"That Vicky's brother. Jeremy. He got hooked on drugs. Ms. Tiffany had him in and out of rehab but it did no good. He O.D.'d in college. I knew it was gonna' happen. You can tell the ones that can't feel the beat in life, so they think they need more. Jeremy was like that. He wanted to feel more. And sometimes he wanted to feel nothin'."

"You seem to know Jeremy pretty well."

"Jeremy gave me my first hit. Started with pot at thirteen. Up on the roof just outside a second-story window. It went on from there to bigger shit. Up 'til then I never took it from the dealers in my hood, but it was hard to say no to Jeremy. And surrounded by all that privilege, he made it seem safer than it was."

"But it wasn't safe?"

She searched for a way to explain it. "It make you… hungry?"

"That sounds like weed."

"Not that kinda' hungry." She gave him a sarcastic smile. "Not for food. For more. For less. For… what did he call it? Euphoria. And oblivion. But that boy, his mama think he the sunshine of her life, but he lived always in the shadow of the woods." She shivered.

The Well-Dressed Man swung his chair around to look at her. "You, Tequila Williams, are a poet. Who knew you had such a vocabulary? Such a gift for allusion? You talk like you grew up around 'White folk' and not in the projects."

She gave him a steely glance. "I did. I had two childhoods—one with my broken family and one with Victory's. But it hard to escape the drugs and the crime and the pain of poverty and want and hunger and loneliness. There be just so much fear. It eat at you all the time. There is, well, there was… more to me than you saw in them first clips you showed. But there was no room for all of me with the street life. When you live the street life you fit in or you die. You learn to leave parts of yourself behind."

"So, you code switch." He nodded and then put his fingertips together again, looking at her over them. "You did it and you died anyway. So, I wonder if it was worth it to pretend to be something you weren't, just so you'd fit in?"

"You wrong. I did fit in. That was me, too. It was just a part of me. But there was no place that I ever found that could hold all of me."

"Except with Victory?"

"Maybe with Victory."

He turned back to the images reflected in the white, billowing cloud. A young boy, about twelve years old, was walking into a bedroom. After taking three steps past the door, he stopped and looked down. The floor was littered with tiny high heels, doll dress-up evening gowns lying in discarded heaps, and miniature fancy hats. He brushed his long brown bangs back out of his eyes and surveyed the intensely pink room, his lip curling slightly. It made his flawless features tragically haughty—and even more handsome in an empty sort of way. It was a face that was rarely ever told *no*.

"Vic—your room looks like a Pepto-Bismol explosion. It's disgusting."

Amidst the flotsam and jetsam of the exploded doll trunk lay the two girls, Victory in a pink tutu and a sparkly tank top holding a dark-skinned

53

Barbie and Quila in a fairy skirt, an oversized boy's black tank top, and fairy wings, holding a similarly dressed, blonde-haired version of the doll.

"Yetch." In a much-put-upon voice muttered, "Mom told me she needs to take Quila home in about twenty minutes. You guys need to start cleaning up… is that… is that *my* shirt?"

Quila looked up at him. "What Peppy Bismal?" she asked.

"You're wearing my shirt? That's my shirt!" Jeremy took two more steps into the room.

Quila got up from the floor and sat down on her knees, looking down at her shirt. "Yeah, I think so. I got catsup all over mine at lunch and Miss Tiffany give me this one. She said mine needed cleaning."

"To be cleaned," Jeremy corrected automatically, having been corrected by his mother frequently on this very grammatical point.

"What Peppy Bismal?" she asked him again.

"Peppy-Abysmal is this room. It's a nightmare of pink. It's disgusting. That's *my* Higgs-Boson shirt. You can't wear that. Take it off! Grannie Maude gave me that!"

Quila looked down at the shirt again. Words snaked their way across the front, looping to create a gray infinity symbol, which said, *Higgs Boson: all things ending or beginning? When will the God Particle go BOOM?* She could only read the word *Boom!* "What it say?"

"You wouldn't understand. You take that off!"

Quila stood up and looked Jeremy in the eye; hands balling into fists, she said defiantly, "I didn't steal it!"

"Calm down, Jeremy." Victory was still walking her Barbie around in her evening gown. "Mom handed her that because it was on the top of the pile of clean laundry, just until her shirt was clean. It won't kill you for her to wear your shirt for a while." Then she continued to play, humming a little song.

"Yeah, you got a problem with me wearing your shirt?" Quila stood up proudly, her chest out, shoulders back. She tossed her bushy hair back, her tone daring him to make an accusation. Victory looked up, for the first time paying more attention to her brother and her friend than her dolls.

Jeremy looked coolly down at Quila. "Yeah, I got a problem," he said, mimicking her accent.

"Is it because I'm Black?" Quila's voice rang out. Victory slowly looked at Quila, the collection of Barbies at her fingertips forgotten. Quila looked at Jeremy, who looked back at her, gray eyes meeting green. "Well?"

Jeremy took half a step back, her direct defiance making his confidence falter. "No. No, it's not that. It's the *wings*. You're wearing my super cool Higgs-Boson shirt with… with fairy wings!"

"What's Peppy-Bismal?" she asked, even more defiant, not breaking eye contact. Now that she had Jeremy off guard, now that he wasn't being too cool to talk with them, she felt like she had the upper hand. A rare feeling. She felt expanded by the sensation.

"It's pink medicine," he said, sounding ruffled. Then he took a deep breath and in a rush added, "Mom wants you guys to clean up. Time to go home."

"I'll give you your shirt back when I get my shirt back. What's a…" she struggled to remember the name he had said, "the thing that go boom?" She read the only word she could from the front of the shirt.

"Higgs-Boson. It's physics. You wouldn't know about that. You're a first grader." Theatrically, he leaned down towards her and explained with broad gestures, "It's a particle that's so small you can't see it. It's a speck. And it might blow up and explode the universe with it, destruction coming at the speed of light. You'd never know what hit you. *BOOM!*" He leaned in more closely, his hands mimicking an explosion in her face.

Quila jumped.

He stood up straight and with a flat voice announced, "Mom wants you downstairs." He turned and left.

Victory sighed. "He's got a real problem with girls." She rolled her eyes. "As if a girl would want to have anything to do with *him*."

"He got a real problem with fairy wings, too." Quila looked at her friend, nodding knowingly.

Victory giggled. "Don't worry about the peppy stuff. Ever since he had diarrhea and had to take that pink medicine, he keeps saying my room looks like that and calls it *dis-gus-ting*. He hates anything pink."

"It ain't the drugs I was thinkin' of. I seen a lot a drugs. But not a… a boom speck." Quila looked down at the shirt again, willing herself to be able to read the twisting, snaking words, but all she could identify were individual letters and a few simple words. The BOOM jumped out at her and gave her the shivers. Back in her own clothes, she was very quiet on the way home, not listening to the music playing in the car. Victory was loudly singing, *Don't walk in the middle, in the middle, in the middle, in the middle, in the middle, in the middle of the street* along with the chorus of a *They Might Be Giants* song.

Quila was thinking about that boom speck. Is that what had gotten her daddy? The boom speck? She didn't remember him very well, but she imagined that he would have been a lot like Victory's daddy. Always at work, but when finally at home, excited to see his daughter and always wanting to know what she was up to. Bringing her treats and presents, like Dr. Van Dyke always had for Victory and Jeremy.

Quila's Daddy used to pick her up and swing her around. She could remember that. She could feel his strong arms lifting her up and then he would hold her, singing to her softly. She remembered lying in his arms, feeling the safety of sucking her thumb and twiddling his ear back and forth. But the thing that Quila remembered most about her daddy was his eyes, perhaps because they were gray like hers, and her Grandma Mayme always said that she had her daddy's way of looking at things. She also remembered expecting him to come by at Christmas the year before this last one. She had been a little girl of six. She couldn't remember what she had gotten for Christmas. Maybe there hadn't been anything.

Mama had been around back then. They had eaten Christmas dinner at the food store where Mama shopped but didn't have to pay for anything. Without even closing her eyes she could recall how she waited and waited and finally fell asleep waiting. Waiting for her daddy. It was the crying that woke her up. Her mother and her grandma holding each other, Grandma Mayme holding Quila's mama while she cried and sobbed. Quila didn't know what they were crying about but she knew better than to ask, knew better than to let them know she was awake. Lying on the couch, feigning sleep, she lay still and listened. If they knew she was awake, they would send her to bed and she wouldn't find out what was going on. Her mother never told her anything. She always said it was better if she didn't know.

"He got it in the back. He never saw it comin!'" Rashida sobbed into her mother's arms. "They said they was gonna do it. They said they was. I told him to stay in that place. Even if he had to hurt someone. I told him to hit a guard. Let them beat him for it but to stay in there. At least he was safe there. They couldn't get to him there."

"There, there, sugar. There, there. He a good man. They was gonna' let him out. He couldn't stay." Grandma hugged and rocked her daughter.

"He *wouldn't* stay. He want to see his children. He want to see them at Christmas. He said the bighouse was too shit to stay at during the holidays, what with the fake Christmas dinner and them jive holiday wishes that just mean shit!"

"And he was gonna', he was gonna' be here with his family. In jus' two days he would have been here." Mayme wiped tears from her cheeks with her sleeve, continuing to pat her daughter on the back.

"He never saw it comin'. He thought he could hide, and they wouldn't find him. But Bison found him. He said he would. TaeQuan told me it was jus' BOOM, and it was over. He was lyin' in the street in a pool of his own blood." She sobbed again. "He got it in the back. He never even had time to look around!" She blew her nose on some toilet paper that was lying on the table. "What am I gonna' do now? How am I gonna' feed these children?"

"You find a way, sugar, you find a way. The Lord will look after you." Mayme patted her. "We have to have faith in the Lord." After a while she asked, "And what did TaeQuan say happen next?"

"After he fell, the Crips left, Bison ran oft with his guys. They jus ran oft. TaeQuan, he and the brothers, they check him, and he was dead. They left him in the street before the cops come. You know them cops."

Mayme shook her head sadly. "Any brother will do if they need to charge a body with murder. Any brother will do. They best get outta' there." The two women were quiet for several minutes. Quila hardly dared to breathe. This was her father they were talking about. She was sure of it. And it had been *boom!*

"What will you tell Quila and Rasheed and Deyonte?"

"What can I tell them? That Daddy couldn't come home from college? That Daddy had to stay there for Christmas? That I not sure when Daddy will come home? I can't jus go and tell them he dead. I can't tell them he gunned down by them damn Crips, angry because he ratted one a them to the judge so he could cut short his time."

"Truth will out, sugar, truth will out, like my mama always said."

"Well, maybe after Christmas." Rashida began to cry again.

Quila lay on the couch, unable to listen to them after that. So, Daddy wasn't coming home for Christmas. He wasn't ever coming home from Bighouse College again. Something had happened to him. Something called a crip had gotten him in the back and they left him lying in the street. That much she had understood. That memory stood out for her, emblazoned on her mind. Quila couldn't smile that holiday. She knew. She couldn't turn to her mother for comfort because she didn't want to risk Rashida's temper if she found out that she'd been listening.

Rashida was too distracted by her own grief to pay much attention to her four children. Relatives and friends came in and out of the apartment. Quila noticed they passed around brown paper lunch sacks which were quickly hidden away. Strangers showed up. The police came by and the children were shuttled upstairs. The social workers rang the bell, but Rashida wouldn't let them in the house. "Can't trust 'em. Can't trust 'em," she'd growl. It seemed that everyone shot furtive, sad looks at Quila and her brothers. Many gave them hugs, a few brought them toys that only had minimal signs of having been used by other children. But no one said anything.

Quila knew that her mother was taking medicine that came out of the brown lunch sacks. Peeking around corners late at night, having snuck out of bed to find out more about what was going on, she would see her mother staring at the wall for what seemed hours, a crumpled brown paper bag next to her. Those days she spent a lot of time sleeping on the couch while Rasheed and Deyonte made peanut butter sandwiches and microwaveable mac and cheese to eat. People she didn't know brought over food, and they ate that, too, while Rashida was unable to get up and take care of them. The TV was on all the time. It seemed like an endless haze in which Quila didn't know what to do next.

On a night when Quila's crying made it impossible for her to fall asleep, Deyonte whispered irritably, "What up with you?" She climbed out of her bed and went over the bunk beds her brothers shared, climbing into the bottom bunk with Rasheed.

"He dead, Rasheed. Daddy dead. He got it in the back. He never saw it coming. I heard Mama crying with Grandma."

"Naw, he not. He just had to stay at college." Deyonte's tone was derisive. "He gonna' come home and it gonna' be better. We won't have to live in the projects no more. He gonna' take care of us. He promised! We gonna' get a car! He told me so."

Rasheed looked up at her with his huge brown eyes. "He gonna' help Mama keep straight and strong. Stay away from the paper bags. He come home, you jus' wait and see."

Quila teared up again. "No. He got it in the back. He never saw it comin'. Our daddy dead in the street. The Bison got him."

59

"I don't believe you. Go sleep in you own bed. Daddy fine. You see," Deyonte hissed.

Quila slipped out of the bed and crawled back between her own covers. She could hear Rasheed sniffling from across the room.

"Deyonte?" she whispered. "What's a Bison?"

"I don't know. Go to sleep."

"Quila? Quila, honey! Earth to Quila." Tiffany called Quila back from her memories. *They Might Be Giants* were now singing a song about a clock always saying the time is 4:02. "We're here, honey, you're home."

Quila shook herself and came back to the present. She took a quick breath and said, "Thanks Miss Tiffany. Jeremy, I'm sorry I wore your Piggy-Bison shirt. I hope the wings don't ruin it."

Jeremy was reading a graphic novel, deeply absorbed in his cartoon. "Yeah, whatever. No problem."

Quila turned to her friend. "Victory, I had fun at the playdate." The two girls hugged each other.

Victory took the Black Barbie out of her little backpack. "I want you to have this." She had dressed it in a hot pink evening gown. The figure was wearing tiny little wings and matching spiky high heels. "She wants to be with you."

Quila teared up and hugged Victory. "I love her." The two girls giggled.

"Bye, Quila." Victory was bright eyed. "See you at school!"

"Yeah, see you at school." Quila smiled, and got out of the car, hugging the Black Barbie to her chest.

"Honey, do you want me to walk you to your door?" Tiffany asked. "It looks kind of dark in there. Are you sure people are at home?"

"Mom," Jeremy looked up annoyed. "It must be like twenty feet to the door. She's seven. She's not helpless."

"Jeremy!" Tiffany scolded, but her tone was gentle. "You are twelve years old. I expect you to act it!"

"Thanks, Miss Tiffany, but Jeremy right. I let myself in all the time. Thanks again. I had fun!" She smiled and waved at them.

Quila walked up to her front door. It was unlocked. She knew it would be. Before disappearing inside she turned, waved again and smiled at Miss Tiffany's car. She took a deep breath and stepped inside the smoky, dim interior. She had just left one world—a world of bright pink walls, princess beds, more snacks than you could eat, more toys than you could play with—toys in perfect condition that clearly had hardly been touched. And now she was back in her old world. She took a deep breath as if to bring the fresh air with her. She hugged the little doll to her chest.

Her mother was asleep on the couch again and her baby brother was crying in the playpen. Mama wouldn't wake up. Quila knew she wouldn't. She never woke up when the baby cried. Quila set down her little backpack and doll and helped the one-year-old out of the playpen. Waleed's diaper smelled. She sighed.

"Well, I changed about a million baby dolls over at Victory's. I suppose I can fix you up, too."

The shabby diaper bag was in the corner and she got out the mat, a pack of wipes, a fresh diaper and she did her best. She had helped Rashida do this before, but she'd never done it on her own. After she was done, she washed her hands and got a bottle of cold milk out of the fridge, helping her little brother drink and gently patting him on the back, although she wasn't sure why that part was important. He sat up and looked at her as he sucked away at the bottle, apparently ravenous. She looked over at the couch, surveying the unconscious form of her mother. "Man, Waleed, we both need a mama!"

Chapter 8

The image faded away leaving just the billowing cloud. "Pretty heavy for a seven-year-old." Somehow the man sounded neither sympathetic nor comforting. If anything, she would have called it sarcastic.

She gave him a withering look.

"So that was your mother."

"Yeah. By the next Christmas she was gone. She wasn't much of a mama before Daddy was shot, but she was sure no kinda' mother afterward."

"What killed her?"

"Don't know. Thought you might. You seem to be all knowing here with your weird little fire-pit-shit and home-movie-cloud. We never heard nothin' 'bout her after she disappeared. I told myself she went off to college like my daddy had. It wasn't until I was almost in middle school that I learnt there no Bighouse College. He'd been in prison. Grandma didn't want to tell me. Didn't want me to know. Poor Mayme never wanted me to know nothin'. But truth was Mama spent most of that last year drugged up on the couch. I don't know whether she crawled out the door or if Grandma told her to leave and go die someplace else. My grandma was an old woman by the time I born. She in her late forties there," Quila nodded at the billowing cloud. "But she had diabetes. High blood pressure. Smoked, even so. She'd a hard life and my mama made nothin' easier. Mama had Deyonte, and I never met his daddy. Then Rasheed. His daddy would come and see him for a while. Bobby was Waleed's and my daddy. Until the Bison got him."

"And did you ever learn the difference between the Higgs-Boson and a Bison?"

"Didn't matter, did it? They both go boom. They both end your world. What the difference? Same effect. I like to think that Daddy could have held things together. I know we never would be the Van Dykes. Never would have been Victory's family, but maybe we could been a family? But he was shot dead, boom, left in the street, his friends too afraid to pick him up or they be charged with murder by lazy-ass police who didn't care nothin' 'bout the truth."

"Huh. You had a hard life, Tequila Williams. You never stood a chance."

"Should I say thanks for that?"

"So, what happens to you next?" He stared at her, hard, like he was boring more holes into her with his eyes. As if she needed more holes. From what she could tell, she had plenty and some to spare.

"Does it matter? Like you said, I never had me a chance. Does it matter what happen next?"

"No. I suppose it doesn't. And truth be told, you aren't worth much to me. There isn't much to you."

She thought she should feel offended, but she remembered his delight at Mr. Number Eight in the waiting room with the never-ending panic attack and decided that not being worth much and not being interesting might be a good thing in this case.

The man slapped the desk, making her jump. "Tequila Williams, this is your lucky day! I'm going to make you a deal. A deal you can't refuse." He chuckled. "Quite literally in this case."

She looked at him warily. "What kind a deal?"

"You didn't do much good in your life. Okay, so you changed some diapers while your mother was incapacitated on the couch, but really, other than that you're pretty small time. But that Victory, now she seems to be pretty interesting. *Victoire*, you said? High class. Quite the goody-two shoes. Mission trips. Peace Corps. Enough to make me vomit. I think I'm going to give you a second chance."

"A second chance? A second chance at what?"

"At life."

"Huh?"

"Yes. I think I'm going to send you back. Give you a second chance at your life. Tell you what, I won't send you 'on' as planned and you can go back and try to do it differently, perhaps."

"You gonna' send me into Victory's family? Do I get to live her life?"

He laughed, almost cruelly. "Ah, a real movie-made-in-heaven, huh? No. Your slot is slated for you. What you do *with* it is up to you."

"How can I do differently if you send me back to where I come from? There was no food. There was no help with school. Ever. There was nothin' but bein' 'fraid all the time. Nothin' could ever turn out different if I stuck in that life. You can't climb out of that bucket!" She was seething inside. "What would you know, with your fancy suit and your bad ass office. You ain't never had to crawl out of what I had to crawl out of."

He leaned forward, looking at her with a hungry leer. "Wanna bet? I'd love to show you what I've had to crawl out of." There was something eerie about the way his face contorted when he spoke.

She leaned away from him, realizing she really didn't want to see his life story in that cloud he commanded. She shook her head ever-so-slightly.

He just looked at her with that little smile on his face. "I'm going to send you back *aware.*"

"What in the hell do that mean?"

"What in the hell indeed?" He laughed again. "You have a great sense of humor. I'm going to send you back *knowing*. Being aware."

"Just what good is that gonna' do me?"

"I don't know. I suppose it'll be what you make of it. But there is a catch."

"A catch?"

"Oh yes. You get nothing for free. I'm going to give you a second chance and we'll see what you can make out of it. But I have a price."

She looked at him suspiciously. "And that be…"

"I want Victory."

"You want… what?"

"Not what. Who. I want Little Miss Goody Two Shoes."

"Then why don't you just call her in like you did me when she bites it?"

"Oh, she won't show up here. Not like that. She'll have another review board. They'll watch the scenes of her spending three months of her pitiful salary on a decent burial plot and headstone for you. Or her year in AmeriCorps trying to save inner city kids. And of her eight-year-old self asking for donations to the local food pantry instead of birthday presents. Of her giving you her absolute most favorite Barbie doll when she was seven years old. Revolting really. I'm so glad I'm spared all that sentimental tripe." He looked at her hard. "Oh, spare me," he said as he rolled his eyes. "Now you're getting all sentimental too. But of course. That very same Barbie doll is still sitting in your shoebox of treasures, isn't it? You had so little left in the world when you made your dramatic ending, and that was the one thing you kept for all those years. Why, Quila? Why was that?"

Quila felt naked in front of this man. Everything about her life was laid bare. The conditions. Her hopes and frustrated desires. Even her thoughts and feelings. Quila nodded as she was hit with a wave of something that was hard to name. He would call it revulsion, she was sure. But she thought it might be love. She loved Victory. Her best friend. She felt intense longing for the happiness they had shared all those years of their childhood and a sharp pain at what had happened to their friendship as they grew up. How it had slipped away as the stark difference in their circumstances cut a chasm so deep that she felt drowned by the pain and injustice of it all. "Victory a good person."

"I know. Gross, isn't it? But the good news is that she doesn't have to be! Her kind of soul is rather rare and, if I say so, utterly delicious. You know, those who are truly good rarely fall from the path."

"They do if they the TV preachers Grandma Mayme watches. They was in the news."

"Yes." He gave a heavy sigh. "There are those who use false goodness as a cloak to distract everyone around them so they can cover their tracks. Preachers, politicians, and the self-professed 'saved'; those who use their good deeds like a veil while they rob others blind, cheat their way through, or mimic piety while they satisfy their petty desires… Oh I've got vaults and vaults full of souls like that." He snorted. "Boring. I leave them to my administrative assistants to deal with, as they don't merit my full attention. Of course, to the Junior Ministers those types provide wonderful

67

entertainment, fabulously painful delight to the Junior Ministers. Ravenously hungry, they are." He chuckled. "They always appreciate me passing those types along to them. But if I could get a soul like Victoire's…" He pronounced her name the French way. "Ahhh, that would be something new in my world of endless same-ness. She would be a real delight. Someone *authentic* who fell from the path. The *real thing,* here, in my halls."

Quila shivered at the sound of his voice. "Victory is the real thing. Wait a minute? Did you just tell me you have a bureaucracy here? Junior ministers? Administrative assistants?"

"Of course! You think all this runs itself? I tell you, leadership is like a plague. If they had told me how much paperwork there was, I never would have taken the job. And now I'm stuck with it for all eternity. All predictability and so little fun. But Little Miss Victoire could be quite fun."

Quila shook her head. "I spent nearly my whole lifetime with her. She won't change. She be who she be."

"She would do it for you," he gave her a look. "She could fall like you did. It would only take a little push. She could live a life as desperate and depraved as yours was, Tequila Williams. It wouldn't take much. It never does. No one is actually Job. They can't endure the plagues and remain faithful. They all turn. And you can turn Victory. You know her better than anyone. You can turn her towards me. And then, when I have her, just maybe I'll let you go."

"What would you do with Victory?" Quila asked. She was shocked. She was offended. And afraid. Afraid for Victory.

He was quiet for a moment, and then answered, "Whatever I like. Oh, it would be delicious to have Ms. Goody Two Shoes in my realm. Someone so pure and mighty to have fallen to, well, to your level."

Defiance and anger swelled up in Quila. She felt like a Mama Tiger. "You can't have her! I won't do it!" Quila tried to stand up and resist him, but she was stuck to the chair. She struggled and squirmed.

He laughed, rocking with the enjoyment of watching her. "You don't have a choice. You will go back. But about that little gift. Some tokens to remember me by. I'll give you wisdom. Memory. Insight. You'll be armed with those. Knock her off her path. Send her to me. And we'll see what you can make of yourself. You just might be able to escape your fate after all."

"I ain't gonna' sign no contract with you!" She struggled in her chair, imagining him producing some fancy scroll that she would have to sign in her own blood.

"Quila, my dear, that shit is only in the movies. Signing a contract." He sneered. "How human. My 'contracts'," here he used finger quotes, "are much more binding than your signature."

"No! You bastard! You can't make me! I won't do it!" Quila continued to struggle but all she could hear was his laugher. It grew louder and louder, echoing around the room. She put her hands over her ears to block the sound. The whole time the white cloud seemed to boil and billow furiously, expanding in space, and soon it surrounded her. She couldn't see the well-dressed man anymore, or his desk or office. She couldn't see anything but blinding whiteness.

Chapter 9

    Quila felt like she was floating around in a sea of whiteness. She tried to feel her bullet holes again, but she couldn't seem to move her arms. She wondered if she was in the hospital, hallucinating weird scary dreams about the Devil and her regrets in life. Sure, she regretted that she'd been born poor. To a drug addicted derelict of a mother. Sure, she regretted that she'd been born with every obstacle in front of her. She never stood a chance. Her zip code had more to do with her destiny than anything she could ever do. There was no way out of that hole and maybe there was no way out of this haze either. Then she heard a voice and thought maybe she really was in an ICU and hovering on the verge of consciousness. She listened. It didn't sound like a nurse. She couldn't understand why it was a little girl's voice. There shouldn't be a little girl here.

    "Don't want!" the little girl screamed. "Don't want!"

    "Victoire, honey, they have a painting area. Don't you want to go and paint? You love to paint."

    Quila knew that voice. So patient. Not like most of the voices that she heard around where she'd lived as a little girl. But that voice had been incredibly patient and kind to her, too. She felt surprised at how she yearned to hear it again. This was definitely a dream. Or a memory.

    "Honey, it'll be fun. I promise. There will be other little girls to play with."

The mist started to thin and Quila could make out the nice car with the small child in the car seat in the back. She was clutching her doll, had her thumb in her mouth and was shaking her head back and forth rapidly. Her mother was trying to coax her out of the car, to no avail. Quila felt a pull and the scene seemed to get closer... or she came closer to it. She wasn't sure. What she was sure of was that little girl was her Victory... as a preschooler. She had to be four years old. But of course, that was when they first became friends. She wondered why she was seeing this scene and if somehow the Well-Dressed-Man's creepy old movies were starting up again. But she was *inside* the cloud this time. She wasn't sure what was going on. Then she heard another voice.

"I like your dolly. I never had a dolly, but that a one nice."

Quila turned her focus to that voice and a little girl came into view. She had dark skin, very white teeth, and two puff ball pom poms on either side of her head. "Oh my god, that's me," she said aloud, but wasn't sure if there was anyone there to hear her or indeed, if she was actually speaking at all. Surely all this was going on in her head. Pharmaceutical grade painkillers could really trip you out.

"My name Tequila Williams," her little self said.

The grown-up White lady looked a little surprised. "Te...quila?" Then she looked around her quickly and met the gaze of the woman with little Tequila. "Oh, uh, what a pretty name!" Her recovery was acceptable, if not smooth. Quila gazed into the face of her mother. She looked healthy. She looked focused. She looked clean. She had a little baby in her arms all dressed in pink. Quila always fantasized she'd had a little sister but thought that was a dream. There she was. Quila was amazed. Was this the life she remembered?

Quila reached out for her mother, wanting to freeze this moment forever, to keep her mother safe in this in-between place, this island of relative healthiness, this short time when she had a mother who acted like a mother. This was a time when Bobby was around, before he'd gotten laid off and things had become desperate. Before her mama had started crying all the time and holding onto a pink blanket. Bobby tried to make things better but then he ended up going off to Bighouse College, leaving Mama pregnant yet again with Waleed. Mama cried and cried and Quila hadn't been able to reach her. And there was no little sister for her to play with.

Before he went away Bobby was sad too, but he kept things together in the family. Kept food on the table. He was organized. He wanted the best for little Tequila. He had signed her up for this "Blended Head Start" program. Quila remembered how she loved that school, those teachers. Every day that was where she wanted to be. She thought that if she could just grab her mother that she maybe, just maybe, could hold her here, in this moment and protect her. She reached out and just as she touched her, Quila felt a sucking feeling, like she was getting pulled into a rip current and being drawn away from Rashida.

"Nooooo…."

Then she smelled it. It was the way Mrs. Van Dyke's car always smelled. She called it "new car smell". Quila remembered finding little cardboard cutouts shaped like drawings of pine trees under the seats. They seemed to reek of that smell that Mrs. Van Dyke liked so much. Then suddenly Quila felt it, a crushing weight of pressure on her chest like she was drowning. She struggled and fought and then sucked in a huge breath and started coughing.

"Honey! Are you all right?" the nice lady with the funny smelling car asked her and started patting her back.

"She got a bit of the asthma, but she be all right. You all right, Tequila?"

"Yes, Mama," Quila heard herself say and then realized that she was saying it. She looked around her. Everyone was so tall. Why was she so short? She looked down and saw tiny little feet in tiny little sneakers. She quickly felt her body and with shock realized that she was a child. She was a four-year-old child.

I'll give you a little gift. A token to remember me by. I'll give you wisdom. Memory. Insight. You'll be armed with those, she remembered him saying.

"I'm back."

"Glad to hear it, baby!" her mother said and then she turned to the other mother who was trying to reason with her preschooler. "My name Rashida. This be Tequila. And this here be Little Rashida."

"Oh, hi." The White lady sounded a little unsure of herself. "My name is Tiffany. Tiffany Van Dyke. This is my daughter, Victoire. She's a little shy about starting a new school."

"Vic-twah?" Rashida asked.

"Yes, it's French. *Victoire*."

"Naw, Mama. It be Victory! Everybody gonna' call her Victory!" Quila turned to the little girl. "That a funny name, but I like it! Hey, do you wanna' be my friend?" Quila heard herself say this, but was also caught by Little Rashida, the baby. With every passing second she could feel herself sinking in deeper and deeper, getting under the skin of her younger self. The cloud was nowhere to be seen now. Her awareness of herself as an adult was quickly fading with it.

The little girl in the car seat looked wide-eyed at Quila and then nodded.

Quila reached up and took the little girl's hand. "Good. Hop down and let's get goin', girl. Everybody wanna be friend with a girl name Victory!"

Victory nodded to her mother, who could finally pop the car seat buckle now that she'd been given permission. She helped her daughter down.

Quila took Victory's hand again and smiled at the little girl. "Don't you worry 'bout nothin'. I got you." That was what Bobby, her daddy, always said to her. "I got you." She felt little Victory squeeze her hand and hug her dolly tighter with the other arm. "And you got dolly. We good to go." Quila's voice had the squeaky sound of a four-year-old. She was full of confidence and bravado. Leading Victory by the hand, she started heading into the school. "Oh, you gonna' love this. This be the best school ever. These be the best days we ever know."

Tiffany turned towards Rashida as they followed the girls. "Have you been here already? Did she come last year?"

"Aw, nah," Rashida answered. "This her first day. We got here 'bout twenty minutes ago. Her brother in the classroom, playing. But she got a bug in her ear to come outside. Made me come with her."

"How funny!" Tiffany looked like she was trying to figure out what to say.

"She said she needed a friend." Rashida shook her head. "Then she saw you all and she run right over."

"Oh." Tiffany seemed surprised. "Did she see us out the window?"

Rashida just shrugged. "She say lot of strange things. She a wonderful strange lil' girl." Rashida laughed and rocked the baby in her arms.

"How old is… Little Rashida?" Tiffany asked.

"Four months."

"She's lovely."

"Thanks. She a lil' one. Got some struggles, but she be strong and growing stronger. Every day growing stronger. My lil' Rashida. God givin' her the strength to keep fightin'. We so blessed."

The two women chatted as they all walked into the school. Quila stopped listening to them. Her little heart was beating so fast. Memory was fading quickly and for the moment, all she knew was being Tequila Williams, a four-year-old child who was eagerly dragging her new best friend, her only friend, into the safety and magic of school. They entered the doors and walked down a long hallway past many other classrooms. At the end of the hallway was a room with a brightly colored sign that neither girl could read. *Welcome to Head Start* it blared out in primary colors. Quila led Victory into the room.

Four little boys were playing over in a corner on a rug that depicted a town layout. A small black-haired Asian boy was driving a toy truck on the cityscape woven into the bright pattern. "Shudong driving! Shudong driving!" he kept repeating excitedly. Two other Black boys, one obviously older and not a Head Start child, were racing toy cars down the rug-street, while another red-headed boy with a lot of freckles was holding onto a station wagon and trying to keep up. Their laughter dominated the room as they drove outside of the road lines, through the park, through buildings, making loud crashing noises.

They were attended to by a large African American woman. Quila thought she looked lovely, like coffee with just a hint of cream, a lot like Rasheed's coloring. The woman had jet black hair that wasn't frizzy at all, quite unlike Quila's. The woman was sitting in a chair and correcting the boys when they crashed into one another.

"Now Lamont and Henry, drive next to each other, not over each other. Do your parents drive like that, Henry?" The question only resulted in more laughter from the two little boys.

Victory stared at them, speechless, her thumb going back into her mouth.

The woman looked up at the newcomers. "Hello again, Mrs. Williams. Tequila, I see you've brought a friend. My name is Miss Amy. What's your name?"

Victory sucked on her thumb harder, her eyes wide.

"Her name be Victory. She a winner, ain't you, Victory?" Quila said in her squeaky little girl voice. "C'mon. You gonna' love Miss Amy. Everybody love Miss Amy!" Quila dragged Victory over. She climbed up in Miss Amy's lap and snuggled herself into the vast softness of the special education teacher. "C'mon Victory. This is a lil' bit of heaven."

Victory blinked and looked around and then followed Quila's direction, climbing up into Miss Amy's plentiful lap. The woman cooed and rocked as she held the two little girls, humming a little song. Quila felt all was right with the world. This was where she wanted to be more than anyplace. It was warm. It was safe. It was magical. She could see Victory relax and start to smile. Her thumb came out of her mouth. After a few minutes Quila climbed down and then gently guided her new little friend over to the dress up area where they started to play.

"Well, that was… unexpected." Mrs. Van Dyke sounded shocked. "I've never seen Victoire take to anyone like that. You must be a very special person."

"You must be Mrs. Van Dyke?" Miss Amy asked. "Good. I've gotten all the paperwork and Victory's, uh, I mean *Victoire's* I.E.P. I run the classroom."

"Oh yes! I read that you have a master's in special education!" The relief in Mrs. Van Dyke's voice was palpable, as if finally she was working with someone who might be able to help. "I hope you can make a difference for Victoire." She looked around the classroom. "Do you manage all these children by yourself?"

"Oh no, you'll meet my two assistant teachers soon. Victoire will work with all of us, and she'll meet with specialists, Fannie and Grace, generally twice a day."

"Oh, that's wonderful. I'm so grateful for this special class." Mrs. Van Dyke looked at Shudong who was continuing to shout out emphatically, *Shudong driving! Shudong driving!* and refusing to engage with the three other little boys, who were basically playing around him. "Do all the children get the same special therapy?"

"Each child receives the special focus that they need, depending on their individual education plan. In this Blended Early Head Start there are four children who have I.E.P.s, while the other eight children don't have that."

"Oh. that's right. You have four, um, what are they called, bio-normal children?"

"Bio-typical," Miss Amy answered with a smile. "It's a wonderful experience for them, learning that the world holds all kinds of people in it and that we all have meaning and roles and can be friends."

"I'll be glad for Victoire to have friends. She never did well in the playdates. The other mothers don't seem to want to have their children come over anymore." The mother spoke softly and kept an eye on her daughter to make sure the children didn't hear her.

"She'll do just fine here. She seems to be making a friend already." Miss Amy smiled broadly as she looked over at Tequila and Victory who were playing while Rashida and her tiny namesake watched over them.

"Yes."

"Tell me, Mrs. Van Dyke, you seem hesitant? May I ask what's concerning you?"

"So, four children have special needs. Four are bio-um… typical. And the other four?"

"The other four have risk factors for other reasons, economic factors that put them at risk."

"Oh!" Mrs. Van Dyke seemed relieved. "It's just that they're poor." She laughed lightly. "When Drake and I were first married, we didn't have two pennies to run together. I had to be really creative while he finished medical school and his residency."

Miss Amy nodded her head slowly. "Economic risk factors make children eligible for this class as well."

"I'm just so glad to know it's not… oh, never mind." Mrs. Van Dyke smiled tenuously at Miss Amy. "I know Victoire will start screaming if I leave…"

"I think she'll be fine. You can go if you have places you need to be."

"Really?" The woman looked around. "Really? I can just… go?"

Miss Amy nodded.

"I can go?" Tiffany looked around her, as if dazed. "I'm not sure what to do with myself. I'm… free?"

Rashida walked over with the baby. "C'mon, Rasheed. It time to go wait for the bus."

The larger Black boy on the rug looked up at his mama. "Can't I stay? I want to play here too. I want to go to school here too!"

"You be six years old. You start kindergarten tomorrow. You a big boy and gonna' ride the bus!" She laughed at him.

Mrs. Van Dyke did a double take. She looked at Rashida. "This is your son?"

"Yeah, he Rasheed."

Mrs. Van Dyke looked confused. "Oh, Rasheed and… Little Rashida."

"Yeah, that right."

"Oh, okay then. Family name." She didn't ask it as a question and Quila's mother didn't seem to feel a need to answer.

Before lunchtime came around, Quila and Victory were best friends. Quila had even gotten to hold Dolly, who rarely ever left Victory's grip. As days turned into weeks and weeks into months, Victory's confidence grew under the encouragement of Quila. She started to laugh. She started to talk. Sometimes she even sang. Still shy around the other children, Quila jumped in as her social broker, speaking for her and pushing her to speak for herself. The two little girls became inseparable. Victory's mother volunteered as a type of room mother, bringing supplies to the classroom and organizing special events. A string of musicians gave concerts to their miniature audience. A magician and a juggler entertained. Many times Quila overheard her say to Miss Amy that Quila was a miracle for her little Victoire, as she always called her daughter that funny sounding name. Miss Tiffany said she had a hope she hadn't felt in a long time.

Miss Amy would just smile in her soft, comforting way and say, "Yes, Tequila Williams is a very special little girl."

The days passed by in a happy haze with the hot months finally easing into cooler weather where the trees turned the color of Quila's favorite crayons. And then all the colorful leaves were gone and everything faded into grays and light brown and beige colors. It was like the life drained out of the world around them just like the warmth drained out of the sun.

The onset of the cold weather meant that Tequila would wake up at night, hearing her parents walking about, tense voices, and strange activity. At nine years old, Deyonte could sleep through anything and he never woke up. Rasheed was the same way. But she would wake up and hear her mother's anxious voice and the baby's weak cough.

Then one night there was shrieking. Her mother was shrieking and Quila pulled the covers over her head. It woke up Rasheed and he climbed into bed with her. She could feel him shaking. Deyonte refused to join them but she could hear the tremble in his voice as he told them to grow up.

"I'm gonna' find out what goin' on," Rasheed finally said and started to get out of bed.

"Don't you!" Deyonte barked from his upper bunk. "You stay right there. You don't wanna' go out there while she upset like that."

So they stayed put. They never saw their little sister again. A few days later, Grandma came and stayed with them while Daddy Bobby and Mama dressed all in black and left the house for a few hours. They never talked about Little Rashida again. It was like she had never been. But Quila could see how it left a hole in Mama. She cried and cried.

Bobby took Tequila on the city bus ride to school. The big boys could ride the school bus, but the Head Start kids had to come by other ways. Then one night, flashing lights were outside the apartment and some men in uniforms came and took Bobby away. Grandma didn't go back home that time. Mama just lay on the couch. She said she was tired and she was sick. She threw up a lot.

"Why can't Mama take me on the bus to school no more?" Quila asked Deyonte one day. "I want to go back to school!" She was insistent. Little paper bags started to show up in the apartment. Grandma would shake her head sadly, pick them up, and throw them away.

"She depressed," Deyonte answered her with a shrug. "I seen this before. She use those little brown bags to feel better but I think it make her feel nothin' at all."

The days were boring. She missed school. Then one day there was a firm knock on the door. She went to answer it. It was Miss Tiffany, her classroom-mama.

"I'm here to take you back to school, Quila." For some reason, Miss Tiffany had given her this nickname. She never called her Tequila. The new name stuck and now everyone at school called her just Quila.

Quila invited her in, although her mama was sleepy on the couch again. She hid around the corner to the kitchen and listened to the parts of the conversation she could hear between Miss Tiffany and her own mother.

"If you don't take her back to school, they're going to give her place away to another child."

Rashida didn't answer for a while. Her voice sounded slow and groggy. "She be okay here with me."

Quila could hear Miss Tiffany give a heavy sigh. "My daughter is not okay. She's regressing without Quila."

"Tequila. Her name Tequila."

"Tequila," Miss Tiffany acquiesced. "I need her there. Victorie needs her there." There was silence.

"Who Vick-twah?"

"My daughter. Quila, I mean Tequila… calls her Victory." Mrs. Van Dyke looked thoughtful. "Tell you what. If I pick her up every day, and bring her home, will you allow her to go back to school? She needs to be at that school, too. She's starting to learn her letters and numbers and to read. She needs to be there. She's such a bright little girl. So smart."

Silence again.

"You wouldn't have to do anything. I'll take care of everything. It would give you a chance to rest more."

At last Quila heard her grandmother say, "Rashida, babe. You need to rest. You need to be strong for that baby. Chil', Tequila don't do nothin' but sit around all day. Let her go to school. It good for her."

Rashida finally relented. Quila got herself up every morning, got dressed. There was nothing to eat for breakfast, so she just went outside to wait on the little stoop that served as a kind of front porch, waiting for the car with the new car smell and her best friend in it to pick her up.

Chapter 10

Quila looked around her and saw nothing. Everything was whiteness, like she'd been sucked back into the Well-Dressed Man's cloud again. But when she strained she could hear something. It sounded like people shouting in the distance, calling to each other on the street. Far away voices. As the whiteness faded to gray, forms started to take shape out of the mist. A dingy section-eight apartment came into view, the living room full of furniture that was paid for in a by-the-month plan at interest rates so high that they would never be wholly owned. There was a little girl lying on the couch, asleep. The formless Quila moved over to take a look, quietly so as to not wake the child. "Oh my god… it's me." She whispered the words, feeling like her heart should be racing, but she didn't seem to have a heart. She didn't seem to have anything at all. Looking down at her hands, she could almost make them out, but they were blurry and gray and transparent. "I'm a ghost. I'm a ghost in my own life." She could see the cloud still and also the shabby apartment where she had grown up.

The little girl opened her eyes and looked around. She was lying where she had apparently fallen asleep. Quila remembered that the couch usually offered a quieter place to sleep than her bedroom, which she shared with her brothers. All the children slept in one room, except the baby, who spent all his time in the slightly broken thrift store playpen. Her grandma, who was now the official resident of the apartment, had one room and her mama, when she was around, would share that or more often sleep on the couch.

Grandma's domain was the kitchen, although her eyesight was bad enough that Quila had never really known her to cook anything. She mostly sat there and drank instant coffee and watched church services on a little TV set. Mama's domain was the living room, where she slept a lot. Or sometimes she would sit on the couch and just stare, not awake but not asleep either, her cigarette lying on the rented coffee table, leaving little scar marks as it slowly burned away. She would murmur like she was dreaming though. But not today. Today Mama was gone.

Quila floated around the room and tried to figure out when this was. Baby Waleed looked to be about a year old, maybe a bit older. There were crumpled paper bags in odd places about the room, so Mama had been there, her trail of drugs and booze lying in evidence. Deyonte usually came by and picked them up, trying to make a buck selling off any remnants that might have been missed. There was a picture of Bobby in a frame over on a table. Quila drifted to it and saw several cards set around. Sympathy cards. She knew exactly what day this was. Yesterday had been the funeral for Daddy. Even Rasheed accepted the fact now that Bobby wasn't coming back, but he wouldn't talk about it. In fact, he refused to speak to anyone. He just went into a dark place somewhere deep within. Deyonte's reaction was different. He'd just shrugged. Mama's men came and went. He'd seen a lot of them. It was hard to get attached to someone else's daddy.

The baby fussed in the playpen. Her younger self yawned and stretched. Then she got up and went over to her little brother. "Yup. You need a new diaper." She played with little Waleed's fuzzy hair. Quila's ghostly heart filled with compassion for this little girl, her six-year-old self, who was taking on responsibility that never should have been put on her shoulders. Formlessly, Quila's older spirt drifted over to her younger self and reached out to touch the little girl's cheek, wanting to stroke it tenderly like a mother should have. Suddenly she heard a sucking noise and felt herself solidify. Now out of her eyes she saw the hand of a six-year-old child playing with the wiry hair of the baby. She lifted up her hand and stared at it. She looked down and saw the body of the little girl. Her hands went to her face. She felt the face of young Quila. More than anything now she smelled the apartment. Old smoke and baby diapers. A musty smell like no kind of deep cleaning would ever overcome.

"He put me here," she said aloud. "He want me to do something." What had she done back when she was six? She could remember her childhood like it was etched into her mind. Love from Grandma. Horror from Mama and her string of druggie friends and dealers. Fear from the neighborhood. And a dream world from Vicky's life. But she couldn't remember anything significant happening the day after Bobby's funeral. Her mother had disappeared on a drug binge for some weeks after that, too overwhelmed and too frightened to be in reality with her children.

The baby fussed again. Little Quila looked down. "You need a new diaper." She picked up the toddler. He should be heavier than he was. "Waleed, I tell you what you need. You need a home to grow up in. Someplace with parents who be there for you." She stopped suddenly, remembering a dream that shook her. She turned around and looked back at the couch where she had just been sleeping. In her mind she could see her little brother, still just a toddler, playing in a dirt yard where grass would never grow. She was supposed to be watching over him. He stood up, excited to show her something he'd found in the dirt when a stray bullet hit him and he fell. He cried out just once. He was just a bystander. Just a kid. But he fell over and he was dead within minutes. In that fuzzy dream her mama had yelled and yelled at her for not watching the toddler, as if there had been anything she could do about a stray bullet. But it had been more than Mama could take. Losing Bobby and then losing his son and then she lost herself deep into that dreamland she wanted to be in more than she wanted to be in her life. And then Quila never saw her again.

Quila turned back to the baby. She could almost hear the echo of the Well-Dressed Man's words, *I'll give you a little gift. A token to remember me by. I'll give you wisdom. Memory. Insight.*

85

"That ain't no dream." She knew without a doubt that her baby brother's clock was running out... unless... unless she could change something. Quila's hand stopped, resting on Waleed's head. "No, that don't feel like no dream." She lay the baby down on the floor and pulled the diaper bag over to her, pulling out what she needed. The social workers came by every so often and they would refill the bag. It was running really low on supplies. She sighed. As she finished the job she sat Waleed up. "He sent me here. He gave me gifts. And one of them is my memories. Since I know, there got to be somethin' I can do." She looked around her. She had no idea what a six-year-old could do. Even when she'd been twenty-five she would've had no idea what to do. The situation was overwhelming. How could you even begin to make a change when everything was against you?

The door rattled with a strong knock. She picked the baby up and put him back in the broken playpen. Since it seemed like no one was going to answer it, she walked over to the door. By the time she got there they had knocked four times and were now headed back down the walkway.

"Hey! Did you want somethin'?"

The two ladies stopped and turned around. "We're here to visit Rashida and her children," one of them said. She was a middle-aged Black lady who looked big and soft and friendly. The other lady was a younger Chicana dressed in a bright floral print that Quila thought looked beautiful, even under her open cold weather coat.

"She ain't here. But I'm Quila. Rashida my mama. You ladies bring the diaper bags, right? We need more. I just changed the baby's diaper and I didn't know what I was gonna' do next time. There ain't nothin' left."

The two ladies looked at one another.

She thought of playing tea party with Victory. "Why don't you ladies please come in?" Quila said, trying to sound as grown up as she could, to sound like Miss Amy had when she played tea party with them back in pre-school. The two women followed her into the house.

After the ladies sat down, they brought out their checklists. Quila brought over the diaper bag.

"Thank you, honey. Yes, I can fill this back up again. Where's your mama? Or your grandma?"

Quila looked the woman right in the eyes. "I don't know where Mama is. From what I remember, she won't be back for a couple weeks. Grandma is having a terrible time with her blood pressure. Make her awful dizzy. And her blood sugar giving her fits. She probably lying down. Let me get you the baby." She went over and pulled Waleed out of the playpen. He started to cry.

"Hush now, Waleed. This for the best. These ladies can help you. Hush now."

The older Black lady smiled at Quila. "How can we help you now, honey?"

"Me? I'm beyond help. He already got me." Quila said, all matter-of-fact. The two women looked in alarm at one another. "But baby Waleed, he got a chance. He need a family. A home. A real home. If he stay here, he be dead in under a year. Little Rasheeda didn't make it. Bobby didn't make it. Mama ain't gonna' make it. Waleed ain't gonna' make it either."

"Miss Quila," the woman said in one of the softest ways Quila had ever heard. "Why don't you sit down and tell me everything you know?"

It was a nice visit. The ladies were very patient and didn't seem to judge anything she said. They just took a lot of notes. They stayed for two hours. Grandma had come down by then and they sat with her for a long time while Quila took the baby over to the corner to play with him. The Chicana lady gave her some books, which she worked hard to read. She wasn't very good at letters, but this book was pretty easy because there was a picture and a single word on each page. "Apple," she read to him and tried to memorize what the word looked like. It was frustrating that if she had, what did he call it? *memory, insight and wisdom* then why wouldn't she remember all her reading and math and history and science? If he was going to make her live her life over again, why would she have to go through the torture of school again? "Oh, torture the point of it, ain't it?" she whispered to the baby, who cooed back at her and said, "Apple" clearly enough that she could understand it. "Oh Waleed. You really smart! I gotta' get you outta' here. You gotta' have a shot."

As the ladies started to leave, she walked outside with them. Before they got into their car she tugged on the soft lady's dress. "Can I ask you a question?"

"Sure thing, Miss Quila," the lady said as she leaned over.

"Can Waleed be adopted by some family? Some family who want him? He still a baby. He smart. He can talk and say words on the page. He need a foster home. Or a real home. But he can't grow up here." She handed the Chicana lady a brown paper bag. "I don't know if Mama will ever be back, but she has lots of these around. This might help you find Waleed a real home."

The lady looked into the paper bag and gasped. She almost dropped the bag as she handed it over to her companion. Her voice was shaking slightly as she asked, "And, Niña, how does this help us find a home for your brother?"

Quila gave them a steady look. "People want babies. Nobody want to adopt a kid who old like me. They think we ruined already. People want babies who will forget where they came from, who will only remember they new families. That bag is bad stuff. I heard Mama say that you can't see the bags or you take us away from her, like her other children."

"What other children, honey?"

"I overheard her tell Grandma that she moved from another city because the social workers there took all her children away from her. She came here. She had new children. She said you all so liberal here that you would never do nothin', that any mama better than no mama. But that other city was mean. They took away all her other kids. That why Rashida never let you in."

"And do you want to grow up in another family? Do you want a foster family?"

Quila thought about that. "I think I already have one." She nodded. "Yeah, I think I got that covered."

Quila was surprised at how fast things moved after that. Her mama finally reappeared and it was like the social workers were lying in wait to catch her. When confronted with the evidence she crumbled and almost with relief signed the papers that allowed little Waleed to be adopted out. He was gone in two months, given to a gay couple who had not been able to get a child. Quila sighed. It was better for Waleed but it stimulated the same downward spiral Quila remembered from her previous childhood when Waleed was shot in the yard. It wasn't long before Mama was gone, too. But no one ever showed up to take the older children. Quila had been right: there was no place else for them to go.

She lay in bed at night thinking about what she remembered. The longer she was little Quila, the fuzzier her memories became. When school started, she and Victory were in the same class. She knew Miss Tiffany would offer her books. This time she took them, as many as anyone would give her and then she asked for more. The little apartment started to fill up with books. Mama wasn't there to spend drugged out days on the couch anymore. Grandma just watched the television all day in the kitchen, slowly smoking the precious few cigarettes she could get her hands on. That fit the pattern Quila remembered. Now Quila would read to her brothers to pass the time and to keep them at home. Learning to read had been such a struggle before, but now she had books that were interesting and she had her brothers to practice on. It still was a lot of work. "Too bad wisdom don't give you skills," she lamented to Rasheed one day as she struggled over a word.

"Huh?" Rasheed loved for her to read to him. Deyonte pretended like he didn't care, but she could tell he was listening.

"It ain't nothin', never mind." She turned back to her book. "Oh, I got this word. *Pur-ga-tor-y.*"

"What that?" Rasheed asked.

"Hang on. I gotta' look it up." She was reading them a scary story because Deyonte wouldn't listen unless the story was slightly creepy. He loved getting the shivers down his spine. She put her copy of *Goosebumps* down and took a dictionary that Miss Tiffany had given her from the shelf. "Purgatory. It mean 'a state of suffering for a soul who is working off their sins before they can get into heaven.'"

"What does that mean?" Rasheed asked.

"It like detention," Quila answered.

"It like our life now," Deyonte said bitterly. "We in-between. They came and took the baby but ain't no one gonna' want us 'cause we too old."

"Waleed went from no daddy to two daddies. And we got no mama and no daddy," Rasheed whined.

"No," Quila nodded. "But we got each other. And we got Grandma. Now that the drugs are out of the house, they won't take us from Grandma. We be all right if we can just stay together."

"Quila, does that book say how long purgatory last?" Rasheed asked.

She shook her head. "It just a dictionary, Rasheed. It don't tell us nothing but the meaning of words. Not the meaning of life." She picked up their story and started to read again.

"The meaning of life? What the meaning of life?" Rasheed asked, his brows furrowed.

"Get all you can 'fore you die. That the meaning of life," Deyonte answered, his voice harsh.

"Deyonte!" Quila snapped. "Don't you say such things. Rasheed, life is about doin' the right thing, doin' things that help. Doin' good."

"Don't listen to her. They ain't no heaven and they ain't no hell. Nothin' matters. Jes get all you can before you bite it like Bobby did."

Rasheed started to cry. Quila went and put her arms around him. "Rasheed, I don't know nothin' about heaven and hell. But I tell you what I do know: do good. Do all the good you can, even if there ain't no purpose to it. Even if there ain't no meaning to it. Do it just to piss off the Devil even if he don't exist."

    Deyonte snorted. "Quila, you a rebel with no cause."

    "Oh, Deyonte, I got a cause all right. I surely got a cause."

Chapter 11

Quila opened her eyes and found herself surrounded by the billowing cloud; she was engulfed in the white undulating mass. At first she thought she would find herself back in *his* office. Not that she could have done much. She'd hardly been back in her own life at all. Besides, she'd only been a little kid. While she waited she started to wonder if she was in purgatory, but what sins had she committed this time? *I broke up what family I had. I sent little Waleed away and quickened my mama's decline into despair and drugs.* She was sure that had been a sin on some level, but if it saved her baby brother, it was one sin that was worth committing.

"Why did you put me there?" she asked aloud. She didn't get an answer. She didn't actually expect one, so she wasn't disappointed. Victory hadn't been the central figure in her life at that point. A frequent a playmate, yes. "I mean, not much happens when you're just six or seven years old. Children are powerless. It's not like there was anything I could do… like you told me to." Again, there was no answer. *What if I don't do anything? What if I don't turn Victory to him? What if I just live my life and make different choices? I can't change much but maybe, maybe I could just do the things in front of me.*

That man, with his 'deal she couldn't refuse' was a real devil. She paused. Could she cheat the Devil? Could she double cross him when he'd sent her back with a mission she didn't want? One she hadn't agreed to? She wasn't sure what she was capable of, but she knew she could try. She could surely try. And if double crossing the Devil was added to her sins, well, she didn't have much to hope for anyway, but she could prevent Victory from ever showing up in his office. She could do that much. And it seemed to be the thing that was right in front of her.

The cloud started to thin out and there she was, riding in the back seat of a nice car with Victory. Victory had one of her ever-present Barbie dolls and the two girls were playing. She had no idea how old she was here, but it had to be about second grade. She had a Barbie in her hand, too, and the girls were laughing at some silly joke one of them had made. This day was like a hundred others. She had no idea why he put her here or what he thought a seven or eight-year-old girl might do to her playmate to throw her under the Devil's influence. She didn't know what to do, so she just observed. She tried to hover and not touch her child-self after what had happened last time. Maybe she could just watch, learn, or advise her younger self? She didn't know how this ghosting thing was supposed to work. "It would have been helpful if all this had come with instructions," she said into the ether. It was as though she could hear a distant laugh. "I'm gonna' do the best I can. I'm gonna' do the thing right in front of me."

The car pulled up in front of the Van Dyke's house and everyone went inside. After the girls hung up their jackets, Victory turned to Quila and said, "C'mon, let's go upstairs and play Barbies! I got new dresses for her."

Quila observed her child-self glance down at the backpack and then longingly at the doll in Victory's hand. There were no Barbie dolls at Quila's place. "Choose homework, choose homework," she coached little Quila.

"Okay, let's play," little Quila said.

"Let's try a different answer." Quila moved into her child-self and experienced that sucking sound and the solidification that came with embodiment. The house smelled of vanilla, like scented candles had been burning. Quila dearly loved the scent of vanilla. "Sure, let's play, but first I gotta' ask your mama to help me with a question." She turned to Mrs. Van Dyke. "Miss Tiffany? Would you help me with my homework?"

Mrs. Van Dyke turned and looked at the little girl. "Of course, yes, of course. Let's go sit down at the kitchen table. Come on, Victory, you, too." Mrs. Van Dyke walked through the house and disappeared.

"Homework? What fun is that?" Victory rolled her eyes. "Kids our age should *not* have homework!"

"We have plenty of time to play. It just a quick question. I know you don't need help. I see you in class. You understand everything, but me, I gotta' work at it. I got no one at home who I can ask for help."

"Oh, all right," Victory said, but she sounded fussy. Reluctantly she grabbed her backpack and trudged into the kitchen, saying loudly, "We'd better get a really good snack for this!"

"Of course, honey-bun," her mother answered.

Quila watched her friend disappear through the house. "Wow, snacks." She felt a thrill in her heart at the sound of the word.

A couple of hours later the girls were playing Barbies up in Victory's room. "Vicky, why you mama have me over so much?"

"I think it's to teach you to use verbs," Victory said as she focused on dressing a doll. "She's really big on grammar."

"Use what?"

"Mother says you speak and skip your verbs. Like 'why you mama'. It's supposed to be 'why *does your* mama…'. I heard her talking about it to Daddy. She wants to teach you to use verbs."

"Verbs." Quila said the word but didn't know what to think.

"Yeah, she's going to put on School-House Rock for us later. Don't worry, you'll like it. It's from when she was growing up. She'll make popcorn."

"For popcorn, I watch anything." Quila smiled.

"I'll watch anything," Victory corrected automatically. "Not *I* watch. *I'll* watch."

"I'll watch anything," Quila repeated. "Verbs. Okay. For popcorn and snacks, *I'll* use all the verbs she want me to!"

95

"All the verbs she *wants* me to," Victory didn't take her eyes off her doll. "Verb tense is a thing too."

"*Wants* me to. Okay. I got it. Wants me to."

As second grade passed into third, and third into the fourth, the pattern became a regular one, with Quila coming home with Victory most days. Homework was the first order, although that was never Victory's preference. The girls would either be working on homework or plopped down in front of educational television. It wasn't long before Quila had memorized the entire series of School House Rock videos and found that she knew her multiplication tables better than either of her older brothers. She would dance around singing, *"Verb! That's what's happening!"* When grade cards were sent home, she eagerly showed hers to Miss Tiffany. While Grandma Mayme would be proud of her, Quila knew she would pat her on the shoulder and then tell her to put it away and not taunt her brothers with it. She would tell her that boys didn't like to be showed up by little girls. But not Miss Tiffany. Quila knew her reaction would be totally different.

"Miss Tiffany. We got our grade cards today. Would you like to maybe see mine?" She was careful to use her verbs around Victory's mother.

Mrs. Van Dyke stopped what she was doing and came over to sit down by Quila. "I would love to see your grade card. Victory didn't tell me it was grade card day." She took the proffered manila envelope from Quila, whose hand was shaking ever so slightly. Mrs. Van Dyke was careful when she opened the envelope and gently slid out the folded-over paper. "Oh, my goodness! Quila! This is fantastic! You got A's in math, science, reading. You got A's in almost everything. Just one B." She smiled at the little girl and gave her a hug. "I am so proud of you. So proud of you, Quila. This is the result of a lot of hard work. Oh, Quila, you'll be able to do anything in life that you want. I hope you're proud of yourself."

Quila nodded. "Miss Tiffany, thank you for having me over. I like coming here. I like that you help me with my homework."

"You're welcome, Quila!" Mrs. Van Dyke beamed and blushed at the little girl. "You know, I think I would have liked being a teacher. I gave up working to be a mom and while I love being a mother, now that Victoire is in fourth grade and Jeremy is in his last year of middle school… and so independent." Then she muttered to herself, "if still so immature." Returning her attention to Quila she said, "I just have so much time on my hands."

"Well, thank you for spending your time with me." Quila felt warm all over at the attention Mrs. Van Dyke lavished on her.

The older woman smiled at her again. "I think we got lucky that you're able to spend so much time with us!"

That was true. There really wasn't anyone at home who seemed to miss Quila when she was away. It seemed to just make everything easier on Grandma Mayme.

"Why don't you go and watch a National Geographic special. I saved some. You know how to pull them up. I want to talk with Victoire."

Quila did as she was told and was really getting interested in a show about the history of civilization when she heard an argument boiling over in the kitchen.

"She's my friend and you're ruining her!"

"Honey-bun, helping her with her homework is *not* ruining her. It's good for her and it should be good for you, too." Mrs. Van Dyke sounded a little exasperated.

"I do fine on my own."

"Victoire, honey, I've told you I don't appreciate that tone in your voice. And you are not doing fine on your own. I would like to see you put in a little more effort into your homework. I'm getting a little concerned."

"Concerned about what?" Victory sounded plainly defiant. Quila shrunk. It brought up memories of harsh criticism from her own mother when she had been around. She didn't want to hear their argument, but she also didn't know where else to go. She wondered if she should turn up the TV some more, or whether that would be obvious and rude.

"Concerned about your grades, for one." Mrs. Van Dyke didn't sound happy.

"My grades are fine."

"Actually, they aren't fine. This isn't fine, Victoire. You have two B's and the rest are C's. I know you can do better than that. Your father and I are getting a little worried. I'd like to see you focus more. You need to apply yourself."

"Focus more? Apply myself? More like Quila?"

"Well, yes, if you want to put it that way. More like Quila. That girl has nothing at home. No one who can help her. I'm not even sure her grandmother can read, to tell you the truth. Now don't you go and tell her I said that! But she comes here and she is focused and dedicated. I'd like to see a little bit more of that from you, young lady."

"Oh, so you like Quila better than me. You wish she'd been your daughter."

"Victoire! How could you say such a thing? Of course, I love you. You're my daughter. Quila is a fine girl and it's amazing given what she's come from. Probably exposed to drugs while her mother was pregnant. What a way for a child to start out. And just look at her now. She's a bright little thing. She needs more love and TLC and we can give it to her."

"Daddy's just embarrassed that you got stuck with dumb old me!" Victory bit off the words. "Me with the I.E.P. who's too stupid for school."

"Honey, having an I.E.P. doesn't mean you're not smart. It just means you learn differently..." Quila decided to go to the bathroom. She didn't need to. She just wanted to get away from the argument. She wondered what TLC was. She knew what THC was because Deyonte had told her, but she was pretty sure that wasn't the kind of thing that Miss Tiffany would be referring to. She washed her hands just to waste time and then opened the door to see if she could still hear them. It was all quiet. When she came back to the living room, Victory was there in front of the television, but she was looking daggers at her mother. Quila didn't know what part of their conversation she had missed, and she surely didn't want them to know that she'd been listening to any of it at all. She sat down next to Victory and they started watching the show. Slowly, she reached out her hand and took Vicky's. Her friend clasped back, almost desperately clinging on to Quila.

Chapter 12

Quila became aware of the brightness around her and figured she'd been kicked out of her own life, once again. She'd been there pretty long that time, nearly two years. She thought maybe she was getting it right and was going to be allowed to stay, but no.

Her immersion back into what she referred to as "Quila 2.0" had been long enough to notice subtle differences between her real life and this new fantasy one she was living. Last time around school was a tedious chore and she thought that Mrs. Van Dyke had seen her mostly as a charity case. This time around she thought that just maybe she'd had that wrong and that Mrs. Van Dyke really did like her. Really did see her as one of the family. Maybe she always had? And in school Quila got the fundamentals, which made school not only easier, but fun. She found she was something of a celebrity. "Girl from the projects at the top of her class", like she was some kind of prodigy. If they'd only known. Working at it sure was easier when you had memory, insight and wisdom.

As she waited in the in-between, formless, image-less world in which she intermittently found herself, she wondered how Quila 1.0 could have found the path that seemed to be evolving for Quila 2.0? There were no responsible adults in Quila's home life in any existence that she knew. Her grandmother's health was fragile at best. Once she got some food on the table, when she could, she had nothing left to give the little ones in terms of help with school. Rashida had given her will and voice and power over to the drugs, abandoning her children in order to chase something no one else could see. In Quila's world, there wasn't enough food. There wasn't a doctor when you needed one. You just got better on your own, with time and Mayme praying over you. There was trash and needles on the playground. Children couldn't fix these things. Children couldn't overcome these things.

One thing Quila could see clearly now: children needed someone to show them the way, to help them, to guide them. Children needed things that had to be provided. If a child were so gifted, so talented as to make it out of the projects on her own, well, she wasn't that child. She was lucky that she lived where she did and she was one of the token few unprivileged kids in a wealthy school district, partly accounting for the poster-child status of Quila 2.0, star student and role model. What happened this time around that hadn't the first time? She'd asked for help, yes, but it couldn't be that simple. *Maybe it's the butterfly effect*, she wondered. *Maybe the changes are so small, but over time they compound and grow? Maybe a small step in a different direction leads to a wholly different path?* She thought she could hear him saying *You're a poet, Tequila Williams* once again. She wondered how she might test her theory, but from up here in the cloud she hadn't a clue. What was the use of memory, insight and wisdom if you didn't know how to use them?

"Quila, why you home?"

It was Rasheed's voice she heard. Quila tried to peer harder into the cloud, tried to get a glimpse of her brother. Slowly he came into view. She loved Rasheed. He was getting tall. He did look like he was gonna' be a tall one, but she never had the chance to find out how tall before because he started racing the odds every day, living on the razor's edge of guns and gangs and danger by the time he was fifteen. He went down in a shoot-out right after he'd turned eighteen. Her grandmother refused to let her know the details. Made her promise she wouldn't go looking them up for herself, as if she had any idea of how to look something like that up. She looked harder at the boy in front of her now. His face was so lovely without all those scars on it; those scars that were waiting for him in street fights in his future.

"Why you home?"

"Why *are* you home. Rasheed, verbs matter. I'm home after school because Victory's family is off to Italy for a week. Can you imagine going to Italy?" The solid and real Quila sighed heavily.

"Where dat?"

"Where's *that*. It's in Europe. Over the Atlantic Ocean. It's a world away from here." She turned her gaze back to her brother.

Quila's spirit floated closer to this scene. She had no memories of this at all. This wasn't her former life. It was *like* her former life in that Rasheed was achingly jealous of the time she spent at her friend's house, knowing that she got *snacks,* those mythical wonders that he could only dream about.

"I wish that Miss Tiffany would take me over there, too." Rasheed sounded dejected.

Quila's ethereal heart broke for him, seeing him so young and tender, and knowing that he had such a road of fear and peril in front of him and maybe five years left to live. From her very center she reached out to him. The first thing she noticed was the musty smell. She looked around her and realized with a shock that she was back in her body, back in her own story again, and that their apartment smelled musty. Like mildew. She remembered that well enough. "Children need a clean place to grow up. They can't get that for themselves," she said aloud.

"Yeah, dat why I wish dat Miss Tiffany would take me wit you."

Quila looked at her brother. "Rasheed, we're gonna' try to butterfly effect you."

"Huh?"

"Nothin'. You trust me?"

"Yeah. You my sister."

"Then I want you to do as I tell you. It won't be easy but it will make it better in the long run. Will you? I want to save your life. I know you've been talking to the Reds."

Rasheed just looked at her with big eyes. After a while he said, "Quila, you got some magic I don't know 'bout? Cause you say and do shit that don't make no sense, like how you know things. They don't come in no books."

"I don't know how I know, but I just know. So, you gonna' trust me? You gonna' let me save your life?"

He looked at her for a long time. Then he nodded.

"Good. 'Cause I don't want to lose you again." She instructed him to get his backpack and they started to go over his homework. It was far beyond his comprehension.

"I see we're going to have to go back a bit. Hmmm. Let me run upstairs and get something." She came back down with her hands full.

"What dat? Playing cards?"

"What's that. Say *that*."

"What's that?"

"Good." She nodded. "Like I said, verbs matter. You're gonna' need them. And as long as other people than us have power, we're gonna' learn to fit in with them. We'll keep working at it. One thing that you need to know is math. Your multiplication tables. These are a different kind of playing cards. They're flash cards. You, Rasheed Williams, are going to learn math."

"What? I don't want to learn dat!"

"Say *that*."

"That. I still don' wanna' learn *that*."

"But you do want a jellybean?" She pulled a sizeable bag of candy out of her backpack. Miss Tiffany loved to pack up generous snack bags of treats as rewards. It was about the only way she could motivate Victory. "I know you love games, so this is a game. And jellybeans are the prizes."

They worked at it every day. She knew her brother well. Rasheed did love games. And even more than that, he loved jellybeans. He learned quickly. After several weeks she told him, "You know, Rasheed, given the right incentive, you're a really good student. You're catching on fast. I think you know the whole math deck now!"

He beamed at her. Feeling competent was a new experience for him. She could see the success of learning flush his cheeks. He looked radiant with her praise and his accomplishment. She showed him how to start working on the math in his own class, which was easy for her because she was in advanced math and he was in remedial, so they were basically learning the same things. Over the course of the year, he moved from barely scraping by to being a very solid B student. Quila would come home from Victory's house in the early evenings, sometimes even in time for what little dinner was served at home. Then she would spend the next two hours working with Rasheed.

One day when they were in the middle of studying together, Rasheed leaned over and whispered, "Quila, can you help Deyonte?"

She looked towards the living room. Deyonte was watching the television. It was a new television, which pleased her grandmother no end, but Quila knew it hadn't been bought. Deyonte said it was a gift from a friend, but she was sure it was hot. "I'll try. He doesn't seem to be too interested though."

"He likes it when you teach him math."

"Yeah, he does seem to think numbers are important." She looked down at her papers. "But I think that's so he can make sure he's not getting ripped off."

"I'll talk to him." Rasheed got up and left the table. In a few minutes he was back with his older brother.

"Rasheed said you wanted to see me?" Deyonte looked at her as though she had interrupted something important.

Quila shot Rasheed a look. "Well, it's just that Rasheed and I thought maybe if the three of us studied together that it would help. All of us. It would help us to have our big brother here with us. Helping us."

"You sweet, Quila. But I know you tricks. Now let me show you one of mine." He pulled a wad of cash out of his pocket. "This be five-hundred dollars."

"Bro, where you get cash like dat?" Rasheed asked

"Rasheed!"

Rasheed looked at both of them, sizing up which one to be more afraid of. Then he asked, "Deyonte, where'd you get cash like that?"

Deyonte just laughed. "I'm not big time, but I got a start."

Quila looked at her oldest brother, wide-eyed. "What do you mean, you 'got a start'?"

"Well, when Mama was here, she leave around all her little paper bags. I wait until she be really gone. Then I sneak in and clean out whatever left."

"Aw, I knew that. I saw you do that like a million times." Rasheed was clearly unimpressed.

"What'd you do with her scraps?" Quila asked.

"Depends on what it was. If it could be cut, I'd cut it with sugar or flour from the kitchen. But I'd hitch a ride with some brothers I know and we'd take it over to Southie. While the north side be all high and mighty, Southie got some parks where the addicts hang out."

"You went to Southie? That's dangerous, Deyonte!" Quila had dim memories of him going there but not this early. Not this young. Maybe the butterfly effect worked in both directions?

"That where you can deal with no trouble. Ain't no one want that turf so a start up like mine has a chance."

"Start up. Wow," Rasheed said, his eyes wide.

Quila punched her little brother in the arm. "That is not a startup, Rasheed. Deyonte's just a small-time dealer with no good source and lucky enough that he's under the radar." She turned to her older brother. "Those gang boys will kill you without even asking a question. You best be careful. Why don't you come to the table with us?" She gestured to their backpacks, flash cards, and notepads on the table. "There's other paths to find a way out of this place." She looked around them at the dingy, musty, smoky-smelling apartment.

"Quila, you can talk yourself blue but I gotta' way out. I gotta' source." Deyonte said it with a swagger.

"No shit, bro? What give?" Rasheed was all too excited. Quila kicked him in the leg.

Deyonte seemed to feed off his brother's approbation. "Mama done gave me the idea. All them trippers over at Southie? Well, a lot of them are middle class losers on they way down fast. But they got good shit on them. Once they be off dreamin' 'bout all their high-ass lives didn't give them, they leave half-packs and all manner of shit! I once took the syringe out of the arm of a dude. He'd only put half in, and he was out. I turned around and sold that to another druggie, who shot up the rest of it. They done passed out on top of one another." Deyonte was laughing.

"Deyonte! That's so… wrong," Quila said.

Deyonte continued to laugh. "No, what's so wrong is last week." He was gasping to catch his breath. "Last week I picked the drugs off a sleeping dude passed out on a park bench. At the end of my rounds he'd woke up and he asked me if I had anything I could sell him. I told him I did but that he didn't have any money. So, he pulls out his secret stash, forgetting that I could see where he hides his cash, and get this, he bought from me the drugs I stole from him not an hour before." Deyonte laughed harder and wiped his eyes. "That a beauty to behold. And now I know where he hide his dough so when I see him there beyond any reckoning, I know where to take his begging money from."

"You're just a pickpocket working off of addicts in a park?" Quila blinked a couple of times, feeling bewildered at how out of control this situation had become. "That's not funny, Deyonte!"

He looked at his sister. "Look, Quila. I got zero empathy for them. How many of them steal shit from their folks to pay for they habits? Or leave they children, like our mama done? For what they doin' to themselves and

107

they families, they get what they done deserve. Why you so high and mighty? Quila, you just like one of them born-again nuisances who come knockin' on our door and talk Grandma silly."

Quila didn't know what to do about the story he'd just told or with his accusation. They never went to church, although Grandma would try to make up for that by attempting salvation via the television. And those Jehovah's Witnesses always came knocking at the door to share their version of the truth. "I'm no kinda' Christian, Deyonte." She wondered if religion might help her in her particular—and rather peculiar—situation, but then she thought the Well-Dressed Man probably didn't care what you called yourself. He seemed like the type who could see through the hype and hyperbole.

"You may not be a churchy-ass Christian, sis, but you sho' are one a-them-born-again, crazy-ass, lunatics." The tension was building in the room. Rasheed took a step back.

At first Quila was stunned. Then she laughed out loud. "Well, you got me there, Deyonte. You got me there." She had to laugh. "I'm pretty sure that no one has ever been as born-again as I've been!"

Deyonte laughed too, and then Rasheed, looking nervous at first, started to relax and joined in.

Later that night when she went to bed, she felt sad for Deyonte. He was unreasonable. She couldn't get him to even entertain the idea that there might be another way. And his contempt for the addicts and willingness to be a predator of them was a shocking, but perhaps predictable outcome given his considerable unresolved anger at their mother. The only thing she'd ever brought them was chaos.

Later that night she lay in bed and looked at the bunk on top of hers where Deyonte was sleeping. She could hear his soft snores and knew he was deeply asleep. "Well, Deyonte," she whispered. "While I might not be able to help you at school, I certainly am impacting your vocabulary." She giggled. *Empathy. Beyond reckoning. Beauty to behold.* "I don't know what this butterfly is gonna' do for you, but it's doing something."

Chapter 13

Quila woke up looking forward to the end of the school year. No matter what life she was in, the last week of school was the best. Field days. Movie days. Relaxed days. No pressure. Just the bittersweet closure of another year and the opportunity to say a last goodbye to friends before the emptiness and boredom of summer put its stranglehold on childhood. She opened her eyes and felt blinded by the light. She tried to reach for the window shade to pull it down, but realized it wasn't the light of the sun that prevented her from seeing. It was the damn cloud again. She was gone from that life.

Quila got the feeling that one just waited in the white cloud and that, however long it took, eventually something would happen—her life, his office, heaven, or hell. So, rather than the fun and relaxed time waiting until the school year concluded, she just waited. Time was something she had in spades, if such a thing even existed here. Besides, it gave her the opportunity to think. She'd never had time to think when she was alive, to simply reflect on her day, her feelings, or life itself. It had always been about survival. About keeping away from the ones who were going down the drain fast and would grab you like a lifeline, but the end result was that they took you down with them. Of keeping your head down so you wouldn't become the target of someone's anxiety or mischief. Or just finding enough food to eat. She'd spent time in her last year as fourth-grade Quila getting to know the school social worker better. She and Rasheed then came home each weekend with backpacks full of food. Dry goods mostly, and those little containers of milk. Rather a lot of easy-to-make mac-n-cheese and boxes of spaghetti. Never sauce though. Nothing in jars. Donated food was never in jars. She wondered if there were any tuna fish left in the sea or if they'd all been chopped up and put into the incredible numbers of cans that went into those backpacks.

Suddenly she discovered, much to her surprise, that she enjoyed her time in the white cloud just reflecting on things. Just thinking. Just being peaceful. But like all good things in Quila's world, it didn't last. At first, she thought she saw shadows moving about but soon the mist faded away and she could see Victory, already looking every bit like a young Barbie doll, her blonde hair long and pulled back into a ponytail, running over to her bike.

"Look, Quila! Daddy got me this. He said he was so proud of my grade card. Isn't it beautiful?" She stroked the bike.

"Yeah, it's gorgeous." The envy was palpable in young Quila's voice. "You got this for getting As?"

"I sure did. I got A's in art, chorus, theater and health."

"Way to go, Vicky! That's great!" Quila tried to be supportive. "How did math and science and English go?"

Victory hardly paid Quila any attention as she stroked her new bike. "Oh, a B and C's." Then she turned to her friend. "You know, I think I want to take horseback riding lessons. Dad's not a fan. He hates horses and doesn't want me to become one of those horse-obsessed 'tween girls. But I bet I could get a horse from him if I got a few A's in those subjects!"

"Uh oh, you look like a girl with a plan!" Quila laughed. "Maybe it'd be okay to get good grades just to, you know, get good grades though?" She was afraid she was sounding like a nag.

"You're such a goody-two-shoes, Quila. You know that? Such a Little Miss Goody Two Shoes."

The ghost Quila felt a jolt. That was a name that no one had ever applied to her before, not in any kinda' life she ever knew. She was also fascinated by this Victory who was so transactional, so dealing in her approach, like everything had a price tag. Compassion ripping at her heart, she reached out to touch Victory's shoulder and felt the sucking and compressing that always seemed to accompany her getting thrown back into her life and her body again. She had thought it only would happen when she touched the living Quila. But apparently it happened when she made any contact at all with the living world. The garage smelled like paint cans and those odd acrid smells that always seemed to accompany cars. There were a lot of strange things on the shelves that lined the walls in the Van Dyke's garage and bikes hung upside down from hooks in the ceiling. Her Section Eight housing didn't have garages, so she found this space endlessly fascinating.

"C'mon. I want to go for a ride. Asher and Mazie will be down by the park today and I want to rub their noses in my cool new bike. Snub me at her birthday party. Humph. I hate her."

"She had a birthday party?" Quila asked.

Victory gave her the look. "Don't pretend with me, Quila. I know she invited you." She started adjusting things on her new bike, not making eye contact with Quila. "It was nice of you to boycott her party for me. Besides, you would just have been there as the token anyway. To show that she has a Black friend. Everybody wants you to be their friend. The 'amazing kid from the projects'. Geez, you're like a celebrity at school. Don't you get sick of it?"

Quila turned this new piece of information over in her mind. She was… popular? For any reason at all? That was something new. "Sick of being a token or a celebrity?"

"What's the difference? But you're safe. You don't scare people." Victory laughed out loud. "My mom says you're *inspirational*." She snorted. "She wishes you inspired me." She looked up at the bikes on the ceiling. "Let's take the bikes and go down to the park. Asher can drool over the bike and that I'm better friends with you than she is."

"Wait a minute—does that make me your token?"

"Oh, get over yourself!" Victory laughed at her. Together they got down Victory's old bike and the two girls took off. Quila loved riding a bike. Of course, she'd never had one of her own but since she spent so much time with Victory she learned to do a lot of the things that fell naturally into Victory's world. No one was at the park when they went by, which seemed to leave Victory agitated, as if her desire for mischief had gone unfulfilled.

"C'mon," Victory called over her shoulder as she took off on her bike. "Let's head to the shopping center."

Quila biked hard to keep up with Vicky. "Girl, when you want something," she panted, "you like a dog on a bone." A twenty-minute ride saw them to the shopping center, an upper end strip mall with nice stores, a Trader Joe's, and an old-fashioned everything five-and-dime type store that offered a nostalgic soda counter complete with ice cream. They locked up their bikes together and went in. Old Elton was working today, just like always. Quila didn't know what his real name was, but all the kids thought he looked like an old Elton John, so that's how he was known.

"Hello, Elton John!" Victory called out.

"Hello, Blondie! And Tina Turner! Nice to see you in today! You all getting some ice cream?"

"In a minute. We're just gonna' look around," Victory called back. They'd had to look up who Blondie and Tina Turner were after he'd started calling them that. They liked him even better after they streamed some of the old music. Quila loved the idea of her alter ego as Tina Turner, who seemed very elegant and talented to her. A strong Black woman who'd had rough years and made it out. Freed herself from her demons. She followed Victory up and down the aisles. "Did you bring any money?" Victory asked.

"Ugh, yeah."

"How much? I've got forty dollars."

"Oh my god, Vic! That's a fortune. I have twenty." She felt in her pocket to make sure. She worked hard for this helping some daughterless mother clean her house on Sunday mornings while her young boys all sat around and watched TV. The mother paid her twenty-five dollars while they scrubbed the house together from nine-to-noon every Sunday. Quila kept five for herself but twenty always went towards whatever the family needed, which was usually food. She didn't really like the work or that the lady always assigned her the bathrooms and mopping the floors, but she was grateful to have a way to make any money at all. Who else would hire an eleven-year-old kid? And she made sure the lady saw what a great job she did. She was working up her courage to ask for a raise.

"Let's buy a mess of candy."

Quila looked around her at the all the various items on the shelves. There were a lot of things there she'd rather have than candy. "I don't know, Vic."

"C'mon. Don't be such a wet rag! And they have those temporary tattoos. Let's get some of those and put them on tonight. Since you're staying the night, we can stay up late and eat candy and tribe up."

"Aw, you know those things never show up too well against my dark skin." Quila was worried that this slumber party might not turn out to be as much fun as she'd anticipated. Victory was certainly acting like she wanted to make some trouble.

"Then we'll get you the colorful ones," Victory announced definitively, as if the matter was settled. She went to the front of the store and got a basket, then proceeded to fill it with all sorts of candy bars and treats.

"How you gonna' eat all this?" Quila asked.

"Oh, shut it. Just pick out what you like."

"You planning on spending all your money there, Vic? I mean, that's a lot of candy."

"Will you look at that?" Victory noticed that a storage shelf under the candy display wasn't locked and stood open by a crack. She slid the door back revealing broken bags of candy which were spilling their contents, wrapped and unwrapped, onto the shelf below. She had a gleam in her eye. "I think we've found Elton's secret stash! I bet every once in a while, he

115

breaks open one of these by accident. Then he hides them here to take a nip as he likes." She turned towards Quila. "Let's take some!"

"What? Are you crazy? C'mon, Vic. Let's buy this stuff and get out of here."

"C'mon, Quila. What, you afraid?"

"Victory Van Dyke, you got a basket full of candy. Let's go. Look, I'll get this temporary tattoo." She grabbed one at random. "Now let's get back to the house so we can put them on." She grabbed Victory's arm and pulled her to the front of the store.

"My, my, my! You ladies have enough candy for a whole class there!" Elton John laughed as he rang up their orders. "You have a special event coming up next week?"

"Oh yeah, very special." Victory lied easily.

The two girls left with their bags of goods, Victory's laden with candy and Quila's considerably lighter but certainly coming at a dearer cost. She had spent nearly fifteen dollars and felt the loss of each one keenly, but it was worth it just to get Victory out of there.

"I want to go back in."

"You what?"

"I want to go back in. That candy's just lyin' there. No one's gonna' buy it. We should get some."

"Victory, don't you have enough?"

"It's never enough. And it's a lot more fun when it's free. It's a lot more… exciting." Victory had a gleam in her eye that Quila didn't like. "C'mon. We've got our bags. We can fill them. No one will ever know."

Before Quila could stop her, Victory went back into the store. Elton John was busy washing up and didn't see them come back in. Victory made a bee line for the candy section. No one was in the aisle. She got down on one knee and opened the door she knew to be unlocked, reached in her hand and pulled out a handful of candy, sliding it into the bag with all her purchased goods. She looked at Quila, a wild excitement in her eyes. She reached back in and took handful after handful.

Quila felt frozen. She didn't know what to do. Victory wasn't listening to her and clearly couldn't be stopped. She certainly wasn't going to rat out her friend, but she felt uncomfortable being shoved into the role of unwilling lookout as well. She had never been willing to play the edge. This felt like a new low.

"Okay, that's good." Victory stood up. Quila felt a sense of relief. Now if they could just get out of there. "Now you get some."

"What? I don't want any more candy!"

"No, you get some too. Partners in crime, that's us. Besides, you didn't buy nearly as much as I did, so this is your chance. Go on. I'll keep a lookout."

Quila rolled her eyes. "If we can go, then sure, I'll get a piece." She got down on her knees and reached in and grabbed a handful at random, throwing it into her bag.

"Another!" Victory egged her on. She was watching Quila hungrily. Quila shuddered and reached her hand in again.

"Just what are you doing?" Quila froze, her hand full in the cabinet and fingers wrapped around several loose pieces of candy. She looked up at Elton John looming over them, red-faced and angry. Her heart sank. She looked at Victory and could feel the tears welling in her eyes.

"Please don't be angry. We both thought the candy was going to be thrown out because the bags were all broken."

"I don't throw away the candy." His answer to Victory was rather gentle, given the circumstances. He turned to Quila and the harshness returned to his voice. "Have you been tearing open my bags of candy?"

"No sir, I haven't. It's not me." Quila started to wonder if it had been Victory who had been doing that after all? "We just saw the little door open,

117

and then we got curious, and then we, we, just, I made a really bad decision. I'm so sorry."

"Do you know what happens to little kids who steal?"

Quila looked up at him, tears streaming down her face. "Yes." She nodded and sniffed. "I do. They end up getting shot in the street when they twenty-five. They go bad. All their dreams die." She couldn't look in his eyes.

Mr. Elton John seemed taken aback. "Well, uh, um, yes! That's exactly what happens. Stealing is bad, very bad." He looked a little unsure of himself.

Victory pulled on his arm. "Please don't call the police on her. Please! She'll never do it again. I swear. I'm looking after her!"

"Look, Blondie," he put his hand on her shoulder. "You can't control her actions, so don't make promises you can't keep. You're a good girl, I know that. I see you in here all the time. And your mother." He turned back to Quila. "I won't call the police. They won't do anything with you anyway, seeing as you're just a couple of kids. But I *am* going to call your mother."

"She doesn't have a mother." Victory looked up at him with those baby blues, tears now in her eyes. "She's very poor. She never gets candy. She never gets anything, actually. Please go easy on her. Look at her—she's learned her lesson."

Quila felt utterly humiliated and couldn't even look up at the two of them, looming over her. She felt the tears dripping off her nose and could see them splashing on the floor. "I'm so sorry," she whispered.

"Well." He sounded unsure of himself. "Why is she with you?"

"She's spending the night at my house. So she can sleep in a bed she doesn't have to share."

Quila sat there frozen. She didn't share a bed. She shared a room, which Victory well knew. When did Vicky learn to lie so easily?

"Well, um, then I'll have to call your mother. I'll talk to her. Come with me, the both of you."

In the end he talked to Mrs. Van Dyke, who offered to come right down there and pay for all the candy that had been taken and bring the wayward young women home.

"Oh, that's all right. She looks like she's learned her lesson. You don't have to pay for the candy. All the damaged or broken bags I just donate to the food pantry anyway, so no worries. But I would like for you to give her a good talking to, as it sounds like she doesn't have any responsible parties at home."

Before they could leave, Mr. Elton John gave Quila another stern talking to about the troubled life she would have if she didn't learn from this and change her ways. "And I don't ever want to see you back in my store, Tina Turner. You're banned from the premises." Then he turned to Victory. "You, Blondie, you need to find some new friends. I know you feel sorry for her and all, given that she's a, a, well an orphan, but she's bad news. Kids like that don't change. You should find friends more like, like you. Kids who are growing up more like you. Good kids."

Quila swallowed. He was telling Victory that she shouldn't have Black friends. Or at least not this Black friend. The injustice made her want to scream but she was filled with shame at the thought of Grandma Mayme learning about this. It would crush Mayme for her to know what Quila had been caught doing. *He donates the candy to the food pantry? I've seen a candy jar there, but it's only kept for the people who volunteer—not shared with the poor folk who come to get food.* She thought it was a great irony just how many people actually did steal from the poor folk, who had so little to take. Even from the donations made to them.

The girls biked home. Quila was quiet but Victory was elated. "Did you see that! I totally got away with that. That was so cool. He never even suspected me."

"Of course, he didn't blame you. You're White!"

"I know. It's great, isn't it? Gotta love White privilege! Quila we make a great team. I got a huge haul. You had to put all yours back but that's okay,

119

I'll share with you. I got a ton and he never even suspected me. Wow, we're like Bonnie and Clyde."

"They ended up dead. Don't you remember? *You* stayed awake during that movie. *You* thought the ending was cool. I don't wanna' be Bonnie and Clyde. They were shot to pieces." A part of Quila could remember being shot to pieces. It wasn't a fun experience. Even in the relative safety of seeing that kind of violence on a screen, she couldn't appreciate it as entertainment.

"Yeah, but we'd be smarter than they were. They were idiots. They got caught. We didn't get caught."

"You didn't get caught. I got caught. I didn't even want the candy!"

"Yeah," Victory agreed. "I didn't get caught." She pedaled on. "Now we just have to get by Mom." When they got to the house Victory stashed her bag of candy in the garage. The girls put up the bikes and went into the house. Miss Tiffany was waiting for them, arms crossed. She sent Victory up to her room, saying that she was going to speak to each girl alone. Wide-eyed, Victory was reluctant to leave Quila alone with her mother. From behind her mother's back she signaled Quila to zip her lip. *So, she wants me to take the blame. All the blame for this.* Quila didn't know what to do. Didn't know where to turn. If she took the fall for both of them, Mrs. Van Dyke might never want her in her house again. Might never help her with her homework. Might never let her see Victory again. But if she told on Victory she was positive that Vicky would never, ever invite her over again.

Mrs. Van Dyke was stern. "So, I spoke with Mr. Anderson, who owns Suttons Old Time Everything Store. He told me what happened, but I want to hear it from you."

Quila started to cry again. "Well, we were buying some candy. Then we saw the door to the cabinet under the candy shelf was open a bit. Victory said they're usually closed. We were curious so we looked. There was a lot of candy there, just lying about. The bags were broken and I guess Mr. Elton John couldn't sell it."

"Who?"

"Oh, Mr. Elton John. You called him something else, but we thought he looked like an old Elton John, from that record you have that we like to listen to. And that's what we call him. We never knew his name."

"So, you took some? How much?"

Quila swallowed hard. "One handful."

"You took one handful?"

Quila nodded. "Just one. But one or a hundred, what does it matter? He told Victory that I'm not a good friend. That she shouldn't see me anymore. That she needed friends who looked like her."

Mrs. Van Dyke looked taken aback. "He was very upset," she said, but sounded unsure of herself.

Quila could only nod. She found it hard to breathe, much less speak.

"Quila, tell me why, when you'd just bought the candy that you wanted? Why steal more? Didn't you have enough?"

Quila remembered Victory saying, *It's never enough*. But she didn't feel that way. She answered truthfully. "I don't know why I did it. To be honest, I didn't even want the candy. There was other things that I wanted so much more in that store."

This made Miss Tiffany do a doubletake. "Other things? Like what?"

"Well, like spaghetti sauce. Do you know he has like eight kinds of spaghetti sauce over on the next aisle? And mayonnaise. Big jars of mayonnaise. And I even saw a little jar of those pickles, but they're all chopped up and sweet. That's what I really wanted, but we were there to buy some candy and I thought it would be weird if I bought mayonnaise."

"Why would you want those things? Instead of candy? Quila, do you have an eating disorder?"

"A what?" Quila had no idea what Miss Tiffany was talking about. "No." She thought that was the right answer because there was no way she could have something if she didn't even know what it was. "It's just that at the food pantry and at school on Fridays, they give you lots of spaghetti. And cans of tuna. But they never have anything in jars, so there's no mayonnaise.

And you can't make tuna fish sandwiches. I mean, I appreciate the tuna and all, but dry tuna, well, you can get used to eating it. And spaghetti is great, but spaghetti with no sauce gets really, well, boring all the time. And it's really dry. But they never have sauce or mayonnaise, so we just eat it like we get it."

"Doesn't your grandmother buy those things?"

"Most of Grandma's money goes for her medicines. She has diabetes and high blood pressure. It's hard for her to go to the store, so Rasheed and I take the bus and go to the pantry to get food. And school sends us home with weekend food in our backpacks. Those little boxes of milk they have leftover and little boxes of cereal. Before that, we took turns eating." She could feel her lip trembling. "I'm so sorry I took a handful of that candy, Miss Tiffany. I'm so sorry. I spent my money I saved from cleaning houses on candy because that's why we went there, but it wasn't even what I wanted. And I'm so sorry I took a handful of the stuff I thought Mr. Elton John was going to throw away." She burst into tears and put her face in her hands.

To her surprise, Mrs. Van Dyke didn't yell at her or even speak to her sternly. She grabbed Quila and hugged her tightly. "I'm so sorry, Quila. I'm so sorry. I didn't understand. I just never thought… I never knew." She never told Quila what she never knew. She just sent her up to take a bath and to tell Victory to come down.

Quila took a quick, but hot shower. She loved hot water. When she came back to the bedroom Victory was all giggles.

"So, I guess it went okay with your mother?"

"She never suspected a thing. And she loves you again. I reminded her how tough things are for you, so I think she's forgiven you. And the best part, look here!" Victory held up her bag from the store. "I was able to retrieve my stash and she didn't see me. So, it's you and me and this whole bag of candy!" Victory giggled again. She sat down where she was and dumped the bag on the floor, picking up a candy bar and tearing it open. "Go ahead, help yourself," she said around a mouthful as she chewed.

"I'm not sure if candy is what I want," Quila said. "It was kind of a hard day for me."

"Then chocolate is definitely what you need. Here, this one's your favorite." Victory held up a candy bar.

"Well," Quila looked at it. "Maybe just one."

Somehow one became many, as the girls laughed and joked and compared the various candy bars, rating the merits of each. After another hour went by, Quila started to feel queasy. "I don't feel so good." She rubbed her tummy gently. I think I ate too much candy."

"No such thing. This is nothing. You should see Jeremy and me on Christmas morning! Or Easter. Oh my god, Easter. Those huge chocolate bunnies. And all the gooey chocolate eggs!"

"Maybe…" Quila couldn't even fathom what that was like. "But I'm not used to it. We don't get much candy at Christmas and I've never seen an Easter basket. I mean, outside of those big clear plastic wrapped things they have at stores. I mean, I never got one. My mama always said we don't celebrate Easter. And Grandma says church makes her dizzy, so she just watches it on TV." Quila didn't share that her mama had always said *those holidays is for rich folk. White folk.*

"What's church got to do with it? I mean, my mom still does an egg hunt for us in the yard. And we get these huge baskets filled with chocolate. I swear, they only get them for us so they can steal candy and not feel like they bought it for themselves. It's all a game. And we have a ham dinner, sweet potatoes, green beans, potato rolls, same every year." Victory sat back and looked thoughtful. "And Christmas dinner is the same every year. And Thanksgiving."

Quila felt her stomach flip. "I think I'm gonna' be sick." She ran to the bathroom and threw up the chocolate bars and taffy and suckers and mints she had gorged on with Victory. Eventually her friend came in to check on her.

"Are you through yet? God, it smells in here! Yuck!" Victory wrinkled her nose.

Quila flushed the toilet for what must have been the fifth time. Then she fell back and lay on the floor. "I think I got it all out now." She looked at her friend. "Vic, I can't believe you feel fine. You ate more than I did."

"Oh, I've just had way more training than you have. You'll get better with practice."

"Uh… I'm not so sure I like candy anymore. I think I'm through with that. Learned my lesson."

Victory came over and sat down on the side of the tub. "You know, you're gonna' have to wash your hair. You got vomit in it."

"Oh no! This just gets worse and worse," Quila moaned. "It'll go all frizzy. What a pain."

Victory looked thoughtful. "Let's wash it and tell you what, I'll braid it for you."

"That's gonna' take a long time."

"Hey! I'm full of sugar and caffeine. I'm not sleeping for hours and hours! Besides, how long have I practiced on my Barbie salon head? I think I'm ready for the real thing."

As the girls stayed up late and Victory patiently worked on Quila's hair, she said, "You know, I really appreciate you not ratting me out to my mother. I never would have heard the end of that. And I never would have gotten my horseback riding lessons either. So, I want to give you my bike."

"You wanna' what?"

"Don't move your head. Not my new bike, silly. My old bike. The one you rode today. What am I gonna' do with two bikes? And you don't have one, right? Good, it's settled. I'll square it with Mom in the morning."

Quila dearly wanted a bike of her own. It would take her years of cleaning houses to save up enough money for one, so it wasn't even on her wish list, but she didn't like the feeling of being bribed. "You don't have to give me your bike."

"Don't be silly. You earned it!"

It took until 3 a.m. for Victory to finish Quila's hair – she did a passable job, even putting beads on the ends of the braids.

"Mom did bring up something kind of weird, though. She thinks I need a hobby. I mean besides horses. She wants me to start gymnastics lessons."

"Gymnastics? I know that. I've seen that on TV. And we did that in gym class some, too." Quila sighed. "I would love to take gymnastics lessons."

"Well, they're expensive. I don't think I'll be able to get out of it. When Tiffany's made up her mind about something like that, well, it's a done deal. I'm doomed."

Quila fell asleep and dreamed about what it would be like to learn gymnastics.

When they got up very late the next morning, Mrs. Van Dyke was out. The girls made pancakes for breakfast and Quila thought that if there was a food she wanted to eat herself sick on, pancakes would surely win out over candy. When it came time for Quila to go home, Miss Tiffany loaded up the kids and Victory's old bike in the back of her big SUV, along with one of those big re-usable grocery sacks. Pulling up to Quila's apartment, Mrs. Van Dyke waited while Victory walked the bike inside and Quila walked in with her backpack and the big reusable grocery sack Miss Tiffany had given her.

Victory looked around the grounds as they walked in. "Everything is so dead here. I mean they're a few trees but, Jesus Q, it's like nothing grows here."

Quila looked around. "Yeah, I know. Every few years people come and plant bushes and stuff but they just seem to die."

"Huh. I guess no one's got hoses to water them. Dad's watering the landscaping all the time with his sprinkler system."

"The only sprinklers we got here are the boys. They pee on the bushes. And then the bushes die."

125

For some reason Victory thought that was absolutely hilarious. They walked in the door and her laughter died. She parked the bike in the kids' room, looking around the whole time as if in mild shock at where her friend lived. But she had the courtesy to not say anything. Quila thanked her again for the bike.

"Mom totally went for it. Said it was good for me to think of other people for once and to get rid of extra stuff. She called it kid-downsizing." Victory chuckled as if it were a funny joke and then looked around again at Quila's home. Then she gave Quila a hug and went back out to rejoin her mother. Quila went into the tiny kitchen and opened the big bag Miss Tiffany had handed her. Inside she found a half a dozen jars of really nice pasta sauces, all kinds. And five jars of mayonnaise. And even three little jars of the sweet pickles for her tuna fish salad sandwiches. She wiped a tear away from her cheek and put her precious treasures up in the cupboard. There was plenty of space to spare.

Chapter 14

Quila decided that she loved gymnastics and it was all because of Victory. For her part, Victory couldn't have cared less about the classes. If Quila wasn't there, she didn't want to be there. Her performance was unimpressive, her engagement lackluster. The coach didn't want to waste his time on a girl who clearly didn't want to put in the effort. So, Miss Tiffany started looking about for scholarships that could support a poor, parentless Black girl from the projects to take expensive private gymnastics lessons with a bunch of rich, White, privileged kids. When Miss Tiffany had her mind set, Quila thought nothing would deter her. And it worked! As long as Quila was there, Victory did seem to be paying attention and at least trying. The coach adored Quila. Said she was a natural.

This experience was totally new for Quila, who dreamed, slept, and ate gymnastics. Most of her experience in this life was largely the same: same apartment in the small townhome-like Section Eight housing complex, Grandma Mayme and her benign neglect, same teachers, same kids at school. Deyonte was the same entrepreneurial troublemaker he had been the last time. Rasheed was still a comedian, but this time he was following her lead and actually working at his studies. He'd also gotten into a special "AVID" program at school that provided extra help for kids who weren't on a straight shot to college. It was making a huge difference for him. And now gymnastics opened up a whole new world for her.

She carefully cleaned up all the food wrappers, cigarette butts and the occasional discarded needle from a patch of grass in the common area so she could practice. The other little girls in the community would gather around, so she started to teach them what she had learned. It wasn't long before they had all the grass picked clean and she was teaching gymnastics lessons to eight little girls on the weekends and one night a week. She loved it.

What she didn't love was the thought that this second life had come about because of *him*. She wanted to hold on to the fear and hatred of *him*, the very creepiness of sitting in his office and reviewing her life. Of her hatred for this evil mission he had forced her on. She didn't want to even consider the slice of truth that her life was so different this time around *because* of his intervention.

One morning at breakfast Grandma Mayme was washing up some dishes and absent-mindedly said, "Even good things can come from an evil, mmmmm, mmmmm. Can't help itself, can it? The Lord work in mysterious ways. He the source of all. Mmmmmm, mmmmmm."

"Yeah, he's not the only one," Quila said under her breath without thinking as she was wiping dishes dry. It took her a while to figure out Mayme was talking about Waleed's new life and her own daughter's disappearance and abandonment of her children. And good things had come from that. Waleed was in a good place. His two dads kept in regular contact and he was doing great in school. It sounded like they doted on him. Waleed wasn't a part of her life in either round, so she loved the idea that he had a real life and a chance now. The fact that he lived past that fateful date before he was two years old showed her that the trajectory could be changed. It was possible. Things weren't fated and carved in stone. Yes, things were so much better this time around. If that was because of *him* then she wanted to ask, *Well then, where the hell were you last time?* But she got no answer.

"Mmmmmm, Mmmmm. Yes, the Lord is good. Thank you, Jesus, for our blessings."

Quila was lost in thought until she noticed Grandma Mayme giving her a stern look. She tossed out a quick "Amen!", which seemed to be what Mayme was waiting for. At least she continued on with her commentary about their being so very blessed. Although Quila wouldn't say it aloud, she had her doubts about those blessings and wondered how her grandma really felt. Sometimes, she admitted to herself, the praise Mayme heaped on the Lord seemed like it was aimed to placate God, in the hopes of avoiding being bestowed with any more misery.

Every night Quila went to bed afraid she would wake up back in the cloud, which meant she would lose track of her life and then, when it decided to drop her back into the stream of existence, she'd have to figure everything out all over again. But the years went by with her staying with the current of her life and she reveled in it. She hit the books. She went to gymnastics; she coached her girls. And she also stayed away from the people and mischief that had pulled her off course the last time. But her frustrations with Victory continued. And Jeremy was proving to be a real problem.

The peak came one weekend in eighth grade when she was spending the night over at the Van Dyke's for the first time in several weeks. Victory was growing into a little blonde bombshell way ahead of her time, but she had few girlfriends in middle school. She clung to Quila. Tall and gangly, Quila felt like she was the opposite of the blossoming Victory. While Victory lay on her bed upstairs, Quila brought down the empty glasses to put them in the dishwasher.

"Oh, thank you, Quila. I appreciate not having to scour the house to find all the glasses and dishes that seem to disappear. While you're here, can I ask you a question?"

"Sure, Miss Tiffany." Quila was sure this would be about gymnastics. Miss Tiffany was always asking her about gymnastics and how she might get Victory to be more engaged.

"Do you see Victoire having many friends at school?"

"I'm sorry?"

"Friends. Does she have friends? Besides you? Do you have a… a group of girls you're both friends with?"

"Um, well. There's…" and she drew a blank. "I only have a couple of courses with Victory. So, I don't see her in all her classes. We eat lunch together every day, but I don't know about all her other friends."

"Oh, okay. Thanks. It's just you're the only one she ever asks to have over and I know you two are very close."

"Yeah, we're very close. Best friends. Always have been. For like, forever."

"She certainly clings to you." Tiffany turned around and loaded the glasses into the dishwasher.

The interview seemed to be over, so Quila went back upstairs, feeling that was somehow a very odd conversation with Miss Tiffany. When Quila walked into Victory's room, the girl was languishing on her bed reading a Cosmopolitan magazine. Quila plopped down in the beanbag chair and picked up a copy of Seventeen, flipping through the pages, feeling amazed that this was supposed to be interesting to girls her age. "You know, this magazine is just stupid."

"I know. It's so fallen, I mean, who seriously reads that?"

Quila agreed. Not in any life could she find the contents of this thing interesting. Or that healthy for a young girl, she thought, his gift of 'wisdom' giving her insight beyond the years her current body had been living.

"Cosmo—now this is the stuff. This article is about having multiple orgasms when you have sex!"

"Victory! You don't need to be reading that!"

Vic laughed, a rather magical sound coming out of her. Perfect looks. Perfect smile. Perfect laugh. Quila thought that mix could be perfectly dangerous.

"You're such a prude! My boring prude friend!" Victory dissolved into giggles. Quila stared at her thinking that yes, this time around she probably was. Then she, too, succumbed to the giggles. "Seriously Q, you're my only friend. I hate those bitches at school."

"Vic! Geez man, watch your language. Besides, there's a lot of nice girls in our class."

"Well, yeah, if you like hanging out with a bunch of girls called Ashlee, Brittany, Emmie, and the fifteen versions of Kaitlee. Oh my god, they can't even pronounce my name right. It's like they want me to rhyme with them." Victory snorted.

"I thought you liked it that everyone called you Victory? I mean, only your parents call you Victoire."

Victory shrugged and was quiet for a while. "Besides, they're all boring."

Quila looked at her sideways. "Wait a minute… I thought *I* was boring?"

Victory gave her a big smile, the kind a future fashion model would shine on an adoring camera. "Yeah, but you're my special boring friend. You fill the space. I don't need any others 'cause I got my Q!"

Quila thought about Vic at school. They hung together during the few classes that they shared, but she started to wonder if it was more like clinging, now that Miss Tiffany had put that into her mind.

A rap at Victory's window startled them both. Vicky went over to the window, far braver than Quila herself would have been. While she now shared a room with Grandma Mayme, she had of course grown up with Deyonte, who used the bedroom window as his main doorway once the sun went down. Some really scary shit went both in and out of that window. But that kind of thing wasn't supposed to happen here. It was supposed to be safe here. Without a care in the world, Victory opened the window.

"Jeremy! What the hell are you doing?" Victory said as she helped her brother in.

"Duh. Sneaking in. Don't want Mom to know I was out." Then through his laughter he added, "She thinks I'm studying in my room!"

"Where were you?" Quila asked.

"Out. Needed a little pick me up. Hey girls, look what I got." He pulled a lumpy little white stick out of his pocket. "Wanna sit out on the roof and smoke some weed?"

At the same time that Quila asked an astonished "What?" Victory answered, "You bet!" and started to follow him back out. Quila hung back, not knowing what else to do. The memories came flooding back to her, the déjà vu of the moment giving her chills. She had done just this the last time around, following Jeremy out onto the roof, emboldened by all the times she had surreptitiously snuck out after Deyonte. But this time she watched Victory disappear after her brother. After a few minutes she followed them.

"C'mon out!" Jeremy invited, sounding gallant, offering Quila a hand. "Mademoiselle Victoire's room," he said with a fake French accent, "is the best one in the house. It faces the woods." He pointed.

"Uh, nice view," Quila said, not knowing what to say and feeling nervous. The pitch of the roof here did not make her feel safe. And they were high up. It was a really, really, long drop off the edge.

"Oh no, it's the not view. It's what can't be viewed." Jeremy laughed. "The 'rents room is on the other side. No one is gonna' see us up here and they can't smell it being so far away."

"Oh my god, if they did they would totally blame it on the Parker's. They blame everything on the Parker's." Victory turned to Quila. "It's so convenient to have neighbors your parents don't like."

"Yeah!" Jeremy laughed. "Anything they don't want to believe about their own lives they just blame on next door. It provides an expedient way for Mom and our never-at-home absentee dad to maintain their comfortable illusions about their fucking perfect lives!"

Quila was glad it was getting dark so neither of them could see her face. She could remember that Jeremy had done just this in their last time around and offered Quila her first toke of weed back when she'd been thirteen and was already into cigarettes and had no wisdom. Back in that other life, the one where Victory didn't own Seventeen or Cosmopolitan magazines, it was

Vic who had held back. Eventually Victory told her mother on Jeremy, but she had never brought Quila into it, knowing that her mother would put an end to their friendship. Jeremy had been sent to rehab. And maybe that had helped? Quila tried to remember the last time. What had happened to Jeremy? The more time she spent in this life, the fuzzier the details of the last time around became. Sure, she would have strong flashes of déjà vu but mostly the time spent re-living her life dulled the experiential wisdom guiding her. She could conjure up a fuzzy image of Jeremy: in and out of treatment programs, but never a whole person was the best she could come up with. She sat down beside Victory and Jeremy, wondering what to do. Were they some sort of twin Titanics, doomed and unwilling to listen to reason? Victory was inhaling deeply, holding it in, and then letting it out slow as she watched the smoke stream from her mouth. She looked like a pro.

"Nice," she finally said.

Jeremy laughed. "Yeah, it's good stuff. Here, Quila, your turn."

Quila kept her arms wrapped tightly around her legs. The pitch of the roof, the darkness, the clandestine aura; everything about this felt unsafe. "No thanks. I don't smoke. I got asthma."

"But it's not a cigarette. It's weed, man, it's just weed. It won't hurt you." Jeremy snorted.

Memories came flooding back of sneaking out of the apartment at night while Grandma Mayme was asleep. Deyonte did it all the time, slipping out their second story bedroom window. Only he'd stolen a ladder from god knew where and he climbed down. Rasheed had followed him. Then she'd followed them both. Oh, the adventures they'd had. The trouble she got into. The drugs she got hooked on before she was out of high school. She shook her head furiously. She wasn't going back there. She wasn't living that life again. She stared at the gutter a few feet below them. It was clogged with leaves and water. "I'm a gymnast. An athlete. We don't smoke. Vic, you shouldn't. It'll mess you up."

133

Victory looked spacy. "I'm no gymnast. I just do that for you. I hate gymnastics. But you're like the real thing, yeah, the real thing."

Jeremy reached across his little sister, insistent that Quila try it. She got an idea. Taking the joint from his hand she said, "I'm really nervous," and tried to sound the part.

"Just wrap your lips around it and suck," Jeremy said with a smile.

For some reason, Victory laughed hard and then a lot of things started to happen at once. First Victory started to slide on the roof pitch, which caused Jeremy to lose his grip on the steep surface as well. He went spread-eagle flat and stopped moving. But Victory was trying to turn over so she could grasp with her hands and bare feet, but rolling herself into a ball was not helping her gain any traction. She was scrabbling on the roofing tiles. Quila threw the joint into the clogged, wet gutter and grabbed Vic before she slid off the roof and fell two stories to the ground below. Lying on her back, she planted her feet and legs firmly and hauled Victory up by her shirt.

"My joint!" Jeremy said, more concerned about his weed than his little sister. Victory, however, was more than startled with fear. Not as much as she should have been, but enough that Quila was able to drag her back through the window. Jeremy followed them. "You little bitch. You lost my toke." His eyes were slits of anger.

"But I saved your sister!" She puffed up and stood up to him. "You woulda' let her fall off the roof and saved your pot instead? Are you insane?"

"Ugh! I should know better than to waste good shit on little girls!" He stormed out of the room.

Quila could hear Miss Tiffany call up the stairs at the sound of Jeremy's pounding footsteps, asking him if his math was frustrating him and if he needed any help.

"Frustrating. Yes. Help. No," he yelled back, and then went into his room and slammed the door.

Victory was still staring at the window. "I almost fell off the roof. Oh my god, I could have died." Victory was wide-eyed as she turned to Quila. "You saved my life."

Quila put her arm on Victory's shoulder. "That's what I'm here for, Vic. That's what I'm here for."

After her mother went to bed, Victory insisted that she needed some brownies. So, the girls snuck downstairs and raided the kitchen, bringing up a whole plate. Quila ate two. Victory ate six, giggling the whole time and saying how amazing they tasted and marveling at how hungry she was.

"Vic, have you done that before?"

"Done what? Eat a brownie?" She answered with her mouth full.

"No, I mean smoke. You just seemed, well, like you knew how."

"Oh sure. Sure, I have."

"When?"

Victory looked thoughtful. "Well, remember how Jeremy used to be so mean to us? Well, we've been getting a lot closer this summer." She giggled. "I think it's because my room is only one with a window you can use to escape the house. You just climb over the roof line and then you can get down by the corner of the garage. So, he's been a lot nicer to me. And he's let me come along sometimes."

"Come along? To where?"

Victory looked conspiratorial. "Well, last weekend he let me tag along with him and his friends again. I've gone a few times now."

"High school guys?" Quila knew her voice sounded like somebody's mother. Maybe the mother she would be someday, if everything in her world were truly different. She couldn't believe that Victory had kept this from her.

Victory didn't seem to notice. She was full of excitement. Awe even. "Yeah, isn't that cool?"

"I'm not sure, Vic. I mean, what happened? Were they nice to you?" In her experience, high schoolers thought middle schoolers were invisible. And

135

sometimes they shook you up for your lunch money. It made her glad she got free lunch since she wasn't as much of a target.

"Super nice. They shared their beers and joints with me. I mean, I was like one of them. And then we all decided to jump the fence to the swim club in one of their neighborhoods and we all went skinny dipping in the pool at night." She giggled. "Oh boy, if Mom ever found out she'd skin me alive!"

"You broke into the pool? And you went skinny dipping with all those boys?"

"There was another girl there, too," Victory added defensively. "I wasn't the only one."

"Oh my god! Vic, I'm not sure this is something to be, um, well, like, you know, happy about."

Quila was hit by a flashback from another life. It seemed ages ago now, climbing down the ladder and running around with Deyonte and Rasheed. She'd done all kind of things, smoked all kind of things. The memory made her blush now. More than that, it made her afraid for Victory. She could see that her own premature taste of freedom coupled with broad exposure to drugs, petty theft to support their fun, and eventually promiscuity were firm steps towards her premature demise.

"Why not?" Victory looked at Quila.

"Huh?" Quila answered, caught up in her visions of her wayward former self. "Why are we living opposite lives? You're making every mistake I made and I came here to save you. You can't do this!"

"Huh?" Victory asked in return. "Are you sure you didn't take a hit of that toke, 'cause you're not makin' any sense at all!" Victory laughed and ate her seventh brownie. "There's this one guy that I really like. His name is Liam and he's got these killer blue eyes and…"

"And he's in high school?"

"He's seventeen." Victory sighed. "He's sooo cool. Oh my god, Quila, I'm in love."

So many middle school girls fell in love every week, with some cute boy at school or in a boy band they'd seen in a video. This was nothing new to hear about.

"We've been out skinny dipping together twice now," Victory added.

"How do you get there?"

"Oh, he comes by and picks us up. Jeremy and I meet him one block over, so Mom and Dad won't hear the car. And then he drops us off back there too. He always brings the beer and he's always got pot. Says his parents grow it."

"You're drinking beer with them too?" Quila could feel her eyes blinking rapidly. "And smoking his parent's what?"

"It's home grown. Liam says it's for health reasons."

Quila's head was spinning. "Wait a minute, are you thinking this guy is like a… a boyfriend? 'Cause he's not. If he's seventeen and stealing his parent's medicinal pot and bringing beer for a girl in middle school, then he's not a boyfriend."

"Oh yes, he is. We've had sex." Victory looked around, glee on her face and then back at Quila. She whispered, "Twice!" She sighed deeply. "It was amazing. I've been dying to tell you, but I couldn't while we were at school."

"Victory, you are thirteen years old. That's too young."

"I don't look thirteen. Liam told me that. He said my body is a wonderland."

"I'll bet. Oh shit, girl. This is bad. Really bad."

"You're just jealous. He loves me. He told me so."

Quila could remember a lifetime when her older boyfriend said similar things to her. But he didn't stay around long after he got what he wanted. They stayed up late into the night talking about it, but Quila could not convince Victory otherwise. She loved him, she said, he was her forever love and that was all she needed to know.

As the next morning dawned, Quila felt depressed. They were reading about the French Revolution in school, and she thought she understood those people walking up to the guillotine, only in her world it was Miss Tiffany who was the executioner and it was this wonderful second life on the block. She loved Miss Tiffany in any life, but she was afraid to be the bearer of bad news. While Victory was in the shower and Jeremy was still in bed, Quila went downstairs and found Mrs. Van Dyke at the coffee maker.

"Miss Tiffany?"

"Yes, honey?"

"I need to talk to you. I need to tell you something. Something bad. But I'm afraid."

Tiffany turned around. "Did you have a bad dream, honey? Come here and sit down. Tell me all about it." She poured herself a cup of coffee and Quila a glass of milk.

After a stuttering start, Quila finally eked out that Jeremy had offered them both pot the previous night on the roof. She didn't have any idea how she was going to tell Miss Tiffany what Victory was up to.

Tiffany looked tight lipped. "That was a bad dream, Quila. That would be a bad dream for me, too."

"It wasn't no dream."

"It wasn't *a* dream," Miss Tiffany couldn't help her long-practiced habit as she corrected Quila's grammar. "But of course, it was. Jeremy was in his room doing his homework. His math class is really frustrating to him right now, but he's figuring it out. He's a good boy."

No matter which life, Quila knew better. Jeremy was anything but a good boy. And if he did for Victory this life what he had done for Quila in the last, well, that couldn't have a good outcome. But how could she explain that to a mother who blinded herself by her love for her children and her desire, her compulsion, to have a perfect family? "Miss Tiffany, Jeremy came in Victory's window last night. And he offered us a little white lumpy stick. I can tell you just where it is. It fell. I, uh, dropped it. And it fell into the gutter off the roof. Jeremy was powerful mad at us."

Tiffany looked concerned, but not in the way that Quila expected.

"I didn't try it." She looked at Mrs. Van Dyke's hard stare. And then she lied. She wasn't sure why, but heard herself say, "Neither did Victory. But I thought you should know. You know, in case Jeremy needs some help?" She hoped that if Jeremy got help, he might not have the opportunity to be leading Victory out at night. And astray. The look on Mrs. Van Dyke's face melted any of the courage she might have found to tell her the truth about what her daughter was up to.

Miss Tiffany's reaction was instant. "My Jeremy would never…" Then she let out a deep breath. "Get your things, Quila. I think it's time I take you home."

"Miss Tiffany?"

"I'm taking you home. Right now."

"Before breakfast?" Qulia felt stunned.

Miss Tiffany didn't say another word. Quila went upstairs to get her things and before Victory was out of the shower they had left. When Mrs. Van Dyke dropped her off at the apartment, she said, "Oh, and Quila, I'm sorry but I won't be able to carpool anymore to gymnastics. You'll need to find your own ride." She pulled out without another word.

Quila was crying as she went indoors, wishing she could walk through the door and right back into that white cloud. She wanted to be away from this life now. The pain and isolation of losing her best friend, her foster family as she had come to think of them, and losing her mission came crushing down on her. *His* mission seemed to be well in hand. Victory seemed to be on a crash course heading for the office of the Well-Dressed-Man, but *her* mission was to steer Victory well away, to deny him the prize of a corrupted little-goody-two-shoes. If anybody was a little goody-two-shoes now, it was Quila.

She made up for missing gymnastics by holding impromptu extra 'classes' for the neighborhood. She now had fifteen girls she was tutoring in tumbling. And she started homework night in the community center room right after school each night. At school, Victory was grateful at not having been ratted out, as she called it, but added, "Mom is so mad. She said I will never see you again outside of school. Called you a liar. A liar about Jeremy."

"And what did you say?"

"Me? Nothing. I'm not stupid."

"And Jeremy?"

"He just shrugged. He said, 'what can you expect from a…' well, I won't tell you what he said," Victory added, giving it a second thought.

It was two months later that Mrs. Van Dyke showed up at Quila's door, asking Grandma Mayme if she could talk to Quila.

"I thought you forgot all 'bout her. You nearly broke her heart, she been cryin' so much." Mayme crossed her arms, giving Miss Tiffany a most admonishing look.

Quila came to the door when called, nervous that Miss Tiffany might be stern with her again, or worse yet, yell at her, which was something Miss Tiffany had never done in any life. Quila was afraid to hope that Victory would be with her and by some angel's magic, everything was going to be okay. But there was no Victory. There was just Miss Tiffany who looked awkward and uncomfortable.

Tiffany took Quila out for an ice cream sundae and even encouraged her to order the largest one on the menu. Miss Tiffany ordered black coffee. Quila wasn't half-way through when Tiffany said, "Quila, I brought you out today because I wanted to apologize. It's been a rough couple of months for me." She dabbed at her eyes.

Quila froze, the spoon in her mouth. She nodded, having no idea where this conversation was going. She felt a bit numb and a whole lot nervous and didn't want to say or do any wrong thing. She wanted Victory back.

"You see, I was so angry when you told me about Jeremy. And I didn't believe you. I couldn't understand why you would lie to me like that. Of course, Jeremy denied everything. But I wanted you to know I had the gutters cleaned."

Quila nodded again. She thought she understood, but having gutters cleaned where she lived meant a few people from outside the community came in and picked up the debris and trash and old pine needles and decaying leaves from out of the curbs so that the water could flow to the sewer.

"And I asked the men to keep an eye out. And they came and told me they did find an old rotted, um, hand rolled cigarette."

"Oh."

"And then Dr. Van Dyke and I searched his room. And we found, well, more. So now we know. We're getting Jeremy some help. So, I wanted to apologize, Quila, for not believing you. For blaming you. I feel so awful and I hope you can forgive me." Miss Tiffany was seriously crying now and people in the ice cream shop were staring at this White woman sitting there with tears streaming down her face while she watched a Black teenager eating an enormous ice cream sundae.

A woman and her son walked by, staring at them. Quila could clearly hear the son explaining to his mom, "Oh, she probably videoed the bigot in a really racist tirade and posted it."

"Oh, so she's begging for forgiveness?" The mother answered.

"Nah, probably just begging for her to take it down so she'll stop getting death threats."

"What an awful woman…"

And they walked out the door of the shop. Miss Tiffany rubbed her forehead like she was developing a massive headache.

Quila reached out and took the older woman's hand in her own. "Miss Tiffany, you don't have to apologize. I mean I appreciate it. And the ice cream sundae. Man, I never had anything like this before. So, I mean,

141

thanks. I get it. I know how hard it was to hear that about Jeremy. And I want you to save him, too. That's why I told you. And I think he's the kid who was jumping the fence at the local pools."

She could hear Tiffany gasp.

"I don't know more than that. About him. But I think he needs help. I'm glad you're going to save him."

"You have the heart of a lion, Tequila Williams. The heart of a lion. I can't believe you're thirteen years old."

Quila gave her a little half smile. "Me neither. Some days, it feels like I've lived lifetimes."

Miss Tiffany asked if she could take Quila back to gymnastics. She wanted Quila and Victory to maintain their friendship. "I think you are a very good influence on Victory. I'm so sorry I interfered. Please understand I was trying to protect my little girl. But I was protecting her from the wrong thing. I was so blind. Again, Quila, I'm so sorry. So very sorry."

They all fell back into their old pattern of Quila going home with Victory a few days a week and helping her with her homework, going to gymnastics on the weekends, and having regular sleepovers at the Van Dykes. What didn't change was that Tiffany would never let Victory play over at Quila's. She didn't think it was safe. Quila thought it just went to show that the poor Mama Tiger had no idea where the real danger came from.

Quila would come home from doing homework at Victory's and then help Rasheed with his, but he was starting to do pretty well on his own by now and high school was going okay for him. He was turning out to be a solid B-student. A couple of the adults in the complex had picked up on Quila's homework-club-at-the-community-room concept. Even though she was only there one night a week now, it was still going thanks to the dedication of two older moms who were determined to see the kids growing up in the projects finding a different future for themselves.

Quila felt rekindled hope for her mission after all. But she could feel *him*, feel him in the background, and she wondered what kind of curveball he would throw next.

Chapter 15

Quila slowly emerged from what felt like the deepest sleep she'd ever experienced. Her senses felt dulled and she had to fight to actually wake up. It took her a while to realize that the fogginess of her mind was actually the white cloud. "No!" She tried to scream it out, to object to whatever power was toying with her like this. She needed to be back in her life. Well, she needed to be in *Victory's* life. The butterfly effect of gentle nudges might have had miracle downstream impacts on Rasheed's trajectory, but Victory absolutely needed someone sitting on her. She needed Quila. "Please send me back! Please send me back!" she implored to whatever deity was listening. This pull-out felt so deep, it was so *unconscious* that she was afraid a lot of time had passed, maybe years and years, and it would be all too late. Maybe the Well-Dressed-Man thought she'd done a good job of corrupting his prize and he was done with Quila, and he'd just parked her up in his little private cloud for safe-keeping? Maybe she was sitting in purgatory until judgement day? Maybe she would never know what had happened to Victory? That really bothered her the most. Powerlessness coupled with unknowing.

What she did know was that Victory had made horrible choices, just as Quila had her first time around, and now it was like some runaway train that Quila didn't know how to stop. She didn't seem to know where the emergency break was. One thing she was sure of: she wouldn't be able to find any kind of lever from up here. She was no guardian angel with divine powers. For all she knew, she was just a soul trapped like a genie in a bottle, floating in a peaceful ocean of white.

"Why am I here? I need to be down there!" She had no idea if anyone was listening. Then it struck her: Victory wasn't just living the opposite life of Quila. She was living Quila's life. Her first life. Making all the choices Quila herself had made. Despite all her privileges, she was making all those same dumb decisions. Quila felt a heaviness as she thought about what awaited Victory. She was confident she could steer her friend away from those landmines, if only she could get back.

Then she started pondering why she herself was in a different place back down there in her life. The settings were the same. Same family, same house. Same poverty even. But subtle differences came into play and maybe they had butterfly effects of their own? In her first experience, hunger was a constant companion; she had to wait for her day to eat dinner because there just wasn't enough food to go around. She was parentless and adrift far too often. She lived in fear, first of her mama's boyfriends, then of the big boys in the neighborhood, then of just about everybody. Fear took a toll. It ground you down and wore you out. And then you just weren't able to make a good decision from the severely limited choices you had. You became like an old, weathered board, the paint worn off and the wood warped and weak, when you lived in constant anxiety. Then there was nothing left in you to fight the system that built the walls that trapped you there and held you prisoner.

This time around she was still poor. They ate because of food stamps and free lunch, but compared to last time, it was like night and day. Last time they weren't hooked into social services. Not going hungry really changed everything for her and her brothers. Hunger made you fierce. She was still parentless, but this time she had people who believed in her. Who gave her not only chances, but second chances. Miss Tiffany had jumped in early on, just like before, but now Quila had totally different relationships with her teachers. They believed in her. They invested in her. The principal treated her with respect, held her up as a role model. Mothers in the complex asked her questions, seeing how she was so good in school, and called her a leader for starting the homework club and the girls' gymnastics on the grassy lawn. When she looked back each change was so small. But such small changes, like someone important in your life who believed in you and gave you the chance to believe in yourself, well, they all added up to a lot of difference. It made those walls lower and allowed you to jump over them.

"And that difference works both ways." Now, it seemed that Victory wanted to make all the dumb choices Quila had made. "I would do anything to save her," she said, but it was almost like a whisper. "She doesn't deserve my fate. She isn't that person that I was. I'm not that person that I was." The powerlessness covered her like a blanket of snow, freezing her, immobilizing her. Drifting, the thought occurred to her of what she'd heard once. *Thy will be done.* It bothered her that she could yearn to make a difference, was willing to sacrifice her own happiness as necessary to help Vic, and yet the reality was that she was not in control. She could do what she could do when she could do it, but creating the situation was beyond her. She would step up, but some door had to open first. She felt like a passenger on someone else's ride. "I understand I'm not driving this," she said aloud to whatever spirit might be listening. "I understand I'm just a piece in the whole puzzle. A drop in the ocean. I get it, this isn't my game where I can call the shots." That was a bitter realization for her. Even in her disastrous life, she had always told herself that it was her life, she was in charge. She could make her own decisions and control her own destiny. Nobody could boss her around. That false bravado to cover her fear. It was hard to float here and see just how insignificant she really was. "But I want to make a difference. Please, if I'm just a piece on the board, please use me to help. Please."

It seemed like a very long time that she just floated there. Finally, the mist seemed to move and swirl. She waited, trying to be patient, not sure what might be happening. Slowly the mist started to thin and she saw fuzzy images start to emerge. She thought her heart should be beating fast, but here she had no heart or body. Just awareness. It looked like a long hallway. For a moment she was afraid she'd died again and this was that tunnel of light everyone talked about, but she thought it was an awfully dingy glow to be illuminating eternity. Then she could see long lights and thought there was no way eternity would have fluorescent bulbs. No, that looked like what you saw in a school. In fact, it looked like how her old high school used to look. She peered harder at the image and then she was sure it looked like a school. It felt very familiar. At last, the scene came into clarity.

She watched herself walk down the hall. Suddenly she remembered all of this so clearly. The hallway of the high school. The sounds. The colors. But something was missing. She couldn't place it, but something wasn't there that was supposed to be. Her attention was diverted by a young girl walking down the hall. It was Victory. And there, in her wake was Quila. The young Quila looked unsure whether she owned that space, treading in the path created by so much more confidence, by so much more privilege and defiance that was Vicky. When Quila last remembered being present in this life, the self she knew was full of confidence. What could have happened while her spirit-self had been stuck up in that cloud? At least she was still young. And so was Victory. There was still time.

It struck her what this moment was—this was when she got pulled into the gang world. This was the moment. The moment when she would grasp at a place where she felt she could actually belong. Devan would call her out in a second. She and Vicky would have such a fight after this, the old Vicky warning her and the old Quila turning her back and walking away. Quila focused on her younger self, wanting to comfort away the insecurity she could see in the younger girl's eyes. She could sense that feeling of being an imposter walking in her own shoes that she had felt the first time around. What could have happened to shake the confidence of this Quila? She moved beside her younger self and wondered what she could do. She was transparent, like a ghost—obviously no one could see her. It was clear that her younger self couldn't feel her presence. She leaned over to whisper to her that she was alright. She could own her space. She deserved to be here. She didn't have to prove anything to anyone. She didn't need anyone's protection. That Quila was a whole person. She always had been, no matter which life they were talking about.

As she leaned in and her lips touched young Quila's ear, she felt a whooshing sound and suddenly there she was—she was Quila. And she smelled it. That's what had been missing. The smell of the school. With her right hand she pinched her left elbow. *Ouch. Okay, felt that.* She sniffed. *Sure can smell that.* And then excitedly she said out loud, "I'm back! Thank you! I'm back!"

Devan stepped into her path. "Hey, girl. You welcome. You lookin' pretty right. You tight, baby. You tight. Say, whatcha' doin' tonight."

When this had happened before, she couldn't help but smiling at him and his rappin' in the hallway for her, though she knew it was him dealing in the bathroom. She knew it was him who had knocked up Queenie, and then had told her to get rid of it or he'd cut it out of her. And Quila'd been his next girlfriend after that. Like seeing dominoes lined up to fall, she could see the steps of the path in front of her fifteen-year-old self. The steps that led to her being shot in a street in ten years. Of course, he'd been long gone by then. But she'd gone on, getting in deeper and deeper, each step inexorably leading to her doom. And *him*. With those dark eyes that looked like they had no bottom. Like a shark's. He'd thrown her back into the pool and now here she was, haunting her younger self.

She remembered her mission. He'd told her to bring him Victory—a soul worthy of capture. But she was going to defeat the Devil. She was going to save her best friend. The young Quila she'd stepped into might not have much confidence left, but that was a gap she could fill.

"I said, whatch' doin' tonight! Hey, don't you walk by me like you never seen me, bitch." Devan was not a boy who got ignored.

She stopped in her tracks. Slowly she turned. She walked up to Devan and before she knew it, she was aggressively grabbing his collar and pulling

149

him close to her face. She backed him up to the wall and pinned him there. "Look here, Devan, I'm warning you. You are so close to the edge and he's gonna' have you. And you gonna' burn, man."

Devan's smile melted away as he stared at her. "Whatchu' talkin' 'bout?"

"He's breathing down your neck. Can't you feel it? I can see him already, claws in you and dragging you down. I'll give you a tip: quit dealing in the shitter now or Biggie gonna' gun you down when you nineteen. You be layin' in the street lookin' up at the sky and I'm gonna' watch the life bleed right outta' you. And you gonna' be scared. So shit scared that you gonna' look white when the Devil come an' claim you. I'm gonna' stand over you and see the life fade away. Don't you make me do that again! Don't you make me!" She threw him back against the locker with a strength she never knew she had. He slammed into the wall of metal doors and crumpled, eyes locked onto hers. She could see he was scared. Not by what she said. He was scared of Biggie.

She turned around and left him there, in a circle of kids speechless and staring. "C'mon, Vicky. He's a bad man and he gonna' die before he's twenty. Ain't nothin' we can do for him now." Like the other kids, Victory stared at Quila, but she fell in line and followed her. Quila turned back to look at Devan, who met her eye, still sprawled on the floor as though he'd seen a ghost.

As they walked into their class and took their seats, Victory leaned into Quila. "You are such a bad ass, girl! I can't believe you did that. How did you know he was dealing?"

Quila didn't quite know what to say. She was trying to figure out the pieces she was missing. What had happened while she was gone?

"Who's teaching this class?"

"Duh. Mrs. Gradenko. I hate her. She hates you."

"Oh, yeah. She's like that teacher who's secretly a right wing supremacist, isn't she?" Quila looked around. "I remember her. So, this is geography, isn't it?"

"Duh," Victory giggled. Then she looked at Quila, curiosity filling her face. "You're different today. More like your old self. And that locker scene. Hell, Q, you scared the shit out of poor little Devan. Made me feel sorry for him. Say, you aren't gonna' tell the principal that he's been dealin', are you?"

Quila was trying to comprehend what Victory was saying. "Huh?"

"I just mean, since Jeremy was sent to alternative school, and then rehab, I mean, the only source I have is Devan. If you bust him, I'll have to be looking again."

Quila could feel her mouth fall open. "Vic, you can't buy from him. It will ruin you. It will hurt you."

"Nah. It makes me feel good. Means I don't have to listen to my parents' fights. Helps me tune out."

"Your parents' fights? What?"

"Oh sure, I told you. You heard one last time you were over, don't you remember? You know, after I had the, uh, procedure. When Daddy found out. Boy, was he pissed at Mom."

Quila felt her head spinning. "Procedure?"

Victory looked around them, as if to assure herself she wouldn't be overheard. Then she whispered, "Yeah, the abortion. You came over to be with me while I healed up. Man, that sucked. Thanks for going with me. You are the best friend ever. Walking through all those protesters shouting at us, screaming in our faces. Man, I'll never forget what you did for me!"

Quila's heart wasn't just skipping a beat. She was sure it had stopped altogether. She went with Victory? And just what had she done? Pay for it? Force her to go? She couldn't even imagine. "I did something? For you?"

"Yeah! Don't you remember? Jesus, Q, you're the bravest person I know. You squared your shoulders and as those crazy zealots were spitting in my face you told them it was you instead, so they'd leave me alone. Oh shit, they called you all kinds of nasty things."

"They did?"

"Oh yeah. I won't repeat it. Some Christians they were, waving those "Jesus Saves" signs. Name only, man, name only. It was ugly." Victory looked down at the floor. "And I never really said thank you for that. I was so sick, barfing all the time and they were in my face and I… I just want to say thank you for doing that. For getting them off me."

Quila looked at Victory. So, it had already happened. The bad decisions that Quila had made were now haunting Victory and Quila had been up in the cloud, unable to prevent it. Quila could well remember her own 'procedure' from her first life. It was unpleasant indeed. And she hadn't been here to save Victory from following that path. She hated the cloud.

Victory put her hand over Quila's. "You're my best friend. Thanks. I hope it doesn't haunt your dreams anymore." Victory actually looked guilty.

Quila looked at the pale blonde girl sitting next to her. "Honestly, Vic, it's like it never happened. Like it's been wiped from my memory." She looked up as Mrs. Gradenko came into the room. "Just like geography, it's like it never happened."

Quila caught up quickly on the events she had missed in the last year since she hadn't been present in this life. It took a trip to the Open Eye Café and a latte to get Victory to spill about all the events of the past year.

"You know, I can't believe you're sitting there, being so good, listening to all this again. Mom tells me to quit whining. You know, even my therapist says I'm dwelling too much. 'Perseverating' she calls it."

"Well, sometimes you just gotta' get it all out." Quila nodded, grateful for Victory to apparently rehash what they'd been through dozens of times.

"Yeah. Get it all out. That's right. Do you know Dad put a safe in the house?"

"He did?"

"Yeah, a big one. A hidden one. It's installed behind a cabinet door in the basement. Looks just like all the doors covering up the old board games."

Quila knew Dr. Van Dyke made a lot, but enough to need a safe? It wasn't like he made millions. "But why? I mean, what's the point?"

"Jeremy's the point. When Jeremy went to the Phoenix Academy after getting kicked out of school, he was stealing stuff. Most of mom's silver was gone, one spoon at a time, before they caught on. That's how he paid for it, all the stuff he went through. So, when they sent him to rehab Daddy had the safe installed. You should have seen him trying to shove everything precious to him in there. I've never heard him curse like that."

"Wow. That's heavy."

"Yeah." Victory looked down into her half-empty cup. "He didn't know I was there. Didn't know I was listening. But now I know what he's really thinking." She got quiet.

"And what is he thinking?" Quila's voice was almost a whisper.

Victory looked up, false bravado on her face. "That this was not the family he deserved. That it must be Mom's fault, while he was off working that she must have done something wrong. She must have been a terrible parent, a bad influence on us."

"No! Miss Tiffany's an amazing mother. A little too particular about the grammar maybe, but she's been a mother to the both of us!" Quila could feel her hand shaking at such a shocking allegation coming from Drake Van Dyke. "How could he say that?"

Victory shrugged. "Well, he was super pissed when he found out about the abortion."

Quila motioned for Victory to lower her voice.

"And I think Mom's been drinking. She was pretty distraught when she found that her mother's silver had been traded for Jeremy's pastime."

"Habit? You mean his drug habit?"

"Well, to be fair, he also bought some righteous video games as well, so I think pastime is a better descriptor. I mean Mom's always had a glass or two of wine every night, but when Jeremy went to rehab, she started drinking harder stuff. And when Dad screamed at her that it was her fault

153

that we turned out like we did, well, then she started skipping the mixers. But only when he's not around. She really doesn't want him to know."

"Miss Tiffany's hitting the bottle?" Quila struggled with fury at being away for so long but was grateful to have come back at all. Maybe there was still time. She'd missed the unintended pregnancy, though. She wished she could have spared Victory that. "Hey Vic," she changed the subject. "Have you, uh, heard anything from Liam?"

Victory was quiet for more than a moment. "You were right. I've accepted it. He's long gone. I hate him."

"Was he the, uh, father?"

"I don't know? Maybe? Probably?" Victory shrugged.

Quila blinked. "So, are you on birth control?"

"Oh yeah!" Victory brightened. "I went with the LARC you insisted on. That long-acting stuff. Remember, you told me I'd never remember to take the pill every day or even to put on the patch every week." Victory laughed. "I was so pissed at you, but you were right. Once again, Tequila Williams, you were right." Victory sat back and looked curiously at her friend. "You know, sometimes you seem older than we really are. It's weird. It's like sometimes you're just a girl like me, and we're both scared shitless about what's gonna' happen to us. But sometimes you're like…"

"Like what?"

"I don't know. Like an old soul. Isn't that corny shit?" Victory burst out laughing.

Quila laughed too. "It's not the years. It's the mileage, baby. It's the mileage." She didn't think Victory caught the movie reference. Maybe the world wasn't really the same at all… maybe those butterfly effects abounded and lots of little things had changed?

On her bus ride home she contemplated all that had happened while she'd been away. After she'd told on Jeremy and his parents found his drugs, Jeremy went into alternative school and then bottomed out of that too. He would be home from rehab in a couple of weeks. He'd earned a GED there. Tiffany was drinking heavily while Victory was sure her dad was having an affair. Their marriage was more on the rocks than what filled Tiffany's cocktail glass every night. Victory's world was crumbling around her and she was using to numb her pain and sleeping with her dealers to pay for it, given that everything of value was locked up in the big secret safe. Jeremy hadn't been the only one with sticky fingers. Quila might have seemed forgetful, needing to be caught up on Victory's life, but Victory was good at keeping secrets too.

All Quila wanted right now was to hug her grandmother and hold her tight. She wanted to be home and back in her old life where things actually felt safer than the privileged hell Victory was living in. "Grandma! I'm home!" she called out excitedly as she went through the front door.

"Oh, my darlin'! There you are!" Mayme gave her a hug. "You home a bit early. Didn't you go over to that little friend of yours? That Victory girl who stirs up so much trouble?" Grandma Mayme didn't really approve of Quila's best friend and would rarely say her name. She snorted. "Odd name for such a troubled chil' who ain't gonna' win at nothin' in life." Then she softened and said, "Everything all right there, Quila darlin?"

Quila was still holding on to her grandma, not wanting to let go. She knew how short their time was going to be, whether she had her gift of wisdom or not. There were some courses of fate she could not change, like the ravages of diabetes and heart disease on an old body that had seen too much pain and couldn't kick the comfort and companionship of her cigarettes. "I just love you so much, Grandma Mayme. I never wanna' leave your arms."

Mayme patted her on the back and stroked her head. "There, there chil'. There, there. Did that bad little girl upset you?"

Quila struggled to explain what she was feeling. Last time Vic had been able to see what happened to Quila, and she'd learned from the experience of Quila's choices. This time, Quila had turned away from the hard path and it was like Victory then had to experience the darkness for herself. But she wasn't equipped for it and struggled to find her way back to the light. Quila shook her head. There was no way to explain that to Grandma Mayme. The poor woman would think Quila had gone mad.

"No! Nothing like that. She's going through a hard time. And she's not bad. She just… she just didn't have anyone to show her this time, so she had to figure it all out for herself. It's just the circumstances. It's just all that's going on. In another life, she'd be a totally different person."

"Wouldn't we all?" Mayme chuckled and patted Quila on the back. Then she pulled back and looked her granddaughter in the eye. "Now you listen up," she said very gently. "It how you live that matter. The choices you make. If she can only be a good girl because her circumstances are right, then she can't be a good girl at all."

"I don't know about that, Mayme. It seems to me that those circumstances make a lot of difference. And if you change the circumstances, you can make or break someone's very life. Like a butterfly flaps it's wings in Japan and a cyclone hits Hawaii."

Mayme threw her head back and laughed out loud. "Well, I can see that my little philosopher is back. Girl, the things you say would twist the Devil himself up in knots! You been so quiet these last few months, I thought we lost you somehow. I thought you got the depression."

Quila smiled at her grandma. "I'm here. I'm back. And I'm so happy to just be in your arms. Tell you what, let me make dinner tonight."

"Like you do every night?" Mayme laughed. "Lord knows my eyesight so bad, I can't even set the microwave no more. Thank goodness for Rasheed, who heats me up a little meal when he come home from school before he head out to your homework club. Bless him, for runnin' it now that you so busy with all that bending and jumping you doing. Man was born to be a teacher."

Quila felt her heart race. So, Rasheed had not fallen off the path while she'd been sentenced to her time in the cloud! Happiness flooded her. "I'll see if I can't whip up something special." Quila released Mayme and went into the kitchen to see what she might find. Someone had been to the food pantry lately and from the paperwork on the counter, the EBT card had been used to get a community farm produce home delivery. The box looked like it might have arrived yesterday. "I can work with this," she said aloud as Mayme shuffled into the kitchen. "What time will Deyonte be home?"

"Deyonte? Honey, don't you hurt me like that. You know he gone. Long gone."

Quila felt like someone had pulled the plug and everything that had been inside her suddenly drained away.

"Deyonte is gone? Like the Bison got Daddy?" Images of Bobby being gunned down by the Bison filled her mind and tears started running down her cheeks.

"Oh, my goodness, come here, come here." Mayme took her in her arms again. "He not dead. He call last weekend. Didn't I tell you? I'm so forgetful these days. Maybe I didn't tell you! He wonder when you gonna' come an visit him again. He said it lonely there. Two more years be a long time before he get out. I can't make the trip—it too much on me. But he said he love it when you and Rasheed come to visit him."

Quila took in a deep breath. He was in jail. Not dead. In jail.

Mayme patted her on the back again. "You okay, Quila? You look like you seen a ghost. Don't you worry overmuch. Deyonte a smart boy. He know how to survive in there. He not gonna' open his mouth like Bobby did. That boy know how to survive." Mayme went over to the box of vegetables labeled 'CSA Farm to Fork'. She picked up a big bunch of arugula. "I don't know what you gonna' do with this weed to make it taste good. It just bitter. Mmmmmm, mmmmm," she added disapprovingly. "Anything else you need, honey?"

Quila looked up at the ceiling. "A really, really big butterfly."

"Mmmmm, mmmmm. Girl, the strangest things do come outta' you mouth. The strangest things."

Chapter 16

The days and weeks passed by, with Quila going to school, studying hard, dragging Victory to the gymnastics team practice, and making sure Rasheed stayed on track. It turned out he was her easiest challenge. Mayme was right, the man was born to be a teacher. He loved homework club, particularly working with the young kids. He was a senior in high school now and was looking at colleges. He had several of the historically Black colleges on his radar and it was practically all he talked about.

Quila was relieved that her younger self had been engaged in school while she was remanded up to the wherever. Her grades had not suffered while she'd been away and the Quila she was becoming in this life was a star athlete on the gymnastics team. But as her junior year began, Devan started to dog her heels. One day he cornered her during lunch.

"Why you tell me Biggie gonna' gun me down? Biggie my friend. He my man. He got my back."

Quila didn't know what to say. Were there rules to this game? Surely, she couldn't tell him she'd seen him in another life and while the shadows of this life remained unchanged, his destiny was set in cold, hard stone. No, it was too much like a Dickens novel and it was corny, even if Devan would have no idea who Dickens was.

"You answer me! Why you say Biggie gonna' gun me down? Why? What you know? Who you been listenin' to?" Devan didn't just look mad. He looked scared.

"Devan, I can't tell you how I know. No, nobody said nothin' to me so I'm not covering for anyone. Think about it—who ever live long in that world? You know a man over thirty? Over twenty-five?"

"Biggie twenty-five."

"Yeah, and that's mostly because all the boys around him either go to jail or wind up on the news. Either way, that's a dead-end road, Devan. Don't you go down that dead end road. Ain't nothin' for you there."

"And what about the claws? You said claws was in me?" Devan now looked very unsure of himself. His eyes were wide, showing the whites against his dark skin. She could smell fear on him.

She looked at him very seriously and decided it was okay if he thought she was crazy. Maybe sometimes it took a really big butterfly to create an effect. "Okay, Devan. I'm going to take a risk. I'm gonna' tell you to get out. Get out while you can, brother. He breathing down your neck. He gonna' take your very soul. You don't want to go through that door. I've seen it. It cold. Cold like the grave. You can feel it without touching it. And it burns you, it burns. You gotta turn back. Biggie gonna' sell you out. He gonna' feel threatened by you. And he gonna' gun you down on the street. And no one will ever remember your name. You just gonna' be another Black kid on the news. Just a statistic. Your slate wiped clean, but not your fate."

Devan's eyes widened even further the whole time she spoke. His mouth was open and a little bit of spit ran down at the edge. As she finished, he stared at her, mesmerized. Then he straightened up and wiped the drool from his lip. With a nervous laugh he said, "You crazy. You a crazy bitch! Quila be a crazy bitch." He shook a visibly trembling hand at her. "You stay away from me, witch!" And he was gone.

Quila sighed. She hadn't helped him at all. He probably didn't even know what a slate was. She should have said white board. Then he might have known what she meant.

Devan made sure to get his revenge. He started by telling everyone at school that Quila was a witch. That she had a crystal ball and she did spells and she was into voodoo. There was no life in which Quila cared about getting a homecoming date, which was a good thing, because Devan had killed any chance of that ever happening in any life at all. She would hear whispers of "Witch!" and "Where's your coven?" or "Left your broom somewhere?" as she walked down the hall.

Two weeks later, Victory came running up to Quila between classes. "Q! Do you know what happened? Did you hear?"

"No, Vic. Must have forgot my crystal ball today."

Victory laughed. "Hey, you're a good witch. That's cool! Don't worry about what they say. Be like me. You always told me I needed some reputation rehabilitation, but I don't give a shit! But I thought you'd wanna' know: Devan's in the hospital."

"He's what?" Quila's voice was trembling. She looked down. Her hands were trembling, too. She was struggling to hold onto her books. This was too soon. "It's two years too early."

"Two years?" Victory looked confused.

Quila shook her head and waved off her friend's question. "Did Biggie shoot him?"

"Biggie? No. Some other guys, random guys, beat him up. Beat the shit out of him. They don't know if he's gonna' make it." Victory looked around. "Well, gotta' go! See you later!" She was almost cheery as she left, as though thrilled to be the bearer of such dramatic tidings.

Quila went through her day, and the rest of the week even, in a kind of a numb trance. Ten days later she boarded a city bus and went downtown to the hospital where Devan was out of the ICU and in a regular hospital bed prior to being sent to long term rehab. She lied when they asked if she was a relation, saying she was his cousin since they were only letting family in. She sat by his bed reading a book for nearly an hour before he woke up.

"Quila?" His voice was hoarse with disuse.

"Hi, Devan."

"Why you here?" He choked out the words. "Ain't nobody come an' see me."

"Oh. I'm so sorry to hear that. I imagine it's been pretty lonely." She paused, wondering what to say. "I needed to see you. To see how you were doing. You weren't supposed to get beat up like that. You look bad, man. I gotta' say. You look like hell."

"Been through hell." His teeth were almost gritted shut, but she wasn't sure if that was because of his injuries or his anger at seeing her. "Still in hell."

"They sayin' you went to see Biggie."

Devan nodded, just barely. The neck brace prevented him from moving much.

"I'm so sorry. I'm so sorry this happened. I never saw this coming." Quila sat in her chair and looked straight into Devan's eyes. In another life she had been sweet on him. She couldn't say she loved him because she'd had no idea what love was back then. But they'd been close. She felt for him now. She'd never seen him in this kind of shape.

"You didn't make this happen. Biggie make this happen. Had his boys do it." Devan breathed out. It sounded like it hurt to breathe. "But you was right."

"I was right?"

"Yeah. I could feel him. That Devil you spoke about."

"Biggie?" she asked.

"Nah." He sighed more than said the word. "Biggie a bad dude, but what you said, 'bout the claws in me. I was dreamin' it before you done said it. I could feel them. I could feel him breathin' down my neck."

"You could? You could? Oh, Devan…" She didn't know what to say. "Have you seen him? The man in that killer suit? With those dark shark eyes?"

His eyes moved over sideways to look at her. "Don't know who you mean. I never saw no one in no badass suit. Biggie's a red. He don't wear no suit."

She just shook her head.

Devan went on in his weak voice. "Not Biggie. But the breath on my neck. It come every night. I couldn't sleep no more for it comin' at me, I be feelin' it. Like you said at school. I could feel it." He was quiet for a bit and then added, "And the claws." After a long silence he added, "I saw that door in my dreams. That icy hot door."

Quila sat with him in silence for a while. She thought he fell asleep and figured that maybe she should leave. She wasn't sure why she had come in the first place. She was just about to get up when she heard him say,

"I'm glad you came." He seemed to wake up again. "The breath is gone."

At first she thought he was saying that he couldn't breathe. She looked around, sure there was some kind of button she should press to call someone. Then it hit her what Devan meant. "You mean *it's* gone? *It's* not breathing down your neck anymore?"

A slow smile crossed Devan's face. "Right. Bein' here been the best sleep I had, the only sleep I had, in months and months. He been in my dreams." Devan winced. "But it like they beat him outta' me. Tell me, Quila. You a witch. Am I still gonna' die in the street?"

Quila had been leaning forward, her whole body tense. Now she leaned back in her chair. She looked at Devan. He seemed to be in bandages and casts from head to toe, cuts and bruises on any part of him that showed. She couldn't know, couldn't know for sure, but it was a big change, a big change from the last time. The last time Devan had been Biggie's acolyte, more like a pet really. But once his business started to grow and people started to be loyal to Devan, Biggie had ended it. The dude brooked no rivalries. In some ways this was worse, but at least it was different. She laid a comforting hand on his forehead. "I'm no witch, Devan. But maybe if you can't feel him, maybe he gone. Maybe by standing up to Biggie, you changed things."

"But will he still shoot me down? Will I be erased… like you said?"

Quila was once again stuck without an answer. But she remembered something that the old Victory used to say about the importance of being positive. Optimistic thoughts and positive thinking. It used to really annoy her, Quila remembered with a small smile, but she decided to give it a try. "I only know what I knew once upon a time, Devan. But what I can tell you is this: you have already changed your destiny. I believe a new door is opening for you. All you have to do is walk through it. And if you can't feel those claws no more and that breath ain't on you neck, then I think you opened that new door." She was leaning into him now and whispering into his ear. "Walk through that door when it open, Devan. Take the new door. Be brave. Walk away from all you've known. Walk through that door into a new place."

"Excuse me, miss? This is not the time for visitors. I'm afraid I'm going to have to ask you to leave." A nurse with a very stern expression stood in the doorway.

Quila jumped. "Sorry ma'am. I'll be on my way. Good to see you, Cousin Devan. I'll come back."

Devan gave her a pain-laced smile as he said, "Glad you came, Cuz'. Glad you came. I'll look for that door."

As Quila left the room, a huge dark-skinned man in a black suit and white collar walked in. He had a bright embroidered cloth around his neck, like a scarf but short. It made him look like he was ready to give a sermon right there. The pastor sat down in the chair next to Devan. Quila turned to the nurse. "I thought you said he couldn't have visitors?"

"Oh, the Reverend Barberet isn't a visitor. He's just going to sit quietly with the young man."

"I'm here to pray over him," the big man said, his voice quiet and gentle.

The stern nurse shooed Quila along as if she was some little girl. She exhaled deeply. She had done what she could. And, if truth be told, she felt like she was leaving Devan in good hands. Maybe that preacher could help

Devan find some comfort and solace in his pain and fear. As Quila was stepping in the elevator she heard the sound of obnoxious muzak playing through the speaker. Then she caught a glimpse of a doctor as he sauntered down the hall. He had a neatly trimmed beard and dark eyes. Under his white coat he wasn't wearing scrubs like the other doctors. He was wearing a fine suit. She met his cold, dark eyes just as the elevator door closed, shutting her in with those lifeless tunes, and she was whisked away to the lobby level. A hospital security guard with a similar shark kind of deadness to his eyes appeared out of nowhere and escorted her out of the hospital.

    Standing outside the building, she looked up at the windows above. Devan was up there someplace. She hoped that reverend was protection enough.

Chapter 17

Victory plopped down at the table between Quila and an all-black clad, goth-girl named Elvira. At least that's what the girl insisted everyone call her. She was one of Victory's friends, and hence, was almost a friend of Quila's and occasionally joined them for lunch. Victory's lunch tray slammed against the hard surface of the cafeteria table.

"Victory! Where you been?" Quila asked, her voice sounding sharper than she meant it to. Victory didn't respond well to sharp tones and direct criticism seemed to crumble her. Quila heard how Miss Tiffany spoke to her daughter—like she was "walking on eggshells" she called it. You just never knew what was going to set Victory off. And then she'd pout and sulk for days. She might cry or she might scream, but she'd find a way to punish any negativity sent her way. She could sure dish it out, but taking it was not in her area of expertise.

"Where *have* you been," Victory corrected. "Geez Q, it's like you haven't been raised by my mother at all." She turned to Elvira. "Be glad that you weren't raised by my mother."

From beneath raven-black dyed bangs, Elvira blinked the massive eye makeup that stood out against her pale skin and framed her ice-blue eyes. All she said was a slow, "Yeah," in a low and emotionless voice.

Quila sighed and made sure to not roll her eyes. "Yes, *verbs matter*. I can hear Miss Tiffany saying it now. She always wants me to speak like White people." Victory giggled first and then Quila joined in. Elvira just stared at them. Quila continued, "But the question still stands, Miss Evasive. You missed gymnastics practice yesterday! Where were you? And I haven't seen you all morning at school. What gives?"

Victory shrugged as she started to take a bite. "When I found out the Sugarmans could give you a ride home from practice, I didn't see much point in me going." Then she stopped and looked sideways at Quila. "You didn't do anything dumb like call my mom to find out where I was, did you?"

Quila shook her head. She'd wanted to. She'd desperately wanted to, but Victory was funny about people checking up on her. Even Quila. She couldn't stop the school though. Victory was close to being a truant for skipping out so much.

"Good, 'cause she thinks I went. I told her I had a spectacular practice, one of the best ever. Oh, her eyes were all shiny over that one." Victory took another bite of her sandwich and through her mouthful added, "Oh, don't look at me like that. I'm only on the team because my dad bought them a new vaulting horse to replace that old broken thing we used to use. That's the only reason coach keeps me around, because old Daddy-Money-Bags will replace whatever he needs whenever he needs it." She took a sip of her soda. "You know, I have a theory. I think my therapist and the gymnastics coach are in league with one another."

A flat, monotone voice asked, "You mean, like they're secretly dating, and their pillow talk is about what equipment the team needs and how to get that from your dad?" Both Quila and Victory turned towards Elvira. It was the most words either of them had ever heard her say.

Victory burst out laughing. "Right! They're both pretty intense for such dumpy people! Ha! That would be just the kind of pillow talk they'd have. Boy, what they are missing out on!"

"Ooooh! Pillow talk! Do tell!" Tamoya sat down at the table across from Victory. Then Jamoya slid in next to Victory, edging Elvira over a seat.

"This sounds like a good convo to be in. But shit girl, I can't believe you got the perfect Miss Quila to talk smut at lunch." She looked over at Elvira. "And I'm not sure you talk at all."

Elvira rolled her eyes and curled a lip at Jamoya, but she was silent.

Jamoya returned a mean-girl expression to the gothie and then spun back to the other girls at the table. "Naw, shit like pillow talk don't come outta' Quila's mouth."

Tamoya laughed. "You so right, bitch! Listen up, Quila! We gonna' enlighten your pure Oreo ass!" The twins burst out laughing so hard that kids at the tables around them began to look over.

Quila was glad that people couldn't see just how hard she was blushing. It did surprise her. In her previous life she had fairly vast experience by this age and absolutely no hesitation to "talk smut" to gain a laugh or a shock when the opportunity presented itself.

"Yeah," Victory said. "I have some suggestions for them. They could start with what they should really do on those rings…"

"Principal alert!" Quila said quietly. She had been afraid that Victory would start offering some salacious details, but raucous laughter reeled in the lunchtime monitor like sharks to chum. Today it looked like Principal Sanders was on duty—a figure with more than representational authority. Dr. Sanders had true bite and wasn't afraid to use it. The girls calmed down immediately.

"Are you all having a nice lunch?" the principal asked in a calm and friendly tone, hovering over them.

Elvira gave a non-committal shrug. Quila looked up and smiled. She liked Dr. Sanders. Thought she was fair, if strict. Strict was okay.

"Yes, Colonel Sanders," Victory said as sweetly as possible, her million-dollar smile on her face. It took more discipline than Tamoya and Jamoya collectively had, and they broke down into guffaws, nearly choking on the food in their mouths. Even the corner of Elvira's mouth turned up slightly. Quila was flat out staring at them.

After making sure the twins could still breathe, Dr. Sanders said, "Keep it together, girls. We don't want to lose anyone over lunchtime laughter." She gave Victory a rather stern look. Quila deduced that the principal had decided to let Vic's comment slide this time. After giving Quila a friendly nod and Elvira an unsure look, Dr. Sanders moved on to a table of rowdy boys to spread her calming influence.

Victory rolled her eyes. "Ugh, I was in that bitch's office for an hour this morning!"

"I wondered where you were. You missed history. I have the notes for you," Quila said.

"She was with us!" Jamoya grinned. "We decided a girl's meeting over breakfast was in order."

"And weed is a good way to start a stressful school day," Victory said as she stretched back and laced her fingers behind her head, a big smile on her face.

"Vic, you cool. I can't imagine what she say to you, though," Tamoya said.

Jamoya agreed. "Yeah, like she be talking at us like, 'you all need to be strong Black women, and not bein' some stereotype!' Like what the hell she mean by that?"

Quila looked down at her lunch. "I can't even begin to imagine." Her voice was deadpan. She heard Elvira snort, but no one else seemed to notice it.

Tamoya picked up her sister's thread. "Yeah—here this White woman telling two Black girls to be upstanders. I mean, could that just be more awkward?"

Elvira blinked and in her deadpan and stretched out way said, "Well, instead of a White lady the principal could be a White dude. That would have been, like so weird…"

Quila looked at the goth girl in surprise. "Right. You're so right, Elvira."

170

"Riiiight! You so right." Jamoya echoed Quila as she took a moment to look at her. "You know, Quila, I usually don't know what Vic here sees in you. She like she one of us. She be a sister. But you like you all White on the inside. Why is that, Quila? Huh? Tell me, why is that?" She wiggled her long, intricately painted fingernails at Quila.

Quila remembered these girls all too well. Remembered the fight that made those fingernails go flying, along with the braided extensions. In zero of the times she had dropped into this life had she experienced anything close to a fight. When she was imprisoned up in that cloud, who knew? What did her other self do without her? What kind of trouble did she get into that the current Quila might not know about?

She pulled herself up to her full height and, even sitting, seemed to tower over the girls. She reached back into her oldest memories, the ones she had reviewed as the unwilling guest of the Well-Dressed-Man. "Tamoya. Jamoya. Let's be clear. I'm Black as you. More so, I think. I know where you live. I know that sweet little house you live in with you mama and poppy, in that neighborhood where you the only Black folk there. And your parents drive Cadillacs and have steady jobs. Let's see, by now you poppy, you call him 'poppy', right? He's probably made supervisor, uh, huh? Yeah, you seventeen, so that's a big step up for you all, and you didn't need much of a step up. You order your clothes from catalogues. You poor, poverty-stricken bitches have to share a car, that's such a burden! And how you each get an allowance that would make most of the kids in this room turn green with envy, but you mama, she still take you on weekends to do that hair and those nails and she pay for it all. And you eat dinner out three times a week because you mama hate to cook. And you have a pool in the back yard. Yeah, I know all about it. You all is tryin' so hard to be Black, to prove you Blackness, with the shit that makes other people think you Black, but you is livin' just like all the rich White folk. When you home you talk White in front of you parents. Hell, you friends are even White." She gestured to the two other girls at the table.

171

Jamoya and Tamoya looked at each other. Tamoya mouthed, "She a witch!" to her twin, who nodded, wide-eyed.

Quila shook her head in frustration. As she spoke, she changed her dialect to one that would make Miss Tiffany puff up with pride. "Now, me: I'm the real deal. My mama is dead. She died of drugs. Or so we think. I haven't seen her since I was seven. So that's the best we can come up with. My daddy was shot in the street as he left 'college'." She used finger quotes around the word. "I live in the projects. I have to share a room with my elderly, sick grandmother because we only have a two-bedroom unit and Rasheed has the other room. I eat because of food stamps and free lunch. I haven't been first owner of any clothes that Vicky's mom didn't give me. I got it all, girls. I got Black down. I got poverty down. I got the stereotyped world down. But I don't see that as an excuse to let it get me down. I am a strong Black woman. I'm going to defeat any devil who would cast me to the gutter. I'm going to be something."

The table was quiet for a moment. Victory looked dumbfounded, unable to say anything. Elvira remained expressionless and kept eating her potato chips as though nothing had just happened. But Quila realized that she had gotten caught up in the moment, in her passion for finding a way out from the traps laid before her, finding a way to win the ultimate prize by defeating *him*. And she'd been speaking way too loudly. Most of the lunchroom was quiet, apparently waiting in the tension before the storm of noon time fight breaking out.

"Sheeeet, girl!" Jamoya called out so that the whole room could hear. "I am Quila! Hear me roar!" She and Tamoya burst out in laughter and gave high fives around the table, chanting "Hear Quila roar!" Jamoya stood up and led the whole cafeteria in the chant, which went on for nearly a full minute. "Hear Quila roar! Hear Quila roar!"

Victory grabbed Quila's arm and practically dragged her from the room. As they left, Principal Sanders was trying to calm the general mayhem, having stepped out for a moment and missed the start of the chanting. Quila could hear the noise die down as she and Victory scurried down the hall.

"Okay, that was so weird." Victory was breathing heavily.

"Yeah," Quila agreed. "Why are you hanging out with them anyway? Those girls are trouble. Despite the fact they're nearly as advantaged as you are, Vic, they're bad news. Have to be the center of attention everyplace they go. Tornados of drama. They're not who you should be hanging out with." She gave Victory a stern look. "And I'm not too sure about that Elvira either."

"You sound like Tiffany." Victory snorted. "But I have to tell you something."

"What?"

"After all that chanting, like the whole school back there. Jesus, Q. I don't know if I can be your friend if they vote you homecoming queen."

While Quila disliked everyone in the hallways calling out "Roar!" to her as they passed, it did seem to finally kill the whole witch thing. All in all, "Hear me roar" was a way better thing to be teased with. And secretly, eventually, she found that she kind of liked it.

It was a gorgeous fall. Cool, finally, as it was supposed to be. At odd moments she would find a plastic grocery bag stuffed into her backpack or when she opened up her locker there would be one hanging on the hook. The first time it frightened her just what could be in there, but when she opened it, it was a new shirt. A nice one. Funky print in a silky kind of never-wrinkle fabric. She loved it. Tags still on it, as if to prove that she was the first owner. It looked great on her. She wasn't sure who was her benefactor, just who she should thank. This would happen once, and sometimes twice a week, each time making her tear up, if not cry outright. People always took notice of her new clothes, saying "you look hot" or "Quila roars fashion!" Once when she opened her locker there was the coolest jacket there. The only tag said *wear it with Black pride.* She blinked. She couldn't believe these could possibly be coming from Tamoya and Jamoya...

Her grandmother loved the new clothes but was suspicious. "Why people give you new clothes? They don't like what you wearin? Mmmmmm, mmmmmm. But this be nice. But why they sneakin' these clothes in you locker? I bet it that principal lady. She believe in you. She love you. She love a Black girl who gon' be somethin' in the world! A poor Black girl who goin' to college!"

Clearly Mayme was struggling just as Quila had been. "You know, Grandma, in some sort of past life I would have felt humiliated and angered at the gesture, taking it as an insult. But this time around, I see it as people being, you know…"

"What?" Mayme asked.

"Kind. They're trying to be kind."

"Kind…."

Quila looked at the new jacket she was showing Mayme. She couldn't help the circumstances of her life, but these gifts felt like kindness and compassion. Tribute even. "Yeah. I think they say that the kids respect me."

"Respect you?" Mayme sounded puzzled. "These ain't charity?"

"Maybe for some, but you know, once you can actually grasp the idea that other people might really like you, might look up to you, wow, it changes everything. You just see everything so… differently." She smiled at her grandmother. "A little bit of living gives you a whole lot of perspective."

"If you say so, Miss Quila. If you say so."

She felt like a modern-day Cinderella, with mysterious little mice creating her wardrobe. She decided to go to the Homecoming dance. She practically made Victory be her date, mostly so her friend wouldn't end up partying in some drug-fueled binge with the kids who lived on margins. The two girls showed up together with Victory wearing a tux while Quila wore a little black dress that was again a gift from the little mice that miraculously created her new look.

"So, I have to tell you that I was so pissed at you for making me be your date," Victory said as she offered Quila a glass of punch.

Quila took the glass. "Well, I knew who you were gonna' hang out with, so I figured we'd both be better off this way. You'll be alive at the end of the night, and I don't have to come here with any of those guys." Quila nodded to a group of five boys who were each trying hard to catch her eye. She just shook her head and turned back to Victory.

"You're making me miss out on some righteous partying, and for that I might not forgive you. But I found a way to make this almost as much fun."

Quila looked at Victory's head. "Yeah, I can see that. And what did Tiffany say?"

"She screamed." Victory laughed, thinking it a terrific joke. She rubbed her hand over the back of her head. "I love the fuzziness of it. Why didn't I do this forever ago? Girls should have buzz cuts."

"It does go with the tux. What did your dad say?"

"Drake? Who knows? He's gone again. Some conference or other. Besides, I'm eighteen now. I think he's emancipated me." She laughed a little too loudly. "It's another word for abandoned," she shouted. Then she was quiet for a few moments. "You know, I found out that he got an apartment."

"A what?" Quila wasn't sure if she'd heard Vic over the music. "An, an apartment?"

"Yeah. They're doing a trial separation. So, when he's gone, he's not gone all the time on trips. He got an apartment and didn't tell Mom. He just sort of set up a parallel life. Kind of trying it out before he announced it."

"How's she taking it?" Quila wasn't sure what to ask or what to say. This was beyond her experience in any life. Victory was still treating it as though it was some kind of joke. As though it were funny. She must be simply crushed inside.

"She takes everything well with a glass or two of vodka."

"How are you taking it?"

It took Victory a moment to answer. "It's quieter. I don't miss all the fighting. It got a lot better after Jeremy went to rehab, but when he came home it was a mess. Dad just hates the embarrassment of having a druggie kid. Wants to wave his magic wand made of money and make it all go away. Have Jeremy healed. Fixed. But that's not Jeremy."

Quila put her arm around Vic. "Nope. Not in any life is that Jeremy. The magic wand he needs doesn't exist in any place I know of."

"Me either." Victory said quietly. "I've tried to understand him. Tried to see the world from inside his head, but I can't quite get there."

"Don't try, Vic. Let it go. Jeremy's got to live his own destiny. You and I have to live ours."

Victory looked at Quila with an intensity Quila hadn't seen since the last time around.

Quila felt hope, a huge sense of hope upwelling in her.

"What's our destiny?"

"We're making it. Right here. Right now." *Progress! This is progress!* Quila thought to herself.

"Well, we're making history at least. We're the first same sex couple to come to the homecoming dance! And the funny thing is, we're both straight!" They giggled and it felt like old times when they were just small girls. "Oh, shit. It's time. They're calling up the court. We gotta' go."

"It's awkward, you know?"

"What? Having a girl in a tux and a buzz cut for your date?"

"No. That seems totally normal, under the circumstances. What seems awkward is that I'm here as the token. The token Black. The token poor girl. The one everyone feels sorry for. I'm here more as a joke than anything else, or as a way for people to feel better about themselves."

"Yeah. Sucks to be you," Victory chirped happily. "Or maybe you just roared and people heard. Maybe they actually like you. Maybe, like me, they actually love you."

Quila took in a sharp breath. The touchy-feely Victory was the last life Victory, not this newer, shinier, spikier version. "I love you too, Vic. That's the only reason I'm here. The only reason I'm breathing."

Later that night the girls came in laughing. Tiffany was waiting up for them. Quila eyed the half-empty bottle of vodka and the smile fell from her face.

"So, girls, how was your night? Victoire, did you thrill everyone with your radical haircut and tuxedo? Bet you were the talk of the party!"

Victory didn't sound victorious as she said, "Yeah, Mom. Life of the party. That was me."

"And don't you look so nice, Quila! Lovely dress." She took a sip from her glass and then she looked at the dress again. "Wait a minute. Victoire, isn't that the dress I bought you last spring?"

Victory shrugged. "Uh huh. I wasn't ever gonna' wear it. Thought someone should."

Quila looked at Victory, now realizing the identity of at least one of the little mice leaving their secret presents. But of course, Victory would figure out Quila's locker combination. It was Victory's birthdate.

Tiffany downed the rest of the glass. "Sure, why not give away the things I give you. Looks good on you, Quila, even though you're so much taller than Victory. Huh, that's funny how that works."

Quila and Victory exchanged looks. Quila hadn't realized that Miss Tiffany was struggling to this extent. Victory looked away. Quila couldn't read the expression on her face. Quila realized that while Victory had her secrets, Miss Tiffany had been able to keep some from her too.

"So, what else happened tonight? Oh, who was named Homecoming Queen?"

Victory smiled for the first time since they'd been talking to her mother. "Oh, it was spectacular. They named Quila! She's the homecoming queen.

177

So, you see your dress ended up being absolutely perfect! And all the kids cheered."

"I think the commotion was actually about you kissing me," Quila said.

"Yeah, they thought that was pretty funny. Hey, if you'd been smart enough to ask a guy that's what he'd have done. But since I was in the tux, well, I thought it was my duty," she said snarkily. "Gave them all a real shock."

"Yeah, particularly because neither of us are exactly known as lesbians."

"Oh, I'm sure that's what made it all right. Damn prudes can take it as a *joke*, but put anybody up there who was *serious* and that would stress their all pretend little liberal hearts."

"You sound just like your father. And wait a minute, you kissed Quila? Like on the lips when she won?" Tiffany was a little slow to pick up on the conversation, not a surprise given state of her liquor bottle. "Oh, Victoire, what am I going to do with you!" Tiffany continued to sip her vodka as she asked the girls about every detail of their evening—what they served, who wore what, how the kids paired up, were the teachers doing a good job of chaperoning. After an hour and downing two more glasses, they both eased her to bed.

"Okay, that was officially weird," Quila said.

"You get used to it." Victory shrugged. "I'm gonna' take a shower."

Quila took the dress off and hung it up. The old Miss Tiffany would have taken it to the dry cleaners the next day. She wasn't sure what would happen to it now. She ran her hand down the length of the velvet. It sure was a pretty gown. She heard something at the door. This was late for a visitor. Tiffany was out cold and Victory was singing in the shower. She figured she could at least see who was there. Probably some acquaintances of Jeremy's, looking for a late-night party playmate. The late night wouldn't surprise her. The fact that Jeremy had any friends left probably would. When you ran with a crowd like his, it didn't take long to get really, really messed up and really messed up people got left behind pretty fast. No one talked about Jeremy much anymore. Quila figured it was just too painful, and as they'd all learned, rehab didn't work for everyone. Or maybe it would be Drake Van Dyke at the door? He didn't live here anymore. Would he knock? She wasn't sure what to say to him. She thought she would rather see Jeremy.

She opened the door. "Hello. Can I help you?" She looked at the face of a young officer. A woman who actually looked a lot like her.

The woman looked at Quila and then beyond Quila into the house, sizing up the situation but showing no emotion other than a quick nod of appreciation. "Can I speak to the head of the household, please?"

"I'm sorry, it's so late. She's not well and can't come down at the moment. But I can take a message."

"Are you a family member?"

She thought about that. "Yes. Yes, I am a family member." She stood up straighter and spoke with more confidence. "How can I help you?"

"Are you over eighteen?"

"Everyone here is over eighteen."

"Oh, okay, just had to make sure. My name is Detective Townsend. I regret to inform you that there has been an incident. A young man was declared dead at the scene. We believe that this is your family member, but we can't be sure. He had identification items for multiple people on his person. We would appreciate if you could come and identify the body. For confirmation, you know."

Quila felt her whole body go numb.

"Ma'am? Ma'am? Are you okay?" The officer was supporting Quila with one arm as she leaned against the doorframe.

"What? Huh? Oh, yeah, uh…" Quila knew she was stammering and felt like it was hard to breathe. "I'm sorry. What, what did you say?"

"I'm so sorry to be calling on you at this hour with such dreadful news, ma'am, but we believe this to be your family member. Could you come down and identify the body?"

"Yes. Of course, we'll come. Of course. I can drive. We'll follow you. Of course."

The officer looked at her, a little unsure whether Qulia was in any shape to drive. "I can take you, ma'am. We understand how trying and upsetting this all is. I have a list of resources for you as well."

"Yes, yes, of course." She felt like she was on automatic pilot. "Um, won't you come in? I'll need to get my sister. The policewoman waited in the entranceway while Quila, feeling nauseous and shaky, went back upstairs.

"Hey," Victory came around the corner with a towel in her hand, rubbing her newly shaved head. "Who the hell was at the door at this hour? I told those guys I was with you tonight. Oh my god, Quila, you look awful. What happened?"

Quila looked at Victory. She didn't know how to tell her. She could feel a tear slowly falling down her cheek.

"The police are downstairs. It's Jeremy. I think it's Jeremy. We need to go and… and, well… we need to see if it's him."

Chapter 18

Quila gripped the steering wheel hard and took a deep breath, steeling herself for the encounter to come. "You can do this, Q. It'll be all right." She got out of the car and tried to not jump when a car door slammed behind her—after all, she'd been the one to close it. On the brink of hope, hope that Victory would find her path out, hope that Quila would defeat the Well-Dressed Man, hope that the world would be restored, the clouds had opened up and poured on them all. She couldn't believe it. So close… and now so very far. "You got this. Stiff upper lip and all. C'mon now." She walked slowly into the building, hearing her boots crunch on the small stones of the walkway. She entered the building. They asked for ID, and she had to sign in on a computer which took her picture and printed out a sticky badge blaring the name "Tequila Williams" with her face caught with surprise and looking awkwardly back up at her.

A burly and rather intimidating woman led her through a door that looked like it was meant to keep all the bodies on the inside right where they were. It slammed shut behind her with an awful finality. "This way," the women gruffed at her. Quila looked at her nametag.

"Agnes," Quila tried to make conversation. "That's not a name you hear much these days."

"At least I'm not named after booze," the woman shot back, taking Quila's small talk as an insult. "We all know what booze gets you."

Quila didn't say anything but looked confused. Finally, she gave a questioning shrug.

Agnes leaned over into Quila and with stale cigarette breath and a raspy voice said, "It gets you in here." Quila didn't say anything else. Eventually they came to a nondescript door that looked like every other of the twenty-or-so doors they had passed. "It's in here. You'll have an hour at the most." Agnes then left Quila standing there as Quila watched her stalk off down the hall in search of someone else to intimidate.

She took another deep breath and knocked on the door. She didn't hear anything, so cautiously she opened it and went in. "Hello?"

"Oh, Quila! Over here, dear. How lovely that we are running into you today." Tiffany came over and gave her a hug. "What perfect timing! Quila I'd like for you to meet Ashton. Ashton, this is Quila. She's been friends with Victoire since they were in pre-school."

"Charming! How lovely to meet you!" The man named Ashton held Quila's hand in a most genteel way. She couldn't quite place his accent. Not quite British. More like English was a second language but he'd learned it from a British teacher.

"It's nice to meet you, too," she answered, trying to hide her surprise at the fact that Tiffany would show up here with a guy who seemed to be a, well, a boyfriend. Yes, the way she was making eyes at him, Tiffany certainly thought of him as a romantic partner. "I told Victory I would come and see her today."

"Yes, of course. She mentioned as much. She's in the bathroom. She'll be back in a moment."

Quila felt her stomach jump. She wanted to say, "Not the bathroom!" That was where Vic would always go to shoot up after Jeremy had died. The memory made Quila blanch. Tiffany had been too drunk to go, so Quila and Victory had gotten into that cop car, holding hands and shaking with fear the whole way. The policewoman didn't drive them to the hospital. They went to the morgue. Victory had insisted on seeing Jeremy and then had flung herself over him, clinging onto him, begging him to come back, for him to not leave her. He looked awful. Like he'd been living on the street, which he had been. He had been a homeless, nameless, faceless drug addict who refused to come home and absolutely wouldn't go back to rehab. Well, that's where Victory was now, as though she felt compelled to take his place and follow in his footsteps.

"So, Quila, how is college going? You must be in your junior year now?"

Quila nodded. "It's fine. I like it. It suits me."

"What are you studying?" asked Ashton.

"Non-profit management. It just seemed like it was a good fit."

"Oh! So, you're one of those do-gooder types. Well, you'll never make your fortune in that field. I'm in finance. I manage investments. I'm helping Tiffany manage her investments." He picked up Tiffany's hand and kissed it. She blushed like a teenage girl and beamed at him.

"Making my fortune is not actually one of my goals." Quila tried to say it as nicely as she could. She wasn't sure she liked this guy. He seemed kind of like a snake. Like an actor playing a role. She couldn't understand why Miss Tiffany was fawning all over him. He was too young for her, and she hated to admit it, too handsome as well.

"Don't let the love birds make you lose your appetite," Victory said as she joined them. "Mom and Ashton are visiting me before they head off to Europe for a little trip. You'll be gone for, what did you say, three weeks?"

"Yes! I can't wait. I never got to go on the big trips before. I'm going to see so many places I've never been. Rome, Venice, Paris!"

"And you'll love the cruise down the Rhine." Ashton squeezed her hand again. "I'll show you all the museums and oh, the churches! And then the food—I know the best restaurants. You'll have the time of your life."

"That sounds lovely," Quila said. "And expensive." She turned to Tiffany. "Won't that cost a fortune to do all that?"

"Oh, Ashton is managing all my money. He's a genius. We're only spending the profits from his investments. He's keeping the nest egg safe." She lay her head on his shoulder. "I got so lucky when I met you."

Ashton smiled and kissed her on the forehead.

Tiffany turned to her daughter. "I'll send you postcards, honey. And I'll pick up some things in Europe that you'll love! I'll come and see you when we get back."

"Okay, bye, Mom. Have a good time." Victory let her mother give her a big hug and a kiss.

"You be good while I'm gone. Listen to your counselors. Do what they say. And honey, leave your hair long. It's starting to look really nice again."

"You know it," Victory said with a chipper tone in her voice. Then as they were walking out the door, hand in hand, she shot out, "Now you two make sure you're practicing safe sex!" with the same, sweet honey-dripping tone. Tiffany didn't even turn around as she and Ashton walked out the door and let it close hard behind them.

"So, who's the dude?" Quila asked. "And just where is he from?"

"My guess is that Ashton," Victory mimicked his accent, "is from con-man central. I've told Mom over and over again that there is no way a guy that young and handsome would be into her dumpy old ass. Yeah, we had a big fight over that one. But she won't listen. Says she's in love. This is the way it should have been with Dad." Victory guffawed. "While Dad might not have given her the love she needed, he didn't try to bleed her dry."

"You really think he's stealing from her?"

"Guy like him? Heck no. He'd be too afraid of going to jail. He's just living the high life at her expense. Investing. Shit. I bet she's the investment. Not investing her money. Just his time and drooling into her." Victory looked very seriously at Quila. "Q, why is it that you just can't tell people what's right in front of their face? They can't see it? It makes no sense. I keep telling her to watch out, but it's like she's plowing ahead and racing to crash into a huge brick wall. Like she can't wait to get there." Victory looked rather disgusted.

Quila was stunned. "Really? Can't imagine that, huh? Wow. Nope, never seen that happen before."

Victory looked at her and then burst out laughing. "I'm glad you're here. So, what did you bring me this time? I liked the book you brought me. It was fun. Kind of hard to get through but I liked the Elves and the Hobbits."

"I thought you would. It's a classic. This time I brought you something really different. I think it's perfect."

"Yeah?"

"Yeah." Quila handed over the bag she had brought in with her and watched Victory pull out the book.

"Short course on the GED test. Third Edition." Victory looked up. "Q? What's this for?"

Quila sat down next to Victory. "It's for you to start your life again." She looked around her. "I mean, you aren't going to spend your whole life in here. Eventually they're going to kick you out! And it's going to be a whole lot easier with that GED under your belt. I know you can do it. You know you can do it. You only missed a semester, yeah, and a little bit more, of senior year. I mean, it's not like you've got years and years to make up for."

Victory gave her a look that made Quila brace for a temper tantrum. But then she turned back to the book and started to flip through it.

Quila leaned into her friend. "And after you pass that, I thought we could talk about getting a tat to celebrate."

A big smile crossed Victory's face. "I thought you didn't like my tats! Thought you didn't approve of inking up?"

Quila laughed. "Who said you would get the tat? I thought I would get one to celebrate such a major life event."

Both girls laughed and then Victory became more serious. "You would do that for me? You'd ink yourself in my honor?"

Quila nodded slowly. "Yeah. But you'd have to hold my hand the whole time because you know what a weenie I am about pain." She looked down at

185

her arm. "And I'm so dark I don't know how it would show up on me, but yeah. You get your GED and I'll be inked in your honor."

"Bet my dad would be shocked"

"Oh god, you wouldn't plan on telling him that I got a tattoo?"

"Not shocked at you! Silly. Shocked at me. Doing anything good at all."

"Do you hear from him?"

"He's been in to see me. Once. Said he's living with another woman, A nurse from work. He got rid of the apartment and moved in with her. He's living in her house."

Quila nodded.

"I hate that. I still hate that they got divorced. That they couldn't work it out. When I needed them the most, they were all too wrapped up in how much they hated each other."

"Tiffany hated Drake?" That was a surprise to Quila. She'd always thought Tiffany was heartbroken over her husband leaving her, blaming her for how the kids had turned out. "I always thought she was kinda' devastated by it all. That that was the reason for all the vodka, remember?"

"Well, she sure went after Dad for the money. Every penny she could get."

"Exacting her revenge?" Quila asked. "Taking it all in bank notes?"

"Maybe. But there's no greater revenge than the disappointment Jeremy and I turned out to be." Victory shrugged. "Of course, Ashton advised her to refuse the alimony and to take everything at once. Never mind that she hasn't worked a day in her life. Has no idea how to make that last for the next thirty or forty years. But Ashton assures her he'll take care of everything. I bet he will." Victory looked up at Quila, her eyes full of tears. "I can't believe I'm back here. Trapped here."

"Vic, a lot of people have to go to rehab a second time. I don't think it's a one-and-done for anybody. Addiction is a tough, tough battle. It's your Mount Everest. But you're not climbing alone."

"I miss him."

"Yeah, I know you do."

"I feel sunk without him."

Quila thought about that. There was some real revisionist thinking there. Jeremy hadn't actually been that nice to Victory. He hadn't been around that much and when he had, it was let the good times roll and the chips fall where they may. None of that had been good for his little sister. And then there was that whole mess with Liam. In Quila's memory, Jeremy had been pimping out his sister to his friend in order to score booze and weed. And once he found street drugs, well, it had all been downhill from there. "Vic, I don't know what to say. I can't make you feel better. Jeremy was a complicated person. It was like there was never enough for him. I think that you, just maybe, that if he were still around that you might still feel sunk, only this time by him. Not by his absence."

She thought Vic might rail at her, but she just nodded her head. "He wasn't meant for this world."

Quila shook her head. "Maybe not. But you *are* meant for a better world. A better place. And I'm here to see you there, okay? So, will you use the book I brought you? Will you do the GED thing?"

Victory flipped through the pages, not really looking at them. She shrugged again.

"I can come at least once a month to see you. Sometimes I'll be able to be here twice a month. I'll help you work through it. I'm sure Tiffany will help, too. You won't be alone, okay?"

Victory nodded and wiped away a tear. "Jeremy never got to graduate high school either. Not the real way. Not wear the cap and gown. Not march. We're such a pair of losers. Dad, valedictorian that he was, doctor that he is, could never believe that Jeremy could bottom out like that." Victory looked up into Quila's eyes. "Will he love me again if I get it? Even though there's no ceremony?"

"He loves you already, Vic. He never stopped. I think he just doesn't know how to relate to you. But we aren't doing this for him."

187

"I know, I know. You sound just like my therapist. I have to do it for me."

"For you? What the hell?" Quila smiled at Victory. "You're doing it so I have a good enough excuse to get my first tattoo!"

Victory's smile was all Quila needed to see.

Chapter 19

Quila was at her wit's end with Victory. "Oh my god," she said to her reflection in the mirror. She put toothpaste on her toothbrush and shook her head. "Was I this hard on you last time around? Oh my god, I think I was." She hadn't been kicked back out to the cloud for the longest time, which was good. She felt like she really needed to be in this game and not miss a moment of it. Victory needed constant babysitting. She'd been in and out of rehab now three times. She was clean again, but it felt tentative.

"There is a distinct possibility that you are actually taking it a bit easy on me," she said as she thought back on her own path of dereliction in her first time around. "Talk about seeing through the glass darkly." The gift of memory, insight and wisdom also laid a heavy burden of guilt on her shoulders. Now that she could see more clearly, she was in awe of the patience and stamina Victory 1.0 had last time. "Well, I'm not gonna' let you down, girl," she said to her reflection. She just wasn't sure if she was referring to Victory or herself.

She finished brushing her teeth and started pacing around her apartment. What did Victory need? What might make a difference? She stopped dead in her tracks. "Helping. Last time she was always off helping people. Doing crazy stuff for others. Like she'd volunteer at soup kitchens. She served meals on wheels. She went on mission trips. Peace Corps! That's right, she went off to Peace Corps! That must have been after she gave up on me. Huh." Quila thought about that. "Well, no Peace Corps is gonna' take you now. Not in the shape you're in. Oh Vic, but maybe there's another way you can help people." She went to her computer and spent the next two hours researching online.

Two days later she picked up Victory to take her to lunch. She was living with her mother again, sleeping on her couch. Quila was going to make her big pitch. She pulled up in front of the little condo Miss Tiffany now called home and before she could get out of the car Victory nearly ran out of the house. She hopped in the passenger side door.

"Okay, let's go. Let's get outta' here."

"Hi, Vic. What's the rush? I thought I'd say hi to Miss Tiffany."

"Oh, please spare me. I've gotten enough lectures today. Let's just go."

"Rough morning, huh?"

"Rough life."

"I'm sorry you're having a bad day." Quila tried to say it delicately to avoid provoking a reaction.

"I said I'm having a rough life!" Victory shouted.

"You don't need to shout at me. I'm your friend, remember? I'm one of the bright spots."

Victory looked sullen. "Sorry. It's just she's always nagging at me to be more. To do more. Always telling me how I've wasted myself. Like I don't tell myself that enough? It's the last thing I need to hear from her!"

"Well, let's go to lunch and see if we can make today more fun. My treat." Quila tried to sound upbeat and remember her mission. *Man, how did you put up with me before?* This was a total test of her patience.

As they waited for their lunch to arrive, Quila tried to find safe topics to talk about. "So, I like the lavender hair. Really pretty."

"I wanted it to be mauve, but Tiffany said if I ruined any more of her towels, she'd kick me out, so I went for something that matched the towels she already has."

"Oh, well, uh, that was really considerate of you."

"Yeah, really."

"So, how's your mom doing with, with everything?"

Victory played with the straw in her iced tea. She had tried to order a long island iced tea, but the restaurant said they didn't serve liquor until evenings on Sunday. Victory had been most disappointed. "She cries a lot. I think she misses the big house."

"I imagine it would be a hard change." Quila nodded sympathetically.

"Yeah, it's a really dingy little condo. But she's kinda' lucky to have anything. I mean, after that Ashton guy romanced her and spent everything Dad gave her in the divorce settlement. God, that was just so stupid of her."

"She was in a pretty vulnerable place." Quila winced at the memory. Tiffany had hit the bottle pretty hard after Drake left her. She was dry now, but man did she ever lose herself there for a while. "It was all so hard on her." Quila was afraid to mention Jeremy's death. That could always send Victory into a tailspin. Dwelling on Jeremy was not a good idea for any of them.

"Yeah, and that rat-bastard could sniff that out. Woman-of-a-certain-age going through a divorce. Encouraging her to take a single big settlement? He told her taking alimony was just a way Drake was going to cheat her out of what was rightfully hers. And any sentence that had 'Drake' and 'cheating' in it was a particular sore spot for Mom."

"Didn't he say he was some kind of an investment counselor?" Quila sighed. "A guy who's supposed to give people advice on what to do with their money."

"Well, he certainly had fun spending hers. She thought she was healing, what with all those vacations they took. Trip to Europe. Beach trips. The fancy nights out. She thought she'd found love again. But all he was doing was spending her money to support their lavish lifestyle. And his crazy investment? I bet the guy was actually gambling away everything on the side. You know he bought her fancy jewelry? But it turned out to be with her own money. Then when he disappeared, everything was gone with him." Victory snorted. "Jewelry too."

"I'm so sorry he fooled her. It's hard to see through con men. They're really good at what they do, which is to con people."

"Well, Daddy couldn't believe she fell for that. He said that was proof positive that it was her fault we ended up like we did. Couldn't believe he'd married someone like her in the first place."

Quila was stunned. "He didn't!"

Victory just nodded, still staring at the ice cubes slowly melting in her alcohol-free glass of tea. "Yeah. I overheard him tell his new wife."

Quila knew that Victory would never mention that woman's name. Some nurse her father worked with. Victory hated that woman. Blamed her for breaking up her parents which, of course, was much easier than blaming herself or her brother.

Victory nodded. "Back when they would let me come and stay there. Bitch won't let me see my own father now."

Quila didn't know whether she should remind Victory that she probably wasn't welcome because she had stolen from them to support her drug habit. *Nah, probably not a good thing to bring up. She's clean now. Better to keep moving forward.*

"You know, Victory, I had an idea."

"Of how I can get revenge on my evil step-mother?" Victory was all attention now. "She thinks I'm such a loser. Tells Dad I'm such a loser, I know she does. Her, with her two perfect little children. She's afraid I'm going to contaminate them or something. Hey, I'm totally up for revenge."

Quila knew better than to go there. Dr. Van Dyke's 'new and improved family number two' was a painful spot for Victory and Tiffany alike. But maybe there was an angle here that she could use. "Yeah… uh, sure. You know, one of the best ways to get revenge on someone is to be successful. Works every time. And I was thinking that I might know of a way."

"Successful at what? What could I be successful at?"

She couldn't tell if Victory was really interested or not but decided to plunge ahead. "I have this hunch, since I've known you almost all your life," *and a lot longer, if the truth be told,* "that you would really get a kick out of helping people."

Victory looked blank. "Helping people. What does that mean?"

"You know, like doing things for others. I think you'd really find yourself there. Find meaning in life. Your purpose."

"I have a purpose?" Victory looked bewildered.

"Of course you do! Everyone has a purpose."

"What's your purpose?"

"Right now, it's you. You're my purpose. That's what best friends are for. I think about you all the time, Vic. I want you to be happy. That means a lot to me. I want you to find what makes you happy. And I've been thinking about all the long years I've known you. I really am sure that you will find your bliss in helping other people."

Victory looked skeptical. "Like what?"

"Well," Quila ventured carefully. "Like I thought becoming a nurse could be a really good start."

"A nurse! How can I be a nurse? I'm a high school drop-out, remember?" Victory had that defeated look about her again.

"You have your GED! You're a high school graduate now. Look, I've researched the whole path. I know just how you can do it, step by step."

Victory crossed her arms. "Nobody would accept me."

Quila sat back and crossed her arms, a reflection of the woman sitting across from her. "Sure, they would."

A smirk crossed Victory's face. "No one in their right minds would accept me."

Quila burst out laughing. "I can remember another girl, long ago, saying that very same thing about going to college."

"Who?"

"Me," Quila said and shook her head. She didn't mention that it had been in her previous life when their roles were reversed, with Victory imploring Quila to not give up. Oh, but Quila had been snarky and mean.

She thought back on what angle would have appealed to her back then. "Listen, this is a good deal. You can get a nursing assistant certificate in just a couple of months. They make okay money. Not great, but okay. You'd be able to get a place of your own. And you'd get a job in a snap!"

"A place of my own?"

"Yeah, and not living with Tiffany or ever having to ask your dad for a place to stay or for help."

Victory looked interested, even if she was doing her best to pretend to not be.

"And once you're working, you can continue on with school and you can get an Associates in nursing. From the research I did, that will double your pay."

"Double the pay...." She had Victory's attention now.

"Yeah, and then it's up to you. I mean you could go on and get the full RN or a BSN and then you'd not only double your pay yet again but that would really show your dad something, wouldn't it? You'd be independent. You'd be free, Victory. And you'd be helping people. So, like, what's there to lose?"

Victory took a slow sip of her iced tea. "Free. Wow, free." She looked up at Quila. "I could never pay for this." She had that defeated look again.

"You don't have to." Quila could feel the rather mischievous smile on her face. Victory shot her a look. "It's at the community college, so it's not very expensive. And besides, you have a benefactor."

"Look, I'm not taking anything from my rat's ass dad!" she snapped back angrily.

"What? No! Vic, it's me! I'm going to pay for it."

"You? How can you do that? Why would you do that?"

Quila took a breath and thought of a way to explain. "Because it's the most important thing I could possibly do. Victory Van Dyke: you are the most important investment I could ever make. Think it over. It's a good deal no matter how you slice it. And after that you'd be able to do anything, work just about anywhere in the world. You could even do Peace Corps!"

Victory had a look of shock on her face. "Why the hell would I want to do that? Peace Corps?" Her lip was actually curled.

"You wouldn't? I thought you would like that?" Quila drew back, sincerely surprised by this answer. The old Victory had loved Peace Corps. Found herself there. Had talked about it constantly.

"Sometimes I wonder if you know me at all, Quila."

When Quila dropped Victory off back at her mother's condo, Victory turned suddenly just before getting out of the car. "Quila."

"Yeah?"

"So, how do I sign up for this magical mystery tour? The one leading to this perfect life you're promising me? Where do I go?"

Quila's face broke out into a big smile. "I know just the place. I'll take you there. I can go next Monday. Would that work for you? We'll get you signed up. Get you started. I'm absolutely sure you'll love it."

"Yeah. And, uh, thanks. For believing in me. I'm not sure I believe in myself most of the time."

"Well, let's say there's a glass half full here. We can work on making that brimming to the top and overflowing." Quila gave her friend's arm a little squeeze.

"Most of the time I'm just a glass half broken." Victory gave Quila a sad smile.

"I know you might not believe this, but I've been there. I've been that glass half broken and I'm here to say there's a way. I found my way. I know, Vic, I know you can find yours. And I'm here to help you. That's what best friends are for. For helping each other when we're just a little bit side-stepping the path." Now when Victory looked at her, she was almost sure she saw a reflection of the old Vicky in her eyes.

"Or totally fucking lost in space," Victory answered. "But this nursing assistant thing. Yeah, that could be cool. Thanks."

195

Quila had pulled away feeling that at last, at long last, there was hope on the horizon. She felt like she just might defeat the Devil after all. Just maybe.

Chapter 20

"Ladies and gentlemen, we are getting ready for landing," the voice blared over the speaker above their heads. "They've cleared a runway for us to land, but it will be a bit away from the main terminal. I want you to know what's going to happen. We'll be met by emergency personnel, but this is just out of an abundance of caution. We are quite sure that the fire has been completely and totally extinguished. After they check us out, we expect that we'll taxi over to the terminal. We apologize for any inconvenience this has caused you. We should be on the ground in less than ten minutes. We're coming down pretty fast so please make sure your seatbelts are on low and tight. And for heaven's sake, please stay in your seats! Sir! Sir! That means you, too! Yes, thank you." She sounded exasperated. "We'll be back on the ground soon."

"Thank god we're finally going to land!" The woman seated next to Quila was visibly shaking. She moved another rosary bead in her hand. "I've never been so scared in my life! When that horrid smell started and then that fire…" She couldn't finish her sentence.

Quila closed her book for what must have been the thirtieth time on the flight. She took in a breath and turned patiently to the woman sitting next to her. "No worries. It was… dramatic. But they put it out quickly."

"When those alarms went off, that was the most terrifying. Did you see how frightened the stewardesses looked? They're too young to be in such a role."

Quila tried to smile at the woman. "I thought the flight attendants handled it all really well, actually. They might have been a little wide-eyed at first but once they went into action, they were very brave. And very efficient."

"I don't know how you can be so calm!" The lady shook her head and moved a couple more rosary beads in her fingers. "You said you'd hardly ever flown and yet I don't know how you did it, not panicking and all. I was scared for my very life!" More rosary beads clicked through her fingers. "Tell me, you must believe in a higher power." She tried to smile, but her lips wriggled in a most peculiar way. Clearly her fear was close to winning. "You must have a guardian angel or something."

Guardian angel? Not hardly, Quila thought, but she smiled patiently and said, "I guess you could say that I do. I definitely believe there's a higher power looking over me and I just don't believe he's done with me yet. Somehow, I didn't think today was my time." *No,* she thought, *I have at least few more months on the clock.*

"And you won't be scared when you have to fly home? I'm never flying again. Never. I don't have the kind of faith you seem to."

Lucky you.

"It's a gift," the woman with the trembling lips managed to squeak out.

"Excuse me?" Quila asked.

"Your faith. It's a gift. You should be grateful." The woman gave her another nervous smile and gripped the arm rests as she prepared herself for the emergency landing.

Quila leaned back in her seat and said, "Grateful...."

What she was grateful for was this job. She worked for a small non-profit that helped kids from poor circumstances like hers find a way out. She felt like the poster child for that kind of a path but loved meeting the kids. She also liked the job because she felt like it annoyed *him.* Trying to out-strategize the Devil was no easy undertaking, to be sure. She could feel him interfering in her life in so many little ways, just to annoy her or knock her off course. It was the little things she felt most acutely, because they were like a slap in the face, like icy air in winter. Or in summer, floating out in the water in the ocean and being surprised by an unusually big and cold wave making a quick attempt at catching you off guard. The rosary-bead-lady and her near panic attack on the flight was just the latest example. Quila could always feel when the people were actually his players. *Grateful. Right.* It was like she could hear a *ping!* sound as the Devil scored a point. It was like she could hear him laughing.

You just love to stack the cards in your favor, don't you? she asked him in the quiet of her mind. *You think you're so funny, playing out all these little twists.*

The laughing faded away in the roar of the engine's emergency landing.

After the drama of the flight, the trip to Orlando turned out to be all right. She got to present at a conference, which found her actually shaking in her shoes. She didn't think that was a real thing until she experienced it for herself. She also got to go to Disney for a day. Victory had been loads of times as a kid, but places like Disney were just fairy tales to kids from the projects. She decided that it probably was the happiest place on earth. Every story with a guaranteed happy ending. Yeah, just a fairy tale to a kid like her. She didn't have much hope for such an end to her own tale. Instead of Prince Charming, she got *him*. The suit. The desk. The fire pit. The icy hot door to Hell in the background. Very charming.

Quila drove back to the airport and turned in her rental car, happy there were no little surprises from him. No traffic jams to test her. No flat tires to delay her. She walked over to the elevator that would take her to the check-in for her flight. Several options were in front of her: Level One, Level Two, Level Three and Terminal. As she reached for the button, the letters suddenly glowed red. She pursed her lips and gave the button a stern look. She pushed it hard, amazed at how cold it was.

"Ouch!" she cried and then stuck her index finger in her mouth. It was so cold it felt like it burned her. Sucking on her index finger, she could hear him smirking in the distance. "Very funny". *Yes, I'm terminal with a disease that no doctor could ever diagnose.* "It's not over yet, buddy," she said aloud. Then she looked over and realized she wasn't alone. An older lady gave her a look out of the corner of her eye. Quila blushed, but was surprised when the lady said,

"Men! What a problem they can be. I remember when I divorced my third husband. It wasn't over until it was over." She looked triumphant.

Quila looked down at the woman's bag. Coach. When it was over, it must have ended all right. For her, anyway. She looked down at the women's shoes. Probably Etienne's. Miss Tiffany had had some of those, way back a million years ago. You could tell the look once you knew what to look for. And the scarf: totally Hermes.

"So, is he giving you a hard time? Not letting you go? Demanding too much and not willing to give enough back? He's a selfish bastard, isn't he?"

"He's the Devil," Quila answered blithely. She wasn't sure she was supposed to actually *tell* anyone.

"Of course, he is. It's natural to feel that way. You need someone on your side. You shouldn't have to deal with that selfish bastard on your own!"

Quila realized she'd never see this woman again, but still, what spilled out of her mouth surprised her. "I do feel alone."

"You don't have to do this on your own."

Quila sighed heavily. "I'm so outmatched. It's just unreal to fight the Devil, you know? Sure, those Hollywood types fight their demons all the time but it's different to be actually engaging the Big Guy himself."

"Look, honey, what those A-listers have that you don't is a really good divorce attorney."

"Are you an attorney?"

"No. I'm a divorce coach. But I know some really great attorneys. Tough. They'll really squeeze his balls and give the bastard what he deserves." The woman kept pace with Quila as she moved towards the check-in kiosks. "Here, take my card. I've been working with a client here in Florida. She found out that while she was slaving away, running their summer rental empire out on the Outer Banks, he was down in Miami screwing his secretary and downing two-hundred-dollar, three martini lunches. Oh, she's gonna' get it all. The selfish bastard will be eating microwave dinners and popping PBR's after we're through with him."

Quila punched in her city destination and waited for the kiosk to print her tickets, while the lady droned on about what a really good divorce attorney could do for her. The woman's tirade continued all the way to the security line, where Quila had an uncomfortable thought.

"Actually, I'm the selfish bastard." She felt a little bit in shock as she heard her voice utter the words. "I always have been." She looked up at the mystified divorce coach. "It's my fault, really. It isn't over yet, but I made this mess." Quila shrugged. "Now I just want to clean it up."

She could see all the compassion evaporating from the eyes of the other woman. Ms. Make-'Em-Pay's interest waning as quickly as it had waxed.

"Well, good luck with that attitude! You'll never win anything worth having!" She huffed off to the TSA pre-check line and sailed through.

"Honestly, I'm glad to be shod of you," Quila mumbled to herself as she went to stand in line with the mere mortals who didn't have the nearly hundred bucks to shell out to the TSA to pay for the convenience of being a "known traveler". She waited patiently, and when she got to the security screening station, she pulled her work laptop and liquids out of her bag and tugged off her boots. "That lady might have been rich, successful and powerful but there was nothing, and I mean, nothing nice about her," she whispered to herself as she loaded her things into a gray bin and sent it on through.

She saw the lady in the boarding line for her flight as they were calling up the passengers for first class. Quila walked on down the terminal until she came to her own gate, deciding that she was glad she was up against *him* and not her. "Now that lady could give the Devil himself a run for his money." She listened, but this time she didn't hear him laughing in the background.

201

She spent the flight thinking about every selfish, nasty thing she'd ever done. There was no turbulence to distract her from her self-recriminations. No one sitting next to her even. She wasn't even sure the flight attendants offered her anything to drink. It was like she wasn't there. She was in some distant place with her thoughts and memories that were all too acute and clear. Another 'gift' from him. Time and space for reflection. Particularly her first time around, she'd surrounded herself with people who were drowning, like rats in a sewer, and they'd all shared the same fate. It was like her learning had been backwards: rather than learn from them, she learned to be just like them. This time around had been better. She'd done better, but she felt a heavy debt to pay from Quila 1.0. She thought about the things that Victory, the first Victory, had found meaning in. "I'm gonna' do a mission trip," she said aloud.

"What a lovely idea!" A man leaned over from his seat across the aisle. "Here. Take my card. We'd love to have you join us." He handed over his card which claimed he was Cornelius Cumberbatch from an organization called Heavenly Acts. "You're new to mission work? Well, then we have just the place for you in our Act One program. Give us a call or drop us an email."

Quila was surprised at how much the idea stuck with her. She checked them out. They seemed legit, if all far too convenient that Mr. Cumberbatch had been sitting just across the aisle from her on that particular plane flight. But when she would wake up in the morning, she would realize she had dreamed about going. About it being an expedient way to do something good before her clock ran out. The idea would haunt her in the shower. She'd be reading a book and find she wasn't following the words on the page—she was thinking about mission trips. She decided that she needed to give it a try. Doing for others was something which drove Victory in her previous life. Maybe Quila would learn something she could use to help her save Victory now?

One day she couldn't put it off any longer. The time was right. A year ago now she'd literally dragged Victory to the community college and signed her up for those nursing assistant classes. After practically sitting on her, making her do her homework and nagging Vic about her assignments the girl had made it through. Quila was proud as any mama might have been. She'd helped Victory find a job and she was pulling it together. Quila helped her find a place, and Victory was living on her own. She actually seemed happy. Quila was sure that what Victory really needed was to help other people. She would find her meaning there, just like she had the last time around. And now she was back at the Community College and taking classes to become an LPN. So far, so good. If there ever was a time Quila could slip away, it was now. And maybe it would be good to let Victory have a little bit of independence, to show herself that she really could make it? After all, there was a good chance that Quila wasn't going to have a lifetime to watch over Victory. There was a chance she would have just the same twenty-five years she'd had previously, and that Vicky was going to have to learn how to live standing on her own two feet.

So Quila called Heavenly Acts and registered for an upcoming trip. It was a three-week commitment minimum. She hoped everything would hold together while she was away. "Come on, Quila! Get a hold of yourself. What could possibly happen in just three weeks?"

Chapter 21

Quila came back from the mission trip tired but somehow satisfied. She felt like finally, after all these years, she'd won a round. Score one for Quila! Of course, it felt like the Devil had won about a hundred rounds by now, so in the big scheme of things, it didn't really mean that much. She got back into town and hit Starbucks, ordering an iced caramel macchiato with whip and drizzle, which made her think of Victory. Not this Victory of course, but the last one. The one she was really trying to save. Well, she'd made great headway in the last year, so there was light on the horizon. *I'm gonna' see that girl become a nurse even if it kills me.* That thought sent a shiver down her spine.

She started to think about what she should do next. Visit Waleed, for sure. She looked at the picture on her phone from just a couple of months ago. There was Waleed in his cap and gown, his two daddies by his side, bursting with pride. Tiger Mamas, the both of them. Waleed would be moving in two weeks to start medical school and she wanted to see him before he got so busy that she never heard from him again. And Rasheed. She definitely wanted to see Rasheed, find out how his summer break from teaching middle school math was going. Maybe they all could go to dinner?

If only Grandma Mayme had lived to see this day, she would have been on her knees saying the Lord was good, the Lord was so good to them. Lord knows, she didn't have much to thank Him for while she did live. Poor Mayme was distinctly uncomfortable with the idea of little Waleed being raised by two gay men, since she just didn't hold with that. It didn't help that they were White. Quila could still hear her saying, "mmmm, mmmmm" in a most disapproving way. "Garrett and Chad. They even got White names and now they raisin' my little Waleed." But even so, she understood that his new daddies could give him what Rashida would never be able to give anybody: love. And even what Mayme herself was unable to provide: security. "The Lord work in mysterious ways," she'd say to herself as she paced slowly around the apartment, drawing long on her cigarette. While she knew he was doing well in elementary and middle school, since his new Tiger Mamas were good about keeping in touch and sent regular reports, bragging on their little boy, her poor heart had given out when Quila was just nineteen. Mayme never saw Waleed graduate high school as valedictorian or get all those scholarships to college. She never knew he would become a doctor. She never saw Rasheed finally make it through college himself and get his teaching certificate. It had taken him a while, but he'd done it. Quila knew he'd be really good at it. The guy was part comedian, and he really understood the confusion and contortions of pre-teen life. Those kids were so lucky to have him. Grandma had seen Quila graduate high school though. Not at the top of her class, but up there enough to more than satisfy. And she saw her go off to college. Real college. Not code for incarceration. She had been so proud.

"You, Quila, you gonna' make it, girl. You gon' break free. You gon' live another life." Grandma patted Quila's cheek.

"Thanks, Grandma. I think I already am. And I'm excited! I can't believe I'm going to college! To college!" She was trying hard to not jump up and down as she packed her duffel with her clothes. This was exciting no matter which life she was talking about.

"Thank the Lord for all those scholarships." Grandma brought her another shirt to stuff in her duffel.

"Yes! And thank Miss Tiffany for her help. I wouldn't have gotten half the scholarships, or the work study program, without her. She really knows how to work a system."

"You watch out for that woman. She tryin' to make you White," her grandmother growled. "Tryin' to have you replace her own troubled chil'."

Quila had heard this argument a hundred times before. While Grandma was grateful for the help Tiffany Van Dyke had provided over the years, the food, the books, the homework help, she also resented that Quila had spent half her childhood someplace else, not to mention that it had such a profound impact on her, from her language to her experiences to her interests. Or maybe it was that Quila was gone all the time and Grandma was left trying to manage Deyonte, with his wild ways, and Rasheed, the perpetual comedian. It overwhelmed her. They only seemed to calm down for Quila.

Quila put her arms around her grandma. "Don't you worry none. I'm your lil' girl and I'm not leavin' you. I'll be at college but I'm a phone call away. You know that." Somehow, the old woman didn't feel like she was relaxing in Quila's embrace. What neither of them knew was exactly how short their time together was going to be.

Grandma Mayme pulled back and looked Quila right in the eye: "An' don' you let them white devils get to you."

"What, Grandma?"

"They's racist at those colleges. They do bad things and put the blame on you. You be careful now, you hear me? You keep low, outta' sight. Them white devils are everywhere."

"White devils? What do you mean?"

"They's racists everywhere. People who make it a crime to be Black. Shoot our folk dead and get off clean. For walkin' while Black, for talkin' while Black, for sleepin' while Black. It's a crime. It's a sin. And where is the Lord? Why do he let all that happen? Well, Quila, don't you let it happen to you. You stay outta' the sights of the white devil."

Quila nodded mutely, for she had no words. The White Devil had her in his sights, plain and clear, whether she was going to college or not.

She sighed at the memories. She missed her grandmother. Quila wished she'd lived to see so much actually work out all right. Well, not with Deyonte. No one had seen him in years, but with Rasheed and Waleed. And her, too.

Her 'catch a meal out' with all her guys ended up turning into a dinner party over at Chad and Garrett's. It was a nice evening. Those Tiger Mamas were excellent cooks. They decorated their house in a way that would have made Tiffany swoon in any lifetime. Quila was impressed that their house was full of pictures of the extended family. Not just the White grandparents, who honestly looked permanently shell shocked, those frozen smiles staring out of the nice frames as they posed stiffly with their son, his husband, and their Black grandson—but a nice, framed photo of Mayme, too, holding Waleed. And pictures of Rasheed through the years. His graduations and Quila's. Waleed had clearly grown up with his new, middle-class life, but they did all they could to foster strong ties to where he came from despite the relatively few times they had actually seen one another growing up. Something must have worked: Waleed seemed fluid in both worlds. After celebrating Waleed's future, and Rasheed's past year, conversation turned to Quila's experience on her mission trip.

"So, Quila," Garrett asked as he opened another bottle of wine. "You seem to be so quiet about your mission experience. Most of the people I know who've gone are, well, pretty eager to talk about it."

Chad piped in, "No kidding. Our friend Derek will go on for like hours and hours. I think it makes him feel good. Feel holy. Like he can feel heaven's brownie points falling out of the sky or something. Garret, hit me again, will you?"

Garrett, always the serious one, looked at Chad. "I'm not sure you haven't had enough."

"Hey, where am I drivin'? C'mon, sweetie, fill my glass."

Garrett sighed and rolled his eyes good naturedly and filled Chad's glass yet again. Then he turned to Quila and asked, "How did you like the other people who were on your trip?"

"Honestly, I felt like an imposter next to them."

"An imposter?" Waleed asked, curious.

"Well, yeah. I guess they all went for some noble cause, but standing next to them I felt like I was there to just wipe out… karmic debt or something."

"That's being a little hard on yourself," Garrett said and poured a little more wine in her glass. "I mean, you went. That counts regardless of the reason why you went."

Quila laughed, thinking it was sure proof she'd had too much wine if she could laugh at that statement. "I actually went because this divorce coach gave me the willies in an airport a thousand miles from home."

"What you not tellin' us, Quila? You married?" Rasheed's face was full of surprise and concern.

"No, don't be a fool. I'm not married. She was just on an elevator with me and decided to give me an ear full. And believe me, I think I'd rather be up against the devil himself than her. She was a monster."

"So, where'd you go, Sissy?"

Quila loved it when Waleed called her that. She knew it was a Chad and Garrett thing, it was so White, but she loved the sense of family they had now as adults, even though they hadn't grown up together. "You know, it's kind of funny. I had these crazy visions of working with starving children in Africa or teaching school in a developing county so far away that…"

"So far away that, what?" Chad gave her a piercing look.

She had been about to say, 'so far away that *he* couldn't find me', which told her she was indeed drinking too much wine. It was the truth, but not one she could admit. "That I'd be unreachable. Even with, uh, you know, all of today's technology. Step back into a simpler time." She thought that covered it. She hoped that covered it. "But it didn't quite work out like that. Apparently, there is a hierarchy to volunteerism."

"Oh, just like everything else. It's crazy how middle school is just the same way." Rasheed shook his head. "Make me glad I'm painting houses during summer break. Getting away from all the politics."

"So, you didn't get to save babies in Africa?" Garrett asked Quila kindly.

She shook her head. "If you want to save babies in Africa you first have to pay your dues. It was like going to a foreign country was a tourist destination reserved only for 'first class' missionaries. The rest of us just got in line. We still went into a world of abject poverty, but we went by bus, not by plane. The 'Amens' were probably richer though. There were a lot of those. My god, those people were so excited, you would have thought they'd won a trip to Hawaii."

The men around the table laughed. "And the amenities?" Garrett asked.

"Notably missing. But we stayed at the local Red Roof Inn, so we weren't hurting." Quila smiled.

Waleed took a sip of his iced tea. "I had a friend in college who did that once, some far-away place. Slept in cots and had to worry about bed bugs."

"In some of those places eating bugs is a part of the local diet!" Chad added gleefully, thoroughly delighted in this conversation. "And toilets! Well, in those places you wouldn't waste water for that for sure!"

"In the United States, we flush our toilets with cleaner water than most of the world drinks." Waleed nodded sagely.

"So where was this pit of poverty you went to? Baltimore? Selma? Detroit?" Rasheed asked.

Quila hesitated before she answered, not sure what they all would say. "No, not exactly. My bus ride took us to the heart of the Smokey Mountains. I found myself in West Virginia building and repairing homes for poor White racists, actually. Isn't that ironic?"

Garrett looked speechless. Chad, who was never speechless, seemed even more delighted. "Oh girl, do tell. I can't wait to hear all about this."

Rasheed just looked mad. "That sounds like a mission trip to hell itself." Quila burst out laughing. "So right, Rasheed. That's just what it felt like. I was living in servitude to ignorant White folk who loved, yes loved, a Black woman sweating and toiling, unpaid, for their benefit. Made me glad poor Grandma Mayme didn't live to see it. There I was, a young Black woman, building homes for ungrateful Whites. While those people positively fawned over the White folk there to help them out, they treated me as though they were doing me a kindness to even let me walk on their property."

"And you stayed?" Rasheed sounded almost breathless.

"Why did you stay?" Waleed seemed just curious, but he was curious about everything.

"I signed up for the trip. I guess I figured I had to take the ride. I think it was what Miss Tiffany would call 'a stretch experience'. Besides, the bus back didn't leave until the end of the month."

"No need to stretch that far," Rasheed said low.

Sensing the tension in the room, Garrett tried to smooth things over. "And here you are back, no worse for the wear, Quila? What did you take away from whole thing?"

"Besides a workout in 'turn the other cheek' that I was sure would cause my neck to be permanently injured?" Everyone laughed. Everyone except Rasheed. "There was this one really weird week I had. I still can't quite figure it out. Not only did I know absolutely nothing about roofing and repairing drywall, which was a challenge in and of itself, I was working for people who at best treated me like slave labor and who at worst dropped racial insults under their breath. At times I fantasized that I could buy myself a souvenir of this trip—a gold ball stud for my tongue. Surely, I would have taken care of the piercing all by myself."

"Drywall and roofing?" Chad asked, completely missing the larger issues occupying everyone else's minds. "They had holes in their roofs?"

211

"It was extreme poverty, Chad. These people had next to nothing. While we missionaries immersed ourselves in abject poverty by day, by night we escaped to hot showers and ate dinners out at places like Pizza Hut and Subway. Those people we helped, they caught rainwater in pans that dotted their rooms, which tells you a lot about the conditions of the roofs over their heads."

"No running water? In the US?" Waleed seemed surprised and interested.

Quila shook her head. "You know how popular back yard chickens are up here? Particularly where you all live?" Quila looked at the Tiger Mamas, who nodded in reply. "Well, I hadn't actually thought of them as roommates. But there, chickens were very popular, and they lived in the houses with their owners. I had to scoot the feathered flocks out of my way in order to move from room to room. I remember one lady with half her teeth missing—man, my presence seemed to transform her into a plantation owner of old. She might have been receiving charity help with her roof from the mission group, but she was as proud as any pimp with a harem of mules as she strutted around calling her chickens by name."

"And just what can't you figure out 'bout that, Quila? I can't believe you had so little self-respect as to stay!" Rasheed was starting to become very unhappy.

Quila thought back on the memory. "Rasheed, I found myself where I was, and I did what I did. One day I was smoothing out this white paste they told me is called spackle, and I was putting it over the repaired wall where we joined one piece of drywall to another..." Quila knew it was just the kind of experience that *he* would love to see her in. *He* would love to see her squirm and fight herself over the humiliation and taunting that nasty old woman threw at her as Quila worked on her home.

"Yes, and...?" Rasheed looked expectant.

Quila realized that she'd lost her thread there for a moment, thinking about the Well-Dressed-Man. "Sorry. As I smoothed on the spackle, I could feel the old chicken lady's eyes looking at me. I turned around slowly, and she was just staring at me, her eyes boring into me, a smug look on her face."

"The world has gone mad. Absolutely mad, I tell you. What kind of crazy times are we living in? Where in *any* world is it considered okay to act like that?" Garrett said.

Chad nodded in agreement. "Yeah, I want to know who opened the fortune cookie that reads, 'May you live in interesting times'? This dystopian future reality is just not the world I signed up for."

Quila thought about her experience. "I don't think we get to sign up. I think we are signed up. We get what we get. It's what we do with it that matters."

Waleed, who had never really known anything else but living in interesting times, said, "Even though people are divided and it's hard to find how to talk to the opposing sides, people are still coming together in amazing ways. There's more good than bad out there. There's more to be hopeful about than despondent."

Garrett and Chad looked at each other, the pride in their boy brimming their eyes with tears. "Well said, son. Well said!" Chad beamed and wiped an eye.

Still smiling with the pride only a father can feel, Garrett turned back to Quila. "And what did you do?"

"I told that old bitty that she could tell *him* I was doing the very best job for her that I knew how to do. I said 'You can tell him that. Even with your insults. Even with your attitude. I'm still here and even if you aren't going to show me basic human kindness, I'm still going to show it to you. I'm going to show you the grace that you seem to be so unwilling to show me.' That's what I said to her."

"Well, that sounds effective," Rasheed snorted. "And what kind of insult did she serve up next?"

"I more than half expected that, but no, all she did was to huff and shuffle out of the room. I never saw her after that. I don't know where she

213

went, but I never had to suffer her malaise again. Or her chickens, actually. They seemed to wander off right with her."

"So, what happened to the racist old chicken lady?" Chad asked.

Quila shrugged and shook her head. "On our bus ride back, everyone was talking about how meaningful their time had been, how much they had learned about roofing and siding and plumbing and dry-walling and painting and about how touching the gratitude of the people was. I was surrounded by a sea of Amens and back-slapping. I thought they must have been on a different trip than I was."

"It's always a different trip when you's Black." Rasheed nodded. Chad put his arm around him in a show of solidarity, which Quila wasn't sure was quite the right response.

"In the midst of all that, I was sitting next to Aimee on the bus. She must've caught the expression on my face because she asked me what my first mission trip had been like. Had I enjoyed it?" Quila snorted. "I told her I learned a lot about how to do walls and roofs, for sure. I learned that I had muscles I didn't know I had, because they were so sore now. I sure hope I flashed a winning smile." She looked at the faces of her family members, close and extended. "Then Aimee said, it was the people who got to her."

"They gettin' to me and I wasn't even there," Rasheed said.

Everyone chuckled.

"'Salt of the Earth, aren't they? Poor, but salt of the Earth', Aimee said to me. I told her, 'Yeah, they were pretty salty. Particularly that old chicken lady… the one called Yula'."

"So, what'd she think of Yula?" Waleed asked.

"Said she'd never heard of her. I described her and Aimee was just blank, asking who was she? I told her she was the steely gray old lady with the chickens running amok in her house. Aimee was mystified. She remembered this dear old man named Eugene, who had chickens all over his place and pots to catch the rain from the holes in his roof. She said he was a sweetie, always bringing out iced tea for them that they were all too afraid to drink. You know, 'cause they thought it came from those same pans the chickens were drinking from."

Chad, mid sip of wine, started choking and spluttering, the mouthful of red spraying across the table. He gasped his apologies as he coughed out the wine he had inhaled. Garrett and Waleed quickly grabbed discarded napkins and mopped up the mess on the table, while Rasheed patted Chad on the back, in an attempt to help him recover.

When they had all settled down again, Garrett asked, "So, she never saw Yula? But you were working at the same house?"

"Yeah. We all started off at the same place but I wondered where everyone else got off to. And why I got assigned to a house all by myself? Not to mention that I got Yula all to myself." She shook her head and rolled her eyes. "Aimee said Eugene had these big tears in his eyes and he was thanking them all the time. I saw the little old man, but only on the first day. I thought Yula was his wife."

"Well, he disappeared because she run him off!" Rasheed nodded as if that were the obvious explanation.

"Good theory," Garrett added.

"I don't know… I re-read the briefing papers in our packets after talking to Aimee. It said Eugene was a widower. And the address I was at: same as the sweet little old man named Eugene."

Silence filled the table. Slowly people started to look at one another, but uncomfortably. Then Chad broke the tension. "That is the best ghost story I have ever heard!" He slapped his lap in delight. "You should write for TV. You totally had me there!"

Everyone laughed and even Rasheed could find the humor in it, thinking it a great prank on her part. Quila smiled but she didn't really find the experience very funny. She thought that in hindsight, the mission trip had been the most expedient way she could think of to get away from her life and do for others what she so struggled to do for Victory. By comparison it should have been easy to help someone who was starving and whose house

215

was falling down around them, but helping a girl who'd had money, youth, beauty, opportunity and everything under the sun? How did you help someone blinded by privilege? How did you reach someone who had to lash out at every nice thing done for her? And her mission trip hadn't actually turned out to be helping poor White racists at all. No. She'd been sidelined for a personal battle with the Devil. A mission trip to Hell, indeed. But she must have won that round because after Yula left, she hadn't felt him back in a while. Yeah, things had eased up some. She wondered how long that would last. He might go and lick his wounds, but he'd be back. He'd always be back. He wasn't done with her. She could feel it.

Chapter 22

Other than the grand silence when the topic of Deyonte came up, the dinner get-together was one of the best evenings Quila could remember. It was so normal. So ordinary. So precious. Just her and Rasheed with the baby brother they had hardly known until they'd all grown up, and of course his two White, gay dads. Just an ordinary evening in middle America. She smiled as she scrolled through the pictures on her phone. As she drifted through the images, she came upon one of Miss Tiffany. Quila looked up, lost in thought. She hadn't seen Miss Tiffany in a while.

After scrolling through memory lane, she had texted Tiffany and arranged to come by for a visit. Pulling up into the parking lot for the row of scroungy looking condos where Miss Tiffany lived, Quila couldn't help but be struck by the difference between the 'before' and the 'after'. No matter which life you counted it in, the difference was stark. What she had known was the big house, nice cars, and Miss Tiffany with her unusual breeds of fancy dogs. Even this time around it had started out that way, but here was Miss Tiffany living in a tiny one-bedroom condo surrounded by other people who were struggling. Dr. Van Dyke had long gone, frustrated that his perfect life wasn't turning out according to plan, trading in failed family number one for a more promising family number two. The only actor who had seemed unphased and unchanging despite how their worlds turned over was Jeremy.

She knocked on the door and Miss Tiffany came to greet her with the same warm hug she had always known. Walking inside, Quila noticed that Miss Tiffany still had her fine furniture from her married days, but she had too much of it, crammed into the tiny living space. It was like walking through a furniture warehouse or a store. Although only in late middle age, Miss Tiffany was already gray, and something more than fine lines graced her face. The loss of Jeremy had been hard on her. Then the ordeal with Drake. And then that Ashton guy had dealt his own con-man's blow. Quila could only imagine that Victory's meandering path over the past ten or so years hadn't been so easy either.

"Oh, Quila!" Tiffany hugged the younger woman. "It's so good of you to come and see me. How about we have a cup of tea?"

"That would be lovely, Miss Tiffany. And I brought you a present." She handed the older woman a gift bag.

"What? Oh, you shouldn't have." Tiffany peeked inside. "But I think I'm glad you did! Oh, look at this? Carolina Breakfast Tea. My favorite. I haven't had that in, well years and years."

"I remembered that you liked it. And I got you some of those little British cookies that you like, too."

"You're such a dear. I was going to offer you Lipton, but now this will be special! Come, sit down. Tell me how you've been. Tell me everything! Is there a special man in your life?"

Quila laughed at the absolute irony of that question. Of course, there was a special man in her life. She was dancing with the Devil himself!

"I can tell by that laugh that there is!" Tiffany's voice sounded like chimes. She busied herself with making the tea and peppered Quila with questions but didn't get any clear answers. "Why are you being so evasive?"

Quila wondered just how to handle this. "Okay, so there is a man in my life who is clearly important. Actually, he's more important than I want him to be."

"Oh, I know just how that goes!" Tiffany smiled. "So, are things getting serious?"

Way too serious, Quila thought, feeling a little bit panicky. "He's pretty new in my life, so I really don't even know how to describe him." She thought that was true enough, after a fashion.

"Good job?"

"Sits in the fanciest office I've ever seen. Also wears the nicest suit I've ever seen." *Okay, so that's true. And safe.*

"And I bet he's handsome. You're such a pretty girl, Quila. Of course, he's got to be a real catch."

She thought of how much she'd like to throw him back. "Actually, yes. I kind of hate to admit this, but he's really quite handsome." That gave her a shiver, but not a good one. "He's uh, got this goatee that I think he loves because he must trim it every day for it to look so perfect."

"Oh, he sounds delightful!"

Again, Quila felt a shiver.

"So, when do I get to meet him?"

Hopefully never. "Like I said, it's a relationship I'm trying to figure out."

"Figure out? Quila, there's something you aren't telling me. What is it?"

"It's nothing. Nothing. Really." She tried to give a nonchalant shrug but was afraid it might have looked more like a twitch.

"Quila?" Tiffany gave her that hard look that always made Quila crumble and tell the truth when she was little. But this was a truth she couldn't tell. "All right. I'll ask an indelicate question. Is he Black?"

"What?" Quila jumped in surprise. "No, uh, he's White actually." *Of course, the Devil was White. Who else could hold onto power like that?*

"I wondered if there might be something that was bothering you. Honey, don't feel guilty just because you're dating 'out'. It's so common these days. No one will care. You don't have Black guilt, do you?"

"Black guilt?" She laughed out loud. Miss Tiffany was probably the most well-meaning person she had ever known but she could be amazingly blind

219

to being very far off base. "No, Miss Tiffany, I don't have Black guilt or White guilt. I have a lot of guilt but not about anything like that."

"Well, we share that in common." She set the tea and biscuits down in front of them. "I have a lot of guilt too. I've been thinking of Jeremy a lot lately. Next week would've been his birthday, you know."

"Oh. I'd forgotten."

Miss Tiffany was still celebrating her lost son's birthday, but Jeremy'd had no more birthdays after Quila's and Victory's senior year in high school. They'd found him O.D.'d in a park a little less than ten years ago. The police had come by. Tiffany had been hysterical… the next day, when she finally woke up.

"He was such a good boy, you know. That college ruined him, didn't it? All those wild boys corrupting my little man. They destroyed him."

Quila knew better than to mention the times Jeremy had skipped out all night while in high school, slipping out an upstairs window and enticing his little sister to join him. They attended parties and in summer jumped the gates to local pools to take an illicit swim at night, strewing their beer cans all over, thinking it a fine joke to leave for the people who came in the morning to open the pool for the day. She knew better than to mention how it was he who had gotten Victory to try her first weed and to get her first tattoo. After his first rehab stint they had sent him to a small private college, thinking he was all fixed up and ready to go. That hadn't lasted a year.

"Jeremy had a lot of really fine qualities," Quila said. That was true. "He was wicked smart. One of the smartest guys I ever knew."

Tiffany sighed deeply over her cup of tea. "Maybe he was too smart. Maybe that was his problem. He never could seem to find himself."

He lost himself to the drugs before he ever had a chance, Quila remembered. But she knew that Miss Tiffany didn't need any help remembering. She lived with those memories. Quila wondered if she ever let them go. Jeremy had indeed been smart. He thought he could outsmart the gangs, but he didn't account for how vicious they could be. And he hadn't survived it. He'd cheated them one too many times, and they finally sold him product cut with way too much fentanyl. There was just no coming back after that. Tiffany had been devastated at the funeral. Victory had been so high Quila wasn't sure she was even present for it or registering any of it.

"And how is your brother, the teacher?" Tiffany asked her.

"Oh, I saw him last weekend. My two brothers and I got together with Waleed's adoptive fathers. It was good. Yeah, it was great to see them again. Rasheed is teaching seventh and eighth grade math. He's a natural with the kids, so that's a good match for him. They're about at the same maturity level." They laughed. "And my baby brother is starting medical school."

Tiffany was quiet for a while. "I always hoped Jeremy would go to medical school. Or become a pharmacist."

Quila thought that was ironic, given Jeremy's interest in all things drugs.

"Isn't it funny?" Tiffany looked up, her eyes wet.

"What, Miss Tiffany?"

"It's just funny, how my children started out with every advantage. A nice place to grow up. A home. Two parents. Good schools. Lessons. Everything they ever wanted."

"Uh huh…" Quila wasn't sure what to say. That was true. They had every privilege in the book. "It was a great childhood."

"But then it all went so wrong. It went so wrong so fast, and I never knew what to do or how to stop it."

Quila was confused. "What do you mean by 'it's so funny'?"

"Well, just look at your family. You had no real mother. Your poor grandmother, bless her soul and may she rest in peace, but how can a grandmother raise all those grandchildren? I sometimes think what it would've been like if Jeremy or Victory had given me grandchildren? And given how things turned out, what if I had their children living here? How would I manage to raise them and keep them fed and help them with their homework?"

"You were an expert at homework from what I remember."

Tiffany smiled at her. "You always were a sweet girl, Quila." She patted her hand lovingly. "That's very generous of you."

"No, I'm serious. I made it through school, elementary and middle school because of you. Without you, I wouldn't have learned how to study. Wouldn't have gotten into those special classes you signed me up for. Wouldn't have had the chances I did in high school. Miss Tiffany, if it hadn't been for you, I wouldn't ever have gone to college. How can you say that you'd be no good at it now?"

"Well." Tiffany tried to smile. She blinked her eyes a few times. "Things change. I don't have the energy I used to. Once upon a time I really wanted grandchildren, but maybe it's for the best after all." She sipped her tea and smoothed down her blouse. Quila noticed it was stained. She wasn't sure whether Miss Tiffany didn't care or couldn't properly see them. Maybe that was just what she had to wear? "I just mean it's funny how things work out because here you are, a college graduate. Your brothers all doing so well."

Quila thought that it was clear that Victory's mother had forgotten about Deyonte.

"You all had every obstacle in front of you. Everything was against you. No mother. No father. No money. Not enough food. Living in that dangerous complex with needles in the playground. And you're all shining examples of model citizens. Whoever would have imagined it? Whoever could have believed it? It's a marvel to me, a marvel I tell you." Quila was struck dumb and sought for something to say. There was no rancor or jealousy in Tiffany's voice. "It's hard, you know, the sadness. Some days I'm just incredibly sad that my own garden, once filled with sun and fertilized with plenty, withered and died."

Quila swallowed hard. "While a seemingly neglected patch of scratch ground yielded bounty?"

Miss Tiffany wiped a tear away from her cheek. "It's just that my life feels like it has nothing to show for it." She looked at her ceramic rooster, which still brightly gleamed, caught in mid-crow. It was just that now when it sat in this dingy little kitchen, it didn't seem to have much to crow about. "My marriage failed. Drake blamed me for what happened to the children. Said I was an awful mother. Proof was in the pudding. I have no real career. I live here." She broke down into tears and Quila wrapped her arms around the woman. "Everything just seemed to dissolve around me. I never knew what I did to make that happen."

"There, there now. Tiffany, you cry all you need to." Quila held the older woman in her arms and rocked her, patting her back. "You a bit like Job," she said, some of her childhood accent coming back to her as she felt flooded by memories of her grandma holding her just like this. "Don't you lose your faith, Miss Tiffany. I know it seems like everything's against you. I know that feeling. I really do." When Tiffany's sobs subsided a little, Quila continued to hold her and rubbed her back. "I'll tell you something: that scrabble patch grew because you believed in it. And you're right, it was a place where nothing ever should have grown, but it actually produced something. It was you who believed in it. I can't say why Vicky or Jeremy made the choices they did." Inside her head she wanted to scream, *because I failed to save Victory. It's my fault,* but how could she ever explain that to Vicky's mother? To anyone? She certainly couldn't even explain it to herself.

"They made terrible choices." Tiffany sniffed and sat back in her chair, composing herself.

"That's right. They were their choices. Not yours. You didn't force those choices on them. We don't always know the bigger picture. We don't always understand the 'why' behind the 'how' of things happening around us. There's just so much we don't know. But what I do know is that because of you, I was able to make different choices. Because of all the grace you extended to me, I was able to walk a different path from the one I took before."

"The one you took before?" Tiffany looked confused.

"Uh," Quila felt caught. "I mean, no. I mean the one I might have taken otherwise." She struggled to recover from her stumble. "The one way too many kids who come from the projects have to take because it's the only way in front of them. But you reached out. You reached out and this time I took your hand. And I'm grateful, Miss Tiffany. I'm really grateful to be here today and say thank you for what you gave me, because it made all the difference. Not just to me. To Rasheed too. And Waleed. He never would have ended up with his Tiger Mamas if you hadn't been a part of my life. We've all been touched by you." She put her hand on Tiffany's arm and gave her a reassuring little squeeze. "You have more than one garden. I can't tell you why the sadness you've experienced has come to you. You didn't deserve it. None of it. But you should know that you have touched us in such profound ways. I'm part of your garden. And you never know what the future holds. None of us knows what happens tomorrow."

Tiffany lay her hand on Quila's cheek. "And you're like another daughter to me. Thank you, Quila. Oh, my goodness, look at me. I'm a wreck, aren't I?"

"You've been through a lot."

"So, you haven't told me anything about your exciting summer! Your mission trip. Now, I want to hear all about it."

Quila smiled, remembering her conversation with her brothers and the Mama Tigers. She decided it might be better to share only the highlights and leave the existential musings for another time. Miss Tiffany seemed satisfied, delighted even, at how Quila had helped build fences and repair walls for people who lived in such poverty.

"I always hoped Victoire would have experiences like that. I did Peace Corps, you know. I got so much out of that. Where I met Drake, actually. I always hoped that my children would do that, too. I think Victory would have loved it."

"Yes, she would have," Quila nodded and smiled. "I believe she would have found herself there." Quila had to be careful she didn't once again slip and accidentally say something that no one in this lifetime would be able to comprehend. It had been with her so much lately, her two lives. She was constantly thinking about her "mission" and the two journeys she was on, her parallel universes, both of them strange dystopian realities in their own ways. And of course, how to defeat the Devil. She was still stumped by that particular challenge. And her time was running out. She could feel it. "It was because of Victory that I went on the mission trip. She inspired me."

"She did?" Tiffany looked amazed.

"Miss Tiffany, I think it's safe to say that nearly everything I've done in my life has been because of Victory. Because I love her. Because she's my friend. Because she's the closest thing to a sister that I have."

Tiffany looked away for a moment. "I think she's lost."

"What do you mean? She's at the community college. Studying to be a nurse."

Tiffany shook her head. "No. She did that just to be close to the drugs. She was… released… from the program. I haven't seen her for three weeks. She hasn't returned my calls. I don't know where to look."

"She's been gone for three weeks? That was just after I left for the mission trip."

"Oh, I suppose that would be about then, wouldn't it?"

Quila searched her memory for clues that Victory was planning this, planning to cut and run as soon as her minder left town. That it had all been an act, how she'd gotten her shit together.

"I know she's done this before, and eventually she always surfaces. Shows up on my door and stays on the couch for a few months. But this time… I don't know. Quila, honey, it feels different." Tiffany looked at Quila and reached out, putting her hand on Quila's arm. "Could you go and see if you can find her? Bring her back to me? Make sure she's still okay? I wouldn't even know where to start looking."

Quila was stunned. Unfortunately, she thought she knew just exactly where to look. "I'll do my best, Tiffany. My absolute best."

225

Chapter 23

Driving down the street, Quila was amazed at how this town never changed. She should know: she'd lived two lifetimes here now. Well, maybe one for anyone else, since her lifetimes were shorter than the norm. Her circumstances were… special. Miss Tiffany had sounded so old and broken. She'd lost Jeremy. She couldn't lose Victory, too. She had to have her daughter back. What could Quila say? It was all her fault that Victory was in this mess to begin with. If she somehow hadn't gotten caught in this deal with the Devil and had just stayed dead, well then, Victory would have spent these twenty-five additional years living a happy life. She'd probably be living in some fine house having successfully launched her children off into their own lives and now be starting to think about grandchildren of her own. But no, Quila had to turn back the clock and mess it all up.

She'd gotten back in her car and started to troll the meaner streets that she used to know so well. It was a lifetime ago but to her it seemed like just yesterday. She knew just the corner where it all went down. She didn't want to go there again, she never wanted to go there again, so she finally parked about three blocks away and waited. It took a lot longer than she thought it would. About an hour and then she saw a girl with a shock of purple hair in a red jacket running fast.

Quila jumped out of the car and sprinted to catch up. It was easier than it should have been. Vicky was struggling for breath and grabbing a stitch in her side.

"Victory! Victory! Wait, wait up!"

The purple-haired girl looked over her shoulder and stumbled, then fell.

"You alright?" Quila bent down and helped her up. "Man girl, you running like something's after you."

"Quila?"

Quila noticed that Victory's eyes looked fuzzy. Glazed over. "Oh my god, you took a nip, didn't you? Oh, Vicky, you shouldn't be here at all. Not living this life. This wasn't meant for you."

"He's after me. I went to make the drop but I took a nip and now he's after me." The girl looked at her, her eyes moving from head to toe. "Are you really here? Am I dreaming?"

"Oh Jesus, I hope so." Quila looked at her, noticing that Victory had a new tattoo on her neck. "Vic, honey, you're a mess. Come with me. I gotta' get you home."

There was panic in Victory's eyes. "I can't go home. I can't go home! She said I'd stolen from her for the last time. I can't go there. She'll have me locked up in one of those rehab places again. No way." She looked around them both, stealing furtive glances at the alleys and up and down the street. "We can't be caught here. Gotta' go. This is Blues. We can't be here."

Quila looked around them. "Nah. I remember this as solid Red. We're safe here. C'mon. I gotta' get you home."

"No, no. I gotta' make my delivery." Victory started to glance nervously around them again.

"You're still carrying? Oh my god, get rid of that stuff." Quila reached into the inner pocket of the jacket, the secret pocket that was hard to feel and that you could put the thin little bags right along the edging of the jacket. All that bling was great for hiding the deliverables behind since it made it hard to feel in a pat down. Victory was too surprised to resist as Quila whipped out the goods.

"How did you know…" Victory choked on the words.

"Because this jacket used to be mine." Quila was amazed at what she was seeing. "You were never supposed to wear it."

"Huh?"

Quila inspected the bag. It was pretty thin. "How much of this did you take? Oh my god, Victory, they gonna' hurt you bad for pinching the goods."

"I can outrun them. And I paid them last time with some of Tiffany's jewelry. She's got more. She's always got more. He knows I'm good for it." Victory grabbed the bag.

"Girl, you're not making sense. Give me that." Quila snatched the baggie back that Victory had taken from her. She threw it down a sewer drain. "Now that's done, and it's gone. You're coming with me." She tried to drag Victory to her car, but upon seeing the drugs disappear Victory started to scream and dropped to the ground to crawl into the gutter herself.

"No, no, no. He'll kill me." She turned towards Quila, all venom. "You're killing me. It's your fault he's going to kill me."

"Not if I can get you out of here. C'mon, Victory. We gotta' go!" Quila was now lifting Victory physically, holding her from behind, her arms twisted around the other girl's shoulder and her hands laced behind Victory's head. There was little the slighter girl could do, and Quila clearly had the advantage, dragging Victory towards her car.

There was a sudden screeching of tires as a Subaru Impreza pulled up sharply. Quila froze as three men got out of the car all dressed in their badass Blue.

"Well, well, well, what have we here?" The man who was clearly in the lead spoke up while his two cronies echoed him. Quila could see the glint of his gun sticking up out of his pants.

"Jaquan! Honey, I was comin' to see you!" Victory struggled and broke free from Quila's grip. She started to run over to him but stopped short, seeing no welcome from him or his brothers. She started to back up towards Quila, eventually slinking around behind her.

229

"Aw, Vic, now surely you don't 'speck me to believe that. Not while you been carrying for Deyonte. But once again I ask, what have we here? You be… you be Deyonte Williams' little sister? Look dawgs, this be Tequila Williams."

"It's Quila, Jaquan. Just Quila. Been a long time."

He looked at her askance. "Long time? Ain't never been no time, bitch. You never gave me time of day. You all high and mighty, too good for a brother and off to college. Why you talk to me like you know me?"

"Oh, Jaquan Redmond, I know you so much better than you would ever believe."

"Don't talk shit, bitch. You don't know nothin' 'bout me."

"I know you hate chocolate ice cream. That you're allergic to bee stings and walnuts. That you really love old movies. And that you miss your little sister Malejah something fierce." Quila spoke with assurance and felt more confident as she saw Jaquan falter. "And you got a sweet little butterfly tattooed onto your ass." That had been for her last time around. She wondered who it was for now?

"Bro," one of his boys spoke up, "you allergic to bee stings?"

"Dude don't like chocolate ice cream? Who not like chocolate ice cream?"

"A butterfly?"

"Shut up! Both of you." He turned to Quila. "Jus how you know that 'bout me?" He looked at his boys and then back at Quila. "Oh yeah, you a witch." He gave her a funny look. "No matter. It never mind. What you doin' back in the hood? An look at the trash you hangin' out with now? Little Miss Victory. Ain't she jus everyone's favorite little toy. She'll do anything for a dime bag."

"I'd do anything for you, Jaquan." Victory's voice was shaking. She was afraid. She hid behind Quila again.

"So you doin' a deal with Little-Miss-Goody-Two-Shoes-Tequila-Williams? Naw, dawgs, the sister now comin' down to the 'hood for a taste."

He turned to Quila. "You better not be tastin' my goods, sister, not without speakin' to Jaquan first, witch or no."

"I'm not doing any of your drugs, Jaquan. No worries. I just came for Victory."

"Now you on my territory and askin' for time?" Jaquan bit off the words.

"I'm taking her home. Her mama needs her."

At this remark all three young men burst out laughing. "She done stole all her mama's jewelry. Her mama don't want her back less she gonna' press charges," one of the boys said.

Jaquan gave Quila a hard look. "You a pig now, Tequila? You workin' for them?" Slowly he drew his gun, looking at her now full of suspicion.

The roar of an engine made all five of them look up the street. A black Cadillac Escalade thundered up to them and pulled up short, tires screeching. The doors opened and three other young men got out. When they saw Jaquan's group with guns drawn, they drew their own.

"Jaaaquaaan!" The leader dramatically drew out the name, full of confidence and bravado that only came when one was on one's own marked turf, armed, and with backup. "What you boys doin' in the Red zone? You shouldna' be here or bad blood gonna' flow on both sides. You startin' a war or what?"

"I don't want no war, Deyonte. I just want what's mine." He gestured with his gun towards the two women.

"Oh no, Victory is mine." Deyonte's gun glinted in the bright sunlight.

"Deyonte? Deyonte Williams?" Quila stared at her brother. It had been years since she'd seen him. "Everything I tried to do for you, and you end up here in the street with you and Jaquan pointing guns at each other *again*?" Quila could not believe what she was seeing.

This time Jaquan and Victory both said, "huh?" and stared at Quila.

Slowly, as if against his better judgement Deyonte turned his head towards the two women. "Is that? Naw, shit…"

231

Quila took two steps towards her brother and then she turned and grabbed Victory's wrist. She knew that if they could just get in the car, they would be safe. He'd turned that thing into a tank last time; he would've done the same now. She dragged Victory along with her. "Deyonte Williams, I can't believe it's you. I mean, of course it's you. It's the same street. The same day. God, it's good to see you again, even so."

"Tequila? What the hell are you doing here? I thought you was in Africa?"

His surprise seemed to embolden Jaquan. "Well, if we're done with this happy little reunion now, I'll just take back the delivery Victory was making for me and my boys."

Deyonte stepped forward. "Victory don't deliver for a damn Blue!"

Victory cowered behind Quila while the boys started to yell taunts and threats at one another.

Quila still had a vice grip on Victory's wrist. "Oh shit, Vic. I've seen all this before. We gotta' go! We gotta' get out of here. I came here to save you." She started to drag Victory away, but the girl was like a dead weight, just staring at the boys, who seemed to have little interest in the two women at the moment. "Come on!" She began to run, dragging Victory behind her.

She didn't get far before she heard the popping sounds. They grew louder than normal gunfire and reminded her of when thunder rolled in the distance and made the walls vibrate in some kind of demon-inspired low roll. It was like the Devil was hunting you and wanted to devour you alive. In slow motion she turned, just to look over her shoulder, and she saw Victory's arms fling out in front of her as the bullet hit her from behind. One. Two. Three jolts and she was down, her face turned to the side and her blue eyes staring at nothing at all. Quila got down on her knees and scooped up Victory's body. She hugged Victory to her, rocking and crying and saying, "No, no, no! it wasn't supposed to turn out this way!"

Then the crack came like peels of thunder. She felt it first in her shoulder, then her leg, then her neck. After that she didn't know what hit her. The last thing she saw was the bodies of six men lying in the street between that Impreza and that Escalade. Those black cars framing those Black boys and under them all growing pools of blood as red as the walls of the office where the Well-Dressed-Man sat. She could hear him laughing as everything faded to white.

Chapter 24

"Well, well, well. Here we are again. Hello? Hello? Ahh, yes, there you are. Welcome back to my office, Tequila Williams."

It took Quila a few minutes to shake the dizziness and confusion out of her head, but at last her vision started to clear and the room came into focus. The walls were red and now they looked like they might be in motion, like blood was oozing down their surfaces. She turned her head and there he was. The Well-Dressed-Man was sitting behind his desk, a smile on his face. His fire pit was blazing away, but no white cloud was hovering above it just now.

"I'm here? How can I be here? I have to get back. Victory…"

"Oh, Victory. Yes, it was victorious, wasn't it?" He paused to look at her. "You know, I have to admit there were times when I thought you were going to try to go your own way. To try to screw me on our little deal."

Quila tried to struggle in her chair, but she was pinned down. "Let me go," she said through gritted teeth. She pulled and pushed against the force, her efforts fruitless.

"Try all you wish. It is… implacable. Unyielding."

She stopped and looked at him. "What is?"

"That invisible force holding you down."

"What is it?" She looked around herself uncomfortably but could see nothing.

"Death. You can't see it. Or smell it. But you sure can feel it, can't you? I'm always amazed at how something so immaterial, so weightless, can feel so very heavy." He leaned towards her again, a leer in his eye. "And it is heavy, is it not, Quila?"

"It's heavy." She felt panicky. "I can't be here! I did everything…" Then she held her tongue. He was not the type with whom you gave much away. She needed to get a hold of herself and try to think her way through this. She needed to find an angle.

"Yes, you did. You did everything I asked of you. And more. You are such a surprise, Miss Quila. Such a surprise. You had me concerned there for a while, what with your Miss Goody Two Shoes act. I wondered for a bit if you had gotten the seriously flawed idea that you could escape me simply by committing good deeds?" Here he looked at her very gravely. "No one undoes a deal with me."

"No one."

He just shook his head slowly. "But you turned out to be much more devious than I initially gave you credit for. Oh, you'll fit in well around here. And I have to say, that is a different tactic than I have seen deployed before. Of all the many people who have sat in that very chair, begging for their souls," derision dripped off his voice, "I have never seen anyone quite as clever as you."

"Clever?" She was still playing her cards close to her chest. She wanted him to do the talking.

"Yes. To throw Victory off her path of perfection by you walking in the light. It was unexpected. Mostly people are much more direct. They try to overtly corrupt the person who they want to take the fall for them. Throw obstacles in their path."

"Obstacles?"

"Sure."

"Like what? What do they do?" She wasn't sure she actually wanted to know.

"Drugs are popular. I've seen fortunes destroyed. Love lives torn asunder." He cracked his knuckles and looked mockingly sad. "Sometimes they resort to murder or rape. False accusation can have interesting outcomes, particularly when it results in wrongful conviction." He sounded like he was enjoying himself. "But I've never seen anyone try to corrupt another by stopping them from using drugs. Or getting them a useful education that actually meant something. Or keeping them out of trouble. That was an interesting strategy."

"Uh, it was the best I could come up with."

"Indeed. It was a surprise. You must know Victory very well to understand that by you taking up the straight path, she would fall to the darkness. Where you followed in her footsteps from her previous life, she would then follow in yours from your previous life. Ingenious. I can't believe I didn't think of it myself."

"No..." Quila's voice cracked.

"Yes, it's true, even I don't think of every possible turn of events. And I do love to be surprised."

She blinked, not sure what to say, not sure if she trusted her voice. Then she asked, "You do?"

"Oh yes. It's rather tedious here. So surprising me is always a good thing. Always gets rewarded." He looked at her for a while. "But I'm curious."

"Curious about what?" She was cautious. This was another trap and as far as she was concerned, she had done enough damage already.

"Curious about what it was like?" His voice was oily.

"About what... what was like?"

"Living the good life."

"What? What good life? I didn't have money. Or power. Or fame. Hey, I'm still that girl from the projects. What you talkin' 'bout the good life?" She tried to calm herself down. She didn't want to let him provoke her.

"Oh, the good life isn't one of material wealth or endless pleasures. It's living a life where you create good. That must have been an interesting experience… for you. I must say, given your performance the first time around I found it fascinating that you would choose to walk that path. It must have been excruciatingly painful." He was leaning towards her again, looking at her intensely, as if to study her.

She sat as tall as she could in her chair. "It came surprisingly easy. I found I rather enjoyed it."

"Did you now?"

"And there were consequences of my actions."

"Consequences? Say more." She could hear the tone in his voice. It wasn't a request.

"The consequences of my actions. Things changed this time around. Like Rasheed."

"Yes, last time he was an old man before he hit eighteen, and his time ran out soon after. He died—just like you did. Better, actually."

"Rasheed. His name is Rasheed. He was a middle school teacher. This time everything changed. He was a teacher and he was great at it. He loved the kids and they loved him."

The Well-Dressed-Man nodded and looked at his nails, absorbed in giving one a polish to remove an invisible speck of dirt. "Boring."

"What do you mean, boring?"

"Boring life this time. No drama. This time he married. Had three kids. Lived to be an old man. What could be more dreary than that? At least the last time he went down in a blaze of glory. A shoot out after a bank robbery went awry. Very entertaining. All over the news."

Quila was in shock for a moment. She'd never known that part of the story. Mayme wouldn't tell her and made her promise to not go looking for the answer either. That had been easy: drugged up teenagers didn't actually watch the news. So, last time a 'blaze of glory', but this time he'd come out all right. An old man. Children. Family. She felt a rush of joy.

"Oh, stop that. It's revolting. You don't do that *here*."

She thought about the other people she had known. "Devan. Biggie didn't shoot him down when he turned nineteen…."

"No. Just an unintended consequence of your big mouth. It was hilarious though when he convinced all those gullible high schoolers that you were a witch. And that reputation followed you for a long time! I'll have to remember that one. Sending someone back as a witch. That presents just worlds of entertaining opportunities." He sounded delighted again.

"I think I'm not glad that you're finding this so fun. But Devan had a whole different life. He was an Assistant Minister to that Reverend Barberet." She remembered how he never did completely heal. One leg was shorter than the other and his spinal injuries left him in chronic pain.

"Yes, I saw how you threw him into the path of the minister." He held up his hands as if to stop her. "No apologies necessary. After all, it was a hideously painful way to go. I gave you extra credit for that, sending him to face Biggie far too early. And to be fair, I didn't fault you for the effect old Barberet had on him. There was no way you could predict or even understand the power he wields."

She had only seen the reverend once or twice. He was on the news a lot though, what with his social justice work and leading protests down at the State House against new laws that kept people down who were already at the margins of society. "So, what happened to Devan?"

"Oh, he was more interesting. He picked up where his spiritual warrior mentor left off and fought the battle for civil rights for decades."

"I thought you didn't approve of that kind of thing? It sounds just dripping with heroism."

The Well-Dressed-Man nodded. "Right. Dripping and gooey. Not my cup of tea actually, but his end was spectacular! Shot by some hold-out Confederate as he was giving a speech. Oh, the riots were something to behold! Blocks and blocks of the city burning." His eyes were shining with delight. "Like you said, unintended consequences. There are always unintended consequences. I was so proud of you. I lost Devan but gained so much more."

"And Waleed?" She was afraid to ask.

"Yes, that was a brilliant way to destroy your mother. I couldn't believe you had it in you. It was like watching you push your own mother off a cliff. I gave you extra credit for that one. Decided you must have a heart, well, just like mine actually, to take Bobby's only son from her."

Quila knew better than to bring up the fact that Waleed would have perished before he saw his second birthday had she not acted. "And the unintended consequence?"

"I know, don't feel too badly about it. You're just a mortal. How could you have known what the unintended consequence of your interference would be on that boy's life?"

"Why? What did Waleed do? Did he go down in a… a blaze of glory, too?" She was half afraid to ask but couldn't find the discipline to corral her curiosity and shut up.

"Well, not any kind of glory that interests me. He finished medical school and became a doctor. He served the underserved all his life. Married. Had a family. Lived to be very old. Blah, blah, blah. Gave a lot of money to an underprivileged college upon his death. I think they named a building or something meaningless like that for him. Nothing remotely worth talking about down here."

"Wow," she said under her breath. "Little Waleed." Quila furrowed her brow. "Wait a minute. I only got here like five minutes ago. How can they all have become old men already?"

He shrugged. "Time is for the living."

She looked over at him, not sure if he would answer. "Deyonte?"

He had no expression on his face.

"Well? Will I run into him here?"

He said simply, "Blood bather."

"Oh." She felt the weight of death on her even more heavily now. He wasn't going to sit in this chair and review his life. He walked that path to nothingness. He would scratch himself out of existence. She supposed her older brother had probably killed a lot of people by the time they went down in the street together. Mostly brothers. She felt a tear slide down her cheek with the thought of all the wasted lives and devastation that followed on the heels of guns and drugs and young men who had no real options in life.

"Do I taste regret? Remorse?" He sniffed the air, wrinkling his nose.

"Unintended consequences. And some intended ones. But Victory, man what did you do to her?" Quila asked.

"Nothing that she didn't do to herself. She chose her path."

"I did nothing to put her on that dark road." There. She'd said it. The truth was out.

"I know! Inspired genius! Totally surprising. And, if you look at it from the perspective of wisdom, she didn't have the opportunity to learn by your example. That's what you gave her in your first time around. An example of what would happen *if*. You were her 'what if'. What if she followed Jeremy? What if she took the easy path? What if, what if, what if! But this time around you deprived her of all that. So she was left with her curiosity. Insatiable, as it turned out to be. She was left to explore her own darkness. She was left to experience the unintended consequences for herself. And since she was making so many of those choices at later and later ages, the consequences for her were so much larger."

"But that's not fair!"

"True, perhaps, but the world is full of unintended consequences, of both good actions and bad. In decades past, people much like Victory and her parents went to 'third world countries' and vaccinated hundreds of thousands of children against horrible childhood diseases, sparing them and their families the pain and suffering of the illness and death of a child. It was a good thing to do, wasn't it? But when those children grew up, their population exploded. Those diseases had been horrible, but in the cruel way

241

that mother nature works, had kept the population, well, level. Then the miraculously saved children became adults and suddenly there wasn't enough clean water or enough food for them. Insufficient places to live. Inadequate sanitation systems to handle all they produced. Each outgrowing their historical areas, their tribes started to fight over the resources. Eventually war broke out and millions more died from multiple generations. While it was a noble thing to try to save all those children, unfortunately no one gave any thought to the implications of what that meant. They just congratulated themselves on their job well done and went back to their happy homes, leaving all those recipients of their noblesse oblige behind to live in fear and die in anguish. It's a very tangled web indeed. I could explain to you all the downstream effects of your actions but I'm afraid you… well, you might find it overwhelming."

Quila sat back in her seat, feeling utterly defeated. "So why bother trying?"

"Yes, that is the question, isn't it? Just the point!" The Well-Dressed-Man seemed excited, as though she was making scintillating conversation at last. "Why do we bother? Why even try? I suppose that is what we are here to discuss after all, isn't it?" It might have been the first genuine smile she'd seen on his face.

"So, what happens now?" she asked, not really wanting the answer.

"Well, I get Victory. You get time off for good behavior. I'll honor my agreement with you. I always honor my agreements. After all, my 'contracts' are binding in more than just the technical sense."

Quila sat bolt upright. She had the glimmer of an idea. He had said that no one could un-do a deal with him. And from his earlier comments, he didn't seem to find begging to be even remotely persuasive.

"So, all-in-all, well done, Quila! You did a most unpredictable and excellent job. You brought me just what I wanted."

Quila realized that she needed to offer him a new deal. A better deal. And she'd better do it fast.

Chapter 25

Quila took a deep breath and let herself totally relax. That seemed to catch his attention. She smiled at him, and he looked at her with some suspicion.

At last he said, "Yes?" drawing the word out low and slow.

"Let me read *your* fortune for once. You sittin' there in all your fine duds, thinking you own the world, but you don't even know what you want."

"Don't I?" He leaned back in his chair and seemingly unconsciously ran his hand down the front of his immaculately tailored suit. A new level of interest piqued in his eyes. However, the razor of sarcasm was in his voice as he said, "Oh you, who have gone into life-after-death and then come back again, now that you are so wise…" He yawned. "Do tell."

She shifted in her seat, feeling scared to death. She was bluffing. She knew it. He knew it. She took a deep breath to hide the tremble. "You don't want Victory at all."

He snorted. "Then what was the whole sending you back on a mission about?"

Quila had an idea. She was going to run with it, like she'd tried to outrun the bullets in the street. Only this time her goal was different. She wasn't dodging. She was catching. And it was gonna' hurt just as much, damn it, just as much.

"You want me. Victory is just like any other soul now. Troubled. Broken. Diseased. She's not the pure-shining-white glory you were, uh, drooling over at our last visit."

"Oh, no, no, no. Let me be clear. I'm never wrong. I want Victory."

Quila shook her head. "You didn't want me when I was in her place. I wasn't worth it, you said. Wasn't *interesting*. Well now, she's not interesting either. She has none of the qualities that got you so excited before. They all washed away in the maelstrom of her life."

"Maelstrom. That's a big word for you."

"I did go to college. This time, anyway. And don't look at me like that. I'm not smarter this time. I just have more to work with."

"You just lived up to your… potential?" He smirked. "Ah, if only we could help all children live up to their potential." But he didn't say it like he meant it. Not at all.

"You say that like you're making fun of bleeding-heart liberals who want all kids to have an equal chance." She couldn't help but taunt him.

He shrugged, unconcerned. "Nothing's equal. Chances are fleeting. They pass by in a heartbeat and then they're gone." He smiled.

"But there are second chances."

He snorted.

She was filled with indignation. And something else. Hope. "No… No! There are! You gave *me* a second chance and look what I did with it! Yeah, you're like the king of second chances, aren't you?"

She thought for a moment that the Devil actually looked uncomfortable. Like maybe she'd seen some kind of truth he was trying to hide behind that façade of the perfect suit and immaculately sculpted beard. She gave him a more piercing look and decided to run with this idea too. Her insight filled her with confidence.

"Yeah, you gave me a second chance and just look what you created."

"What's that?"

"Duh! Me! I'm way better than Victory."

"Okay, so pride, I always love false pride." He rotated in his chair a bit. She rolled her eyes. "Whatever. Look, you sent me back, so you have a soul here in front of you which was worthless. Dime a dozen, you called me. You thought it would be… uh, delicious, and let me say 'uck', to corrupt Victory. But what you aren't seeing is that what you really want is right before your eyes. She's worthless to you because she's damaged goods. I'm the prize. I'm the damaged goods made whole. I'm the shining star."

"Shining star? You ended up just as dead on the same street with the same bullet holes."

"A lump of coal made into a diamond is worth a lot more than a diamond crushed into dust."

He seemed to take interest in this line of reasoning. "Go on. Tell me more."

She could feel her heart slamming in her chest. A part of her was screaming *You idiot! Get away! Let him take whoever he wants as long as it's not you and get out of here!* But she couldn't do it. This was never Victory's destiny. She had the straight path. A straight path into heaven. Quila might not have started down this road when she was born, but this was the road now given to her. And she'd made some decisions along the way, she'd been her own guidepost, as it were, and she'd taken control of her destiny, to the extent that she could. Well, her destiny had been the same, after all, she was sitting back in this chair. Sure, she was wearing much nicer duds, but with the same bullet holes in her body, as he'd said. So, her destiny hadn't changed but how she'd gotten there was worlds different, and that mattered. That mattered a lot. She couldn't control much, but she could control this.

"Yeah, I'm your shining star. I'm the diamond. I lived and made it out, succeeded against all odds and I lived a good life. I even went to church. Mission trips."

He looked at her skeptically. "Tequila. You cannot try to tell me that you became any kind of a religious convert. You may have gone on a mission trip, but you were no kind of a believer. I was keeping tabs on you, you know."

She gave him a level look. "Believe me, I felt you every step of the way."

"You know, human religion doesn't impress me very much. Just a very short time ago, your kind was worshipping some very severely personality disordered types there, calling them 'Gods'. Looking at the mess you're still in, I'm not sure much has changed."

She sat back in her chair and crossed her arms, wondering how to explain what she was thinking. "Actually, I agree with you. There's a lot of messed up people. Whether they think they're practicing a religion or not, what they're actually *doing* is probably a lot closer to worshipping, well, *you*."

He burst out laughing. "Yes, I see a lot of those types. But tell me more of what you mean by *worshipping me*." Delight played across his face as he taunted her. He was leaning towards her again, intensely interested. He seemed to have this dull red glow about him.

She thought she was on the most dangerous spiritual thin ice possible, but she plunged ahead. Not like there was any choice. "Worshipping you, yeah, well… they value money above all else. And power. They will sell themselves and everything they've ever stood for just to have power. They'll totally switch positions if it garners them more authority or press coverage or fame. The public ones will tell any lie, even lies about their own life, for fame, because to them fame is, well, it's power, isn't it?"

A slow smile came to his face. "Fame is powerfully addictive. Addiction is such a weakness of the human condition." The glee was evident in his voice. "It's wonderful, isn't it? Keeps me in business."

"I can imagine." She took a breath and looked off into a corner of the room, deep in thought. "Not all addiction is alike. There's that money and fame and power thing, but then there's the folk I saw my first time around. That's a different kind of addiction. That's, that's not what I'm talking about. That's oblivion-chasing. It's tragic." She thought about the people she'd lost. The people she'd seen drift off and die. The people who couldn't face their reality so anyplace else was good enough, especially if it was no place at all. For a while there, she'd been one of them, too. "Yeah, it's so sad, but it's not the kind of addiction I'm talking about."

"Of course not. Chasing oblivion would not fit under the category of worshipping me. In fact, I find them just as boring in death as they are in life. They aren't in my jurisdiction, anyway. I gave them up eons ago."

Quila cleared her throat and looked back at him. "Uh, glad to hear it."

"So, go on. Tell me more about these worshippers."

"Okay. Then there are those who don't want to be famous or known, but who want money. They did some awful stuff. Sold awful stuff that they lied about, that they pushed, that they knew was toxic and addictive, but their lies brought them poor suckers who gave over everything they had."

"Oh, those poor unfortunate souls." The look of excitement on his face made her slightly nauseated. "And what were they selling?"

"From what I could tell it didn't matter much. Some lied about pain killers, and addicted millions. Man, that devastated families. You know, it always really seemed to me like one of those plagues from biblical times." She shivered. She thought he shivered too, but probably for a very different reason. "Then there were the pushers: corporate types, who got rich and knew what they were doing all along." She thought about Tiffany Van Dyke, to whom collateral devastation happened on a very personal scale, given how her children fell to addiction. "When I bit it, Miss Tiffany was like this prematurely aged woman. She was living alone in that tiny little condo, scraping by. Still, she had a roof over her head."

"Tiffany Van Dyke? Hmmm, not on my list." He shook his head, not interested.

"Of course not. But there were so many who had their whole lives ripped away from them. Devastated. Thrown into poverty and desperation. From what I can tell, your 'worshippers' knew they were peddling a false future while they lived this crazy high life. So, yeah, I always felt like you had an army of folks who really believed in 'you only live once, so take all that

247

you can'. But aside from the lying, scheming politicians, the fame hounds, and the money addicts, you have a lot of worshippers who think they're being good whatever's, practicing their religion but really putting all kinds of hate out there."

"Oh, those kinds make the news all the time. Blowing up people, weddings, festivals." He seemed only mildly interested. Then she remembered that the blood bathers had no future at all. They scratched their own souls out of existence. They didn't make it as far as this office.

She leaned forward in her chair and straightened out her jacket so it was more comfortable. "I don't mean them. I never went to far parts of the world. I never went much of anyplace. But I saw a lot of people right at home say 'thank you Jesus', but what they were thanking him for was people who stood up for prejudice and division. People who wanted to keep others poor, uneducated, down. People who didn't want to share even a chance for people like me to ever find a way out. They didn't want people like me in their schools or their stores, or even to have stores. I would see them, on TV or wherever, as they would claim their country was for people who looked just like them and only like them. And you know, I always heard your voice in them. And they would scream and rail against being taken over by foreigners and I could feel you every time. It's you they worship really, isn't it? No matter who they pretend their devotion is to."

He looked at her shrewdly. "What they do in the name of whatever God they claim is rewarded by the actions, regardless of the words that come out of their mouths." He nodded, looking quite serious at this moment. "No matter how many words they insist on putting out there. If they do good, but do it in the name of the Devil, it's not he who rewards them, that is true. It doesn't show up on that register. After all, what would be the point of that? Wrong jurisdiction. Doesn't fit—and fit is everything. But you are onto something. Evil done in the name of God or religion or country for that matter, does have its jurisdiction. It has to fit. And evil is not rewarded in the lighted regions."

She thought that was funny how he seemed so bureaucratic about all of this. There were templates and orders of hierarchy and jurisdictions. "The lighted regions?"

"Yes," he said blandly. "Well, they're all lit actually. Darkness is reserved for a very few. But the light is quite… different you would say. If you ever saw the 'lighted regions' I doubt you would call the others 'lighted'. It's just not the same, but I wouldn't expect you to understand. It's an existential discussion beyond your comprehension."

"Okay. Um. So, deeds are what counts, not claims. I like that system, you know."

"I'm so glad you approve."

Man, he could be dry when he said stuff.

"It was interesting to check out religion. Really creepy sometimes. There were so many fakers and haters that it was crazy! You know, in a way you should be proud. Out there, it's like those 'unlighted regions' have a whole undercover following, with lots of loud, grandiose words masking lots of evil deeds."

"Religion was one of the more brilliant inventions. So corruptible."

"Yeah, tell me about it. But you should know, I also met a lot of people from a lot of different faiths who did a lot of good. And you could feel it."

"Feel what?"

"Feel, well, you know… it was like the absence… of you."

He raised his eyebrows at her. "And I thought I'd inserted myself pretty much everyplace."

"I didn't just go to church. I went to Temple. The Mosque. I meditated with the Buddhists. I even hung with the Bahá'í and the Unitarians for a while."

"And this smorgasbord of theological dabbing is supposed to make you a weightier prize than little Miss Victoire? So, tell me, just what kind of enlightenment did you obtain that would make you become that much more interesting to someone like me?"

"No, you're right. I didn't become any of them. I could certainly tell apart the fervently religious who you'll be entertaining some day from the real things. I think knowing you, or at least knowing of you, prevented me from being able to buy into many of the rather simplistic and parental views they were serving up. After all, once you've sat in this chair, you start to get how complicated it all is. It's hard to wrap your mind around. What I did walk away with was that they are basically all the same. They say a lot of the same stuff. You know: do good. Be kind. And I would add 'don't believe your own press', because you aren't nearly as important as you think you are."

He just looked at her without saying anything. She figured if he wasn't interrupting, she would keep going. She wasn't really sure how to do a deal with the Devil, so if they were still talking and he wasn't shoving anyone through that creepy door of his, then that was good. "Take care of the Earth and each other. Even if you are so small and insignificant that you're merely a drop in a vast ocean, do good, if for no other reason than to piss off the Devil himself." She shrugged as she said it.

"I like that. Trying to piss off the Devil." He laughed. "That's funny." He became quiet and looked at her. Finally, he gave a big sigh. "Well, Miss Williams, as fun as this has been, I'm afraid our time together is coming to an end. For now, that is."

Quila could feel her heart in her throat. Just what did that mean? What was going to happen next? She took a deep breath and steeled herself. "Uh, okay..." She thought she should sound sure of herself, confident, even if it was just a bluff, but he was a very hard person to sit across a desk from and keep your cool.

"Tell you what: Miss Tequila Williams, I'm going to take you up on your offer." He reached for a button on his desk that suddenly appeared.

Her heart was racing. Take her up on her offer. Which offer. Did that mean...

He pushed it and a woman's voice answered "Yes, sir?"

"Please send in Victory Van Dyke. I believe she's in the waiting room."

Quila began to tremble. Victory was here? And he was going to let her go? The door opened without a sound and through the opening came a blinding light.

"You are such a show-off, you know that? Turn it down!" the Well-Dressed-Man growled out the words.

The brightness dimmed and Quila could see a woman. She was pale. If she had any hair on her head at all, it had to be short cropped and white-blonde like the light emanating from her. She was dressed in a white suit. Fine, like his. Even with the dimmed light, it still hurt Quila's eyes to look, but she squinted and used her hand to shield some of the brightness. She couldn't look away.

"Sorry. Still too much?" The room dimmed a bit more. "Is that better?"

"Yes, thank you," the man answered dryly.

"Took you long enough." The brightly glowing woman teased good naturedly. "You must have been enjoying yourself for once." She reached back through the door and pulled a young woman through. "Come along now."

Quila stood up. She wanted to run over to hug her friend. Victory wasn't dressed in gang wear, but rather in normal clothes, like she was wearing when they'd had that specialty coffee in what now seemed like more than a lifetime ago. Her hair wasn't a faded, half-grown-out shade of purple. There was no tat on her neck. And most importantly, there were no bullet holes in her body.

"Victory!" Quila called out, her voice cracking as she said the name. She reached out her arm but found that while she could stand up, she could not move or approach Victory or her guide.

"Oh, she can't hear you. You aren't present in her experience," the Well-Dressed-Man explained, uncaring. "After all, she's just passing through."

"Where's she going?" Quila wanted to make sure that if her own soul was being given in trade, that she really had secured Victory's freedom.

"Where she's earned herself a place."

"And where is that?" Quila was insistent, wary of being tricked by him.

The brightly glowing guide turned to Quila. "She's with me. She'll be all right."

Victory looked around her, marveling at what she saw. "It's… it's so… beautiful. I never imagined. It's so beyond anything I ever imagined. And it's so bright."

"Yes, it does seem that way at first, but you'll get used to it," the guide said gently.

Quila looked curiously at the Well-Dressed-Man.

He looked bored. "She doesn't see what you see. Her perspective is different, and therefore her experience is different. She doesn't see you. Or me. No, you can't touch her. You'd just pass through each other. You're on different planes right now."

"But I can see her!" Quila was insistent.

"Yes. You're extending her grace. The biggest grace possible to extend, actually, so it changes your perspective." Then he turned to the brightly glowing woman. "Could you send the others? I think we'll need them as well."

"Of course." She nodded. With a slight laugh she said, "Well, we're all just passing through after all." She started to fade as she moved to the far side of the room.

"Wait!" Quila called out to the glowing woman. "What happened to Victory? Will she remember all that horror and pain? Can I say I'm sorry? I tried, I really did, and still her whole life was ruined. She'd been so happy… the first time."

The glowing woman stopped and slowly became a bit more solid. She gazed over at the Well-Dressed-Man, who rolled his eyes and said, "Oh, go ahead!"

The glowing woman turned towards Quila, which made her eyes squint and water. "Victory Van Dyke lived to be an old woman. She lost her best friend at twenty-five. You know she thought about that girl nearly every day of her life. She understood the powerful impact the girl had on her and her own path. She always wondered what she might have done differently to help her best friend. Her guardian angel, as she thought of her. Always wished she'd found a way. Always prayed that there might be something she could do to help. But she went through her life, had two children, got married eventually even, had a career. She felt powerless to have done anything for her friend, so she poured that into making a difference for others. She was pretty impressive, actually. Touched a lot of lives. And no one ever heard of her. She lived the life of a quiet hero, inspired by her great love for her childhood friend."

Quila watched, mesmerized as the lady guided Victory through the room. As they started to fade and pass through the wall on the other side, into what Quila could not imagine, she called out, "Be happy, Vic! I love you! Be happy for all eternity. You never deserved what I brought you. I'm sorry."

"Touching." The Well-Dressed-Man actually sounded disgusted. "I might throw up."

Quila sat back in her chair. She felt… calm. Really calm. Surprisingly relaxed. And happy. She smiled and looked at the Well-Dressed-Man. "So, Victory got a life? She had a real life? Not the one I knew?"

"Of course. She'd lived her life before you ever showed up through my doors."

"But that was only hours? Maybe days? I was shot. Then I was here." She was confused.

"Time is a concept for the living. It only has limited applications. We've been over this already."

She leaned back in her chair and felt… settled. Victory went to the lighted place. That's where she should be. It felt right. And Quila had played a part of that. Victory got to keep that life. She exhaled deeply. "You know, I'm ready now. Thank you. I know this sounds strange because you're going to torture me for eternity, something awful like that, but I really feel like I want to say… thank you. Yeah, thank you."

"Thank you? Well, that's a new one. Even I have to admit that."

"I know now what it means to escape. What it means to have a chance. And to make choices. And I had the chance to make really different choices, and that changed everything for me. I know I haven't escaped anything, not eternally, not really. But I'll always know that I at least tasted something good. Something real. Something true. More importantly, I'll always know that my best friend will *always* be tasting that. And that wouldn't have happened without you giving me a second chance. Sometimes we just need a second chance. So, as awkward as this is to say, particularly to you, uh, thanks. At least now I know. And I like knowing."

He put his fingers together and looked at her over his fingertips, raising his eyebrows. Funny, she thought he still didn't look very interested. She would describe his look as bored.

"Knowing changes a lot." He nodded. "Some would say that knowing changes everything. But as lovely as this conversation is, I have yet another Number Eight to play with. Lying politicians are so entertaining, and thus our droll little time must come to an end."

In the background behind him, she could see the door to no-place starting to materialize, its outlines coming into focus and becoming clear. It was frightening. It felt icy and blisteringly hot all at the same time, even from this distance. She felt her heart race. She would soon be walking through that door and facing…. Well, she wasn't sure what she would be facing, but she was sure she wouldn't be full of wonder and awe like Victory had been. She could barely move for her terror.

"It's time. Tequila Williams, you lived two lives. One in which you watched and laughed as others drowned, and then you followed that path and drowned just like they did. Like rats in a sewer."

She stood up. She had no choice. It wasn't like she was moving her own body. She felt like a marionette, a puppet on strings, her legs being lifted against the dead weight of her will, and she, powerless, moving through oppressively heavy air to the door to nowhere.

"It's time, Tequila Williams, for you, who lived two lives to enter the doorway. Your second chance, as you called it, brought you the opportunity to buy your freedom, to trade Victory's place for your own, and you screwed that up, too. You just can't seem to get anything right, Tequila. And now eternity awaits you. The eternity you've earned for yourself. I'll see you again. Soon."

The door came closer and closer and suddenly she was standing in front of it. The invisible strings that had forced her to move were gone. She understood: she had to walk through of her own volition. She looked over her shoulder at the Well-Dressed-Man one last time. She gave him a small, half-smile. "Thank you."

"Go on."

She turned and faced that ice cold, burning hot, cruel door. She took a deep breath. Well, he was right. She wasn't worth much, but she'd been worth enough to save Victory. She took a step forward. As she tried to step through the door, she suddenly banged her head hard on the lintel. She fell back, rubbing her forehead and looking at the door, totally confused. "Ow!"

"Well, go on."

She looked over her shoulder at him and he made a little wave with his hand, as if to hurry her along. She took another breath and approached the door more carefully this time. As she got closer and tried to move through, she whacked her shoulder on the frame and fell back once again. She rubbed her shoulder with her hand.

"I can't. It's like a trick door. I can't seem to get through." She tried a third time and it definitely looked like the door shrank as she got close to it. She reached out her arm, trying to put just her hand through the opening, and it quickly shrunk, causing her to stub her finger. "Ouch!" she cried out as she put her finger in her mouth. She couldn't believe you could feel pain when you were dead. It didn't seem fair.

She turned to the Well-Dressed-Man, shaking her head and stammering. "I don't know what to do to. It won't let me in. I can't seem to get through it."

"Hmmmm," he said thoughtfully. "I thought you might be a problem." Then he turned and looked beyond her.

Quila's gaze followed the Well-Dressed-Man's. An older gentleman was suddenly standing behind her. He had ebony skin and was wearing a white suit, very much like the pale lady who had been with Victory. He also emitted a bright, but not painful glow. Quila was amazed that even his dark skin emitted that same kind of radiance. It was a luminosity that was warm and welcoming.

"Thanks for coming so quickly. And for not being such an insufferable show off," the man in the chair said with disdain.

"Not a problem. I got the message that you needed me?"

"Yes. We need some assistance. This is Tequila Williams. She doesn't fit."

"Oh. That is a problem." The man in the white suit was completely calm.

Quila looked from one to the other, not comprehending and feeling her anxiety growing. She didn't understand what was happening or what she was supposed to do now.

The Well-Dressed-Man turned to Quila. "Sorry, honey, if you don't fit, you can't stay with me. You're going to have to go."

"Go where?" She was completely flustered by this change.

"Go… on."

The man in the white suit cleared his throat. "Excuse me, Quila? Shall we?" He gestured to an invisible path, and she found she could take the steps towards him. He put a hand on her arm and suddenly the office around her evaporated and she was stunned by what she was seeing.

"Oh my god," she stammered. "It's so beautiful. I never imagined…"

"No one ever does," he said with a kindness in his voice. "No one ever does." Laughing, the man dressed in white started to guide Quila as she exclaimed her surprise at what she was seeing. Then he turned around and looked at the man standing beside his desk. "Hey,"

"Yes?"

The glowing man chuckled. "Two things: you're a real show off, you know that? Such a flair for the dramatic."

The Well-Dressed-Man just shrugged and laughed. "Gotta' be some way to liven up the work. Make it all bearable."

"And I also just wanted to say, nice job. That was a tough one. Nice job." The glowing man gave him a wink.

The Well-Dressed-Man waved the compliment away. "Nah, she was easy. Just doing my job." Then he looked thoughtful. "You know, she's got real potential."

"Bet," the other man answered. "Might take a little time before she's ready."

A half-smile crossed the Well-Dressed-Man's lips. "Right. That's okay. I can wait. But someday, she'll probably have my job."

The white-suited man laughed, a joyful sound. "Bet." Then he led Quila… on.

The Well-Dressed Man watched them fade out of sight. He sighed and absentmindedly scratched the palm of one hand with the fingers of the other hand. Then he reached for a button on his desk that appeared under his outstretched finger. "Send in that Mister Number Eight. I think I'll work with him next."

The End

ACKNOWLEDGEMENTS

As with any writing project, I am grateful for the support of my family and my reader's circle. Ruben, Alexander, and Ethan have the great pleasure (I hope) of listening to the idea, the initial writing and the twenty-odd rewritings of the story. They are the very embodiment of patience and encouragement! There is no way I could have written this, my seventh completed novel, without their love and support. My Reader's Circle consists of dear friends who graciously read (and sometimes re-read and re-read) my novels in various stages, giving valuable critical feedback every step of the way. Special thanks goes to Dr. Bharathi Zvara for endless phone calls about characters and questions and struggles with my own ability to bring this tale to life. Many thanks go to Angela Rosenberg, Katie Brandert, Erika Lusk, Barbara Marcum, Katie Rosanbalm, Melissa Green, Gary Glover, Adriana DiFranco, Thea Calhoon, Amy Langerfender, Cathy Rohweder, Derrick Stephens, Cheryl Noble, Michelle Abel-Shoup, Linda Peterson, Eve Rittenberg, Dee Colello, and Bekki Buenviaje for their encouragement and feedback. And a special thanks goes to Alison Williams, all the way over in Wales, editor on so many of my books, for teaching me how to write in the first place.

AFTERWORD

Like so many authors, this story came to me in a dream—putting me on a journey that was both exciting and difficult to complete. I was thrilled by the tale and inspired by the heroine, Quila, and yet fully aware that I was ill-equipped to tell her story and needed to learn much more to bring this adventure to life. It is challenging to finally let go and call it "finished", because exploring Quila's world, friendships, courage, and insight is a journey that I know I will never truly finish. Like so many authors, I lived with the constant gnawing struggle and fear that I have not done full justice to the heroism and love that is Quila Williams.

This is a story of redemption and misconception, exploring the meaning of service and sacrifice, of love and attachment. A story of just how far one would go to beat the "Devil" at his own game. It is a story of not only a heroic battle against an ultimate evil, but *the* heroic battles against the everyday evils that people of color, people of poverty, people of addiction, and people of differing abilities face, day in and day out. While Quila's tale involves battles with destiny and seemingly satanic forces, it is also a struggle against isms in society on every level. Ultimately, it is a story of victory. The life experiences of most of the characters in this book have not been mine. I have not lived as a Black woman struggling with poverty or as a White one languishing in wealth. Nor do I have the experience of being a married gay man, a cheating husband, an abandoned wife, an addicted teenager, a devil or an angel. While I think of myself as somewhat philosophical, I must admit that I am not a terribly religious person.

As I mention in the Foreword, *Victory!* is a novel in the form of magical realism. Seeing the story was a true gift, which then led me on a five-year journey of reading and studying, engaging in workshops, working with colleagues far wiser than I am, trying to understand both what Quila would face and how I could even begin to understand her world, much less depict it, given my own biases. None of the characters in this story are real, but nearly all of them are based on real people and many of the events are, sadly, also based on real events. Other real events were just too painful to put into this story. I am forever grateful to those who have shared their intimate stories with me. To ensure their privacy, I won't reveal the families who so graciously allowed me into their lives as they struggled with so many of the social determinants of health depicted in this tale. The poverty, fear, and intermittent homelessness. Living on supplies from the food pantry and having to take turns eating because there just isn't enough to go around. Even as a supporter, I felt overwhelmed by the challenges they faced and how individual efforts could so easily be swallowed by the conditions of society. Painfully, I learned how my best attempts to help—uninformed as they were—could pile on more burden along with those few benefits provided.

Through our friendship with these families, I gained new insights into my own privilege. Before I got to know them, I could easily hear the word "privilege" and think that doesn't apply to me, a mom struggling to cover both the mortgage and daycare costs and keep our growing family fed and clothed. At times I worked two jobs. I didn't own yachts or expanses of land, never went to a private school as a child—things that I equated with the word "privilege" growing up rurally on a farm. I only knew what servants were from watching television. But I began to understand the privilege of living without hunger and without fear, either of gunshots or of being targeted either by shopkeepers, who assumed you were there to steal and not buy, or by law enforcement, who were sure you'd committed some kind of offence even without gathering evidence to support that assumption. I started to understand that there are many layers of privilege and that I benefitted from several of them. I desperately wanted to be an ally to one struggling family in particular, but in hindsight I only knew how to try to be what we now call a "White Savior". I have wondered if my attachment to this story has, in some way, been about emotionally dealing with what I witnessed and learned and felt in an experience where I was so powerless to help in any real and lasting way. Perhaps it was about a fervent desire for there to be some kind of meaning and ultimate redemption for the human experience? I don't know… but I do know that this story has gifted me with hope.

I had other crucial teachers along this journey to whom I wish to extend my gratitude. I am grateful to my dear friends who shared with me the pain and fear of parenting a child who is struggling to find their way and battling the demons of addiction and other serious issues. I so appreciate those friends who have shared their experiences of living in poverty, insecurity, and fear. And my friends who navigated the complexities adopting a child into their same sex parenting household, sharing with me the importance of honoring the race and space from which that child came.

I am in awe of colleague Derrick Stephens, who speaks so eloquently of the value of second chances in his work with children in the foster care system that "second chances" became a central theme of this story. I am indebted to my many friends who are parents of children with special health care needs who have guided and tutored me on my own journey, most particularly my dear friend, Alice Wertheimer.

Quila Williams inspired me as a heroine for today. A heroine for troubled times. Being troubled by poverty is only the start of her journey. Her family, as was the family on which hers is based, is broken by the predatory incarceration of Black men and devastated by the destruction of the Black family. Her world is a victim of the war on drugs, and one turned upside down by addiction. Her shadow and unlikely best friend lives in the opposite of circumstances. Privileged by wealth, education, class and race, Victory Van Dyke's family experience isms of their own, being shunned for Victory's special needs, which leaves its own unique scars. Quila and Victory share a story of the saving grace of friendship across all divisions.

I offer this story up, imperfect as it is, as a hopeful inspiration that we can all find the saving grace of love and friendship that will allow us to broaden our worlds and cross the chasms that divide us. In a world full of systemic issues that oppress all too many people, I believe it is those bonds of love and friendship that will show us a path to healing and give us the courage to make real and lasting change. While I hope this story rings meaningfully with others, nevertheless, I am humbled to have been blessed with the gift of being given the tale to tell. Quila may be a fictional character, but she will ever be a real hero to me.

Book Club Questions

1. Characters in this book struggle with racism (as well as other isms) and a lack of understanding of the challenges and concerns that others face. Where do you see examples of those kind of blind spots, even from well-meaning individuals?

2. In the human experience, it is not uncommon for people to describe "finding their family" in life. This book explores the concept of deep friendship and finding kinship with those whom you don't share a bloodline. What sacrifices do Quila and Victory make for one another, along the continuum from everyday actions to more ultimate sacrifices? Where are their deeds rewarded and where do they misfire?

3. This book illustrates concepts around what are called the "social determinants of health", which are defined by the World Health Organization as "the conditions in which people are born, grow, live, work and age. These circumstances are shaped by the distribution of money, power and resources at global, national and local levels"*. Quila faces many obstacles related to the social determinants of health in both her lifetimes. What is the difference

between the ability of individual choices to alter someone's trajectory versus changing the social determinants of health that affect them? How do the social determinants of health affect Quila and Victory differently?

4. Tiffany Van Drake attempts to make a difference by making a series of individual "good acts". Compare and contrast the kinds of impacts that happen from individual actions versus policy and system level changes. Where do you see the effects of individual actions, collective social actions, versus the effects of policy actions in this story?

5. The Well-Dressed Man makes the point to Quila that Victory learned from Quila's mistakes and that influenced her trajectory initially. However, when she had no such mirror of reflection, she made very different choices as "Victory 2.0". In a very philosophical sense, how does Quila serve as a spiritual teacher for Victory? Given that same lens, how does Victory serve as a spiritual teacher for Quila? How have people in your life served your growth along your own path in the ways that Victory and Quila learned from each other?

6. Imagine: What if you had nothing? Nothing to lose. Nothing to care about. Nothing possibly to gain. What if you were then offered another chance? An opportunity to live your life over? You could right your wrongs. Get even. Get ahead. All it will cost you is the soul of your best friend. How would you try to navigate such an ultimate challenge?

7. Quila muses on what she calls "the butterfly effect". What does that mean in the context of her experiences? How can you observe those "butterfly effects" in your life or your community?

8. The Well-Dressed Man plays a pivotal and rather mysterious role in this story. Just who is he? Is he really the Devil? Or just a devil? Or is he something else entirely? What is his function and role?

9. How does intersectionality play a role in Quila's experience? In Victory's? How does their experience change from their 1.0 lives to their 2.0 lives?

*WHO (World Health Organization). 2012. *What are the social determinants of health?* Available at: http://www.who.int/social_determinants/sdh_definition/en/ (accessed March 31, 2021).

About the Author

Born an urban Northerner, Ci Ci Soleil escaped to plant her own roots in the New American South. While squeezing chickens, a goat, and too many fruits trees onto a tiny farm not-quite-suited-to-the-task keeps her and her family busy, everyone realizes it's really the dogs who are in charge. Ci Ci loves spending her time writing, painting and sculpting, although between her two boys, incredibly supportive husband, all those animals, and oh yes, that pesky day job, there is never enough time. *Victory!* is Ci Ci's seventh completed novel and her first deep dive into magical realism.